BLUE SCORPION

CARTER ONASSIS

Order this book online at www.trafford.com
or email orders@trafford.com

Most Trafford titles are also available at major online book retailers.

© Copyright 2018 Carter Onassis.
All rights reserved. No part of this publication may be reproduced, stored in a
retrieval system, or transmitted, in any form or by any means, electronic, mechanical,
photocopying, recording, or otherwise, without the written prior permission of the author.

Print information available on the last page.

isbn: 978-1-4907-9117-3 (sc)
isbn: 978-1-4907-9116-6 (hc)
isbn: 978-1-4907-9118-0 (e)

Library of Congress Control Number: 2018911586

Because of the dynamic nature of the Internet, any web addresses or links contained in
this book may have changed since publication and may no longer be valid. The views
expressed in this work are solely those of the author and do not necessarily reflect the
views of the publisher, and the publisher hereby disclaims any responsibility for them.

Any people depicted in stock imagery provided by Getty Images are models, and such
images are being used for illustrative purposes only.
Certain stock imagery © Getty Images.

Trafford rev. 10/25/2018

 www.trafford.com

North America & international
toll-free: 1 888 232 4444 (USA & Canada)
fax: 812 355 4082

CONTENTS

Special thanks to my loving family and friends for supporting my dreams of writing professionally. This novel took several years of daydreaming to get on paper. Great effort in many respects. My publisher and editors were too excellent. Thank you again Pepper, Drew, and the team.

PROLOGUE

SELECTED BREED

In a desperate struggle to defeat an enemy of overwhelming strength, atrocities became appealing. Two hundred thousand three hundred forty atrocities were committed in total, not factoring in the collateral victims. The children were taken from their homes, gathered from all over the kingdom. These special children—rich and poor, weak and strong—possessed genes of a far superior race than the invading force. The bloodlines involved in the conflict were related and surprisingly dissimilar. Their designs were comparable, but their abilities varied greatly.

The Arcon (Arconians) possessed great strength and a strong focus. The Harfore (Harforians) manifested great mental capacity and an ability to channel their mental forces to influence matter. The Darcon (Darforians) were benign compared to the rest yet endowed with the greatest potential on all measurable levels. The Pylon (Pylonites) were crooked in appearance and desire; they had the greatest thirst for blood and survival. Of course, the children of those in jeopardy—who had the most to lose—were exempt from the suffering.

The attack was swift. The defenseless home world of a developing youth culture could not imagine themselves to be the target of a seemingly loyal ally. Their defenses fell quickly to a barrage of well-planned and systematic assaults.

Before the onslaught, a messenger of peace was sent to greet the treasures. The magnificence of the beings captured the inhabitants' lust for freedom. The rewards they offered seemed greater than the magnificence of the visitors. The only action they would have to take was to damage the device that was causing them harm yet keeping them from greater misfortune.

They destroyed the unknown object with zeal. A whole universe of resources and enjoyment was much too enticing. These godlike beings had what they wanted, what they needed—a purpose. They shone with the light of the radiant sun, decaying each and every passing moment. They sat on thrones awaiting their paradoxical lies to be accepted as the truth, and by the time they succeeded, their strong mental, physical, and spiritual state had begun to falter. Unable to view the destruction of the device, they fell from their high places.

As the device crumbled, a powerful charge of subatomic energy encompassed the entire planet. As intended, the foreign cells performed apoptosis at an increased rate. Fear consumed the inhabitants as they heard and witnessed the passing of their heraldic visitors. As promised, large ships landed on the planet's surface, allowing hundreds of the captivated people to board. Thousands emigrated from their captivity to the safety and freedom of a new world.

The world was much grander. It was created with them in mind. Their survival and, most importantly, their enjoyment would be fostered. Taken to large structures as they landed on the surface of a rich and sustainable planet, which was more abundant in resources than the last, the immigrants were educated and became well versed in the ways of their new owners. They were taught to worship the royal lineage of their rescuers, who shared similar attributes with the first visitors to their world.

Years of peaceful development and progress passed, undisturbed by heavy violence. The guests invented many new weapons and devices for their hosts. They worked unaware of their slavery, being encouraged and motivated by their captors. Upon the removal of the inhabitants from their home and prison or better termed as jewelry box, they began to explore its surface as attempts to reach the core failed, and many new biological and technological structures were uncovered. The previous inhabitants of the planet designed it to keep intruders out and imprison this unpowered race of beings. They soon learned to exploit their captives, and great secrets had now fallen into their possession. Unimaginable potential lay in the remains of the past and present inhabitants of the planet.

Abruptly and inevitably, the stability and peace of the region ended. The well-adjusted inhabitants were never informed of the many problems the caretakers managed. A war had broken out between the gods and an aggressor. Servants no longer desired to work for their masters and instead intended to surpass them in strength and power. Their most prized secrets had been revealed to them, and emulation grew rapidly.

The anarchy could not be contained or destroyed because high members of the ruling species marveled at the successes of a newly independent lineage of servants and were intrigued by the new ways of thinking that had developed. The alignment of strong powers shifted. The strength and focus of this enemy made them worthy warriors, and the divine beings chose to abandon their unruly servants rather than risk an unprofitable conflict. They preferred to stay peaceful in power and rule at ease.

The gods battled successfully against another more powerful collective aggressor whose attacks were bold, occurring deep within their most protected territories and inflicting heavy damage to vulnerable targets. The gods would have soon triumphed over their foe, but they could not anticipate an overwhelming attack orchestrated by their former servants. Their most developed planets were annexed within the course of a three-month siege and embargo. As their preeminence in the universe began to deteriorate, it became obvious that their incorporation of the peacefully captive race was not beneficial to their cause. They had first sought to merge with the race and share their bloodline. In truth, their plan had been successful but only to a limited extent.

Six rare hybrids were born as a result of a union between the gods and their cherished servants. Unfortunately, they lacked the traits desired in appearance and ability but had increased strength and inner sight. Four of them remained loyal to their destiny. Belligerently, an inability to procreate sufficiently and maintain a population that would ensure their survival had adversely affected their ability to control their empire and led to their weakening military strength. However, the gods remained far more technologically advanced than their newly liberated servants.

A desperate attempt at survival was made. Two hundred thousand three hundred forty children were taken from their parents and guardians. These children had desired traits that the gods also possessed. The willingness of the gods to do anything to survive intensified. The children became genetic experiments, and preliminary studies suggested that it was possible for the products to display miraculous abilities greater than that of the royal gods. The unwilling participants underwent hours of genetically altering treatments, and few were strong enough to survive the initial phases. The cruel and unusual methods of the experimentation remained unspoken, even among the reprobate scientists. Nevertheless, unhindered by the high rate of failure, the scientists continued their experimentation and began to observe some pleasing results.

The initial observation of the first phases of the genetic enhancements was not what the gods sought: one child had superior strength and agility, another was capable of withstanding ninety volts of electricity, another showed increased brain activity, another displayed signs of the ability to suspend propelled objects in space, and one was capable of breathing underwater for more than half an hour. The most successful participants were taken away from the facility and underwent more severe experimentation. As the number of participants began to decrease and an explanation for their disappearance had started to be murmured about by the inhabitants, the planet was invaded by the unruly race of servants.

A war of great magnitude ensued. Destructive explosions and fires shaped the surface of the planet. Millions on both sides of the conflict perished in the struggle. The cherished servants were enlisted to fight the enemies, and when the battle seemed to be favoring the former servants, the gods activated a weapon of immense power and sophistication. The weapon powered down all mechanical ships within the solar system, suspending many battleships in space and causing others to be pulled to the surface of the planets. The effects of the device were temporary, but the recording devices of the ships were completely destroyed. The location of the battle was lost to the enemy, and no new reinforcements could be sent.

Some of the invading forces survived the impact and fled their ships, only to be pursued by the surviving gods. The participants of the experiment went unaccounted for in the confusion of war. Some died from serious complications; some fled, only to be captured again. Others simply disappeared, but some escaped from the holding cells of their experimenters and walked away into the cold streets of the compounds, undistinguishable from ordinary children. There, some stood for hours and were taken away to safety by positive forces.

The child looked outside the window, almost sensing his misfortune. His vulnerable young mind was led to the windowlike wall by a powerful fixation. The sun was high in the sky and revealing the full extent of the destruction that had befallen the city. He observed the tiny children who ran freely through the streets below him. Thick smoke left the smoldering city structures.

His blue eyes electrified as he heard the woman's light steps. The child noticed the reflection of a red-eyed beast in the thick window wall. Red eyes beamed down on him as he gazed up, showing no fear. A strong, tender hand beheld his wrist. The child struggled slowly as she attempted to coax him. He resisted the stranger forcefully. Her mouth formed a dour smile as high volts of electricity bounced off her large frame and around the littered dark hall. Anger entered her features only when a ball of light impacted the gold mask that covered her face. It cracked, and she threw the molten object from her face, revealing true beauty for only a moment. She was damaged and could taste blood.

The bare-chested child retreated to the corner. Smooth, dense, ramlike pearl horns protruded from her hood. She stretched forward again and retrieved the child's arm as he fainted from exhaustion. Black scabs formed on her wounds as she again became hooded. The giant hooded figure picked the child up in her capable arms and began to walk through the halls of her costly laboratory. Her bright red eyes admired his features, envying his blond hair, blue eyes, and fair skin as she calculated his potential. He would exalt the empire of her fathers. She began to think of an explanation for her unplanned adoption as she carried the small frail child through the badly damaged facility.

She broke through many barriers until she created a large enough exit for herself and the child to pass through. Bright sunlight entered the facility. She activated a glowing green beacon in her hands and covered her face with her free hand. A large rectangular vertical black ship appeared from behind a cloud in the sky above the smoke-filled city. The large black-hooded creature vanished in the brightness of the sunlight. The inhabitants of the dying city did not notice the ship that moved over the bright sun.

CHAPTER I

IN DENIAL

Stumbling through the streets of a familiar place, a lost child found herself at the doorsteps of a towering dark structure. Action in the night sky illuminated the burning structures of the city. Her baldness was covered by a hooded red-and-white vial that could not conceal her light blue eyes. Explosions in the sky drew her attention from her desire to arrive home. The streets were colored with the ululations of a disaster. The smell of smoke entered her unconscious mind, and her gaze intensified as she realized that the structure was on fire.

Purposefully, the doors of the structure vanished. Lifting from the ground, the child entered the smoke-filled house. An onlooker noticed the child and ran toward her, intending to retrieve her from the flaming structure for the third time, but he could not pass through the door that appeared invisible. Horrified at the sight of the levitating child and the invisible barrier, he fled in wild amazement. Undisrupted by the heat of the flames and the roar of fire that dimmed, the child moved farther down the smoke-filled halls. There, her search ended as she saw a man lying on the floor, barred by a wall of collapsed metallic building material and high flames. The flames parted as the child entered the room and amazingly lifted the man, who was three times her weight, not with her hands but with her mind.

The structure began to shake, and objects fell from their places. Unable to find her direction, the child grew distressed but only for a moment. Spontaneously, the ground below her began to glow, and the man fell to the ground, regaining his consciousness. Staring up at the child he had so easily given away in his act of devotion, he trembled at the bizarre blue light that illuminated her. The blue light filled the room and reflected off many surfaces. In a flash of bright light, they vanished; and for a moment, he was blinded by the brightness. Opening his eyes, he was in the middle of the street just across from his home. He then realized that he could not find the child. He looked around frantically and found her form in the large smoldering crater beside him. He lamented his previous decision to give her away, and despite his momentary frailty, he lifted her over his arm and fled to a nearby underground tunnel.

Years of reconstruction passed by, uninterrupted by the influences of external forces. The Harfore leadership retreated from the planet and found safety in its orbit. Huge prism structures were built to house the Darcon. The Harfore and the Darcon were now seemingly friendly allies. The environments the planet Darth facilitated and where they inhabited peacefully were now too corrupt and insidious for them to be unsheltered and remain civilized. Foreign beings had adapted to the environment, and it was now hostile and cruel. The climate of the planet shifted from docile to tumultuously unpredictable. Its landscape was littered with rusting and half-buried spacecraft, remnants of the war. The topography and climate of the planet was now just as hostile— desert-and junglelike in the southern regions and oppositely swampy and bitterly cold in the northern regions.

The massive hexagonal and subterranean prisms were surrounded by smooth pavement—six of them in total—scattered throughout Darth's surface; invisible from space as they remained camouflaged, they housed the remaining survivors of the conflict. Less than eight hundred thousand of them were housed in each prism. The inhabitants were educated and trained in various sciences and arts of defense; however, not all six structures were equally made and rationed.

Deep inside the prism, a now adult woman left the confines of her postsecondary training institution. She could have taken some form of transportation but decided to walk. She was brilliant, the top pupil in the classes she liked, somewhat popular, and rather beautiful. She walked down the sunlit corridors of the prism located in the northern top quarter of the world.

The corridors were spacious. They extended fifty meters in width, allowing ample walking space for all pedestrians. The layout of the compound was quite complex. It extended from four hundred meters below the surface of the planet to two hundred meters above. The design of the inside was rather amusing: white marblelike floors, dark-brown woodlike walls, golden lines dividing the floor from the ceiling, and sometimes changing floors in certain places. The decor was only bearable because of the sunlight that shone in through the gigantic sunroof. Some areas of the facility were covered with greenery. Potted red, blue, and yellow flowers appeared at entrances and exits. Walls of plants and rooms of vegetation were reoccurring scenes. No ceiling covered the corridors of the structure. Ceilings were only visible in rooms, residences, gyms, auditoriums, and lecture halls. It was quite a spectacular view regardless of the locale.

The young woman kept up her physique easily and had great intuition. She barely avoided a collision with the children who ran by, unable to tell where they would run; and as if prompted, she remembered her own childhood. She could only remember her first days in the communal facilities, the prism complex's nursery, at the age of seven. Her shyness and sadness overshadowed her willingness to learn, and she was neglected in the facility. She did not remember her parent until he arrived one morning in the late spring. Her father did not hesitate to hug her and told her that she was very special to him. Her stepmother remained distant at first but gradually became charming and very interested in her enough to say that she loved her like a daughter. Her mind fluttered; again, she remembered her uniqueness.

Viewing the time on her wrist, she increased her pace as she walked and tried to determine the quickest route to her destination. Her steps were pronounced by boots with heels. Her clothes were reserved. Her long black hair was held back in a ponytail with no visible holder, her light-red wool coat that just barely passed her knees held together by dark red buttons. A black leather belt surrounded her well-proportioned waist, and low-heel ankle-concealing black boots complemented her fair skin and styled her. Her soft blue eyes gleamed as the sunlight brightened underneath her purely fashionable gray-toned eyewear as they dimmed.

She remembered the many locations of the prism she had grown accustomed to: the communal facility, the recreational facilities, the libraries, the auditoriums, the public spaces, the residences where her parents lived, and the advanced science laboratories. The communal facility was the place where she and all the newborns, children, and nonadults were raised under the state supervision of the Harfore-Darcon planetary leadership. Her parents had the right to visit her anytime they wished; however, they could only take her out of the facility occasionally. At first, they took her to the recreational facilities, where she enjoyed playing in the gravity-free chamber and other simulation rooms. They also took her to the many libraries that were scattered throughout the compound. She remembered the many hours she spent researching in those libraries to complete her theoretical design of a fresh-water-generating device, which she had later conducted further research on for her postsecondary degrees in chemistry and biological engineering. And she concluded that, theoretically and hypothetically, it should function better and use less power than the classified water-creating devices. For this achievement, she received outstanding scientific awards, publicity, and entry into the advanced sciences.

She always felt as if information was being withheld from her when the inhabitants were summoned to the auditoriums to view the latest news, court trials, military performances, and other concerns. It was truly a command environment. The wide-open spaces of the compound were where Cassandra conducted much of her studies, unaffected by the large crowds and events that were held in the vicinity.

When she was finally allowed to visit her father's opulent and spacious living quarters, she realized how comfortable life could be. However, never had she nursed so many bruises, which resulted from an unexpected, intense fight with an instructed android. Having purposely lost the fight, her father looked at her in disbelief. He had known of her gifts and aptitudes and, understanding her pleasant mind-set, knew it was incumbent on him to develop them further. Any other twelve-year-old girl in her position would have resisted his counsel and lashed out, but she didn't. She had a gentle and restrained yet passionate heart.

After her first visit, her father—a high-ranking commander who shared her last name—enlisted her in a rigorous quasi-military service and secret training. She was discouraged from forming any serious relationships with anyone, and that also meant she could not have a serious boyfriend. Thenceforth, the academia and skill building became her interest. Upon her acceptance to postsecondary education, she was given access to the advanced science laboratories and lived in its dorms. There was no party scene, not in the northern prisms. She completed her studies in half the time it usually took but knew that she had to remain unidentified in athletic achievement and avoided the competitions, the fight clubs, the contests, and the sports.

She again smiled as she walked up the stairs into a large building marked "Assessment and placement" and remembered her first visit—the day her father had arrived at the communal facility with flowers for a week-old fourteenth birthday. This was an unusual event because he was typically in a far distant place on her birthday and congratulated her via message or an expensive educational carded gift. So it was natural for her to show excitement when he declassified the vacation that awaited them.

She had needed an access card to visit the even more massive prism complex in the southern region of the planet. Her trip to the transport bay was fascinating, and the sight of the huge circular devices that were capable of breaking particles into electrical energy and recreating them in their physical form bewildered her mind. It was rare for anyone to be given permission to travel, but since her father had such high status within the defense organization and played such a vital role in the construction and maintenance of the prisms, her way was paved as well as driven.

The tropical climate of the southern prism was spectacular and its views enviable. Although the scenery was mostly artificial, it fascinated her, having never seen greenery in its natural state. Cassandra feared the trip was an elaborate trick, a ruse by her father to have her capabilities assessed or to marry her off to someone he owed a great debt. Or perhaps she would see the beautiful jungles and never want to come back to the frigid, mountainous, and seemingly barren environment of the northern prism complex. She had many colleagues and a few friends she kept in touch with, nothing romantic surprisingly. An assessment would be nothing too strenuous, for she had been training secretly for years and could now channel her known abilities.

Interrupted by a familiar presence, she pulled her mind back to the present and joined the line. She carefully selected the most underburdened electronic teller and saw many familiar faces. She decided to let him approach her and be a successful prankster. He was a just a camper and a student of philosophy in her perspective.

"Ms. Vyers," a quick and light-toned voice whispered in her ears as hands were gently placed over her sunglasses.

Without alerting herself, she turned around slowly. "Alex, I know it's you. You didn't have to come here. It's not a graduation ceremony."

"Ah, I am so sorry I missed it," the brown-haired and very handsome young man said sincerely while removing his hands from her face.

Cassandra answered him wholeheartedly, "Oh, it's fine. You're my half brother. I have to love you." They hugged.

"So how are you? You're a medical doctor now, so Dad tells me."

"I told you what I was pursuing years before I started," she declared as she removed her black-gray eyewear.

"You're a surgeon—no, a botanist . . . a genetic engineer," he said questionably.

"I'm a chemical and biological engineer," she said, turning around and grabbing his arm as they moved with the crowded room. She realized her folly. "But you are right, I did tell you I was going to be a lot of things. You didn't come here to see me get my access cards. When are you going to tell me? We talk a lot, but you don't like me this much to show up without flowers to this crowded place." The noise of the room increased, and her last few sentences went unheard. "What did you come to tell me?"

"Huh. Well, I wasn't going to tell you this right now . . . I'm getting married soon," he whispered. "She's here somewhere." He laughed.

Her face showed quick surprise and then slow disbelief and the newness of ecstasy. "Whatever happened to you wanting to marry me?" she joyfully contested. He looked at her, slightly perturbed. "Congratulations. I'm very excited about this. Oh, Alex, I'm kidding. Really, who is she? Is she intelligent? Is she pregnant?"

"You're thinking too much," he said with concern. "Thank you. I knew you'd be supportive and make me feel great about my life finally coming together. She's great. She's an archaeologist and a reporter-writer. She does documentaries."

"An archaeologist. So then she's been on the outside of the compound freely? If she's an archaeologist, she might be in the military. There are too many things lurking out there for any unprotected archaeologist to be digging around. It's lovely, and it's great that she's a writer. Sounds sweet . . . nice."

"Yeah, she is, and Dad is going to envy me," he said with an outstanding pride. "But"—he paused—"don't tell the world." He leaned closer to whisper, but she heard him loudly before he said it. "She is a special forces op."

"How did you manage to find her? How did you two meet?" The line moved faster. Not noticing that her questions were unanswered, she continued. "So where is she?" she inquired.

"Right outside, waiting. I told her about you from the start. She's all about family. She has a twin that she won't stop criticizing. This isn't some plot though, Cass. I came just to see you and congratulate you on your success. But you know, I've been all over since I met this chick, and we've seen each other only three times in the last month. I want to seal the deal. She's here and excited to meet you. You have to meet her, okay?" he insisted.

"How am I going to say no to you? Okay, no, I couldn't. My hair isn't even done. Look at this frizz. I have so many things to do today. This just adds to my anxiety, but I'm not going to be a bitch or a cunt about you choosing to surprise me," she said, shrugging and flicking her hair back in a fake Valley-girl manner.

"Please?" he said, half grinning, tilting his head to the side, and moving nervously in interior lighting, bluish green eyes.

Sensing how much his request meant to him, she couldn't stop herself from conceding. Cassandra reluctantly exhaled, taking a while to make her decision. "Oh, okay, I'm pretty sure I already said yes, all right. But you can't tell her too much about me, okay? Don't make every conversation about me and what I do. Please don't go into too much detail. Let's go meet her in a few minutes. What's her name? You didn't even tell me her name."

"What about you? Her name's long, but everyone calls her Sky. I'm not telling her much about you. You're the last thing on her mind, trust me. You're the only real family I have in the loyalty sense of the word," he said, slightly afraid as she looked up at him crossly. "I won't tell her anything else I haven't already told her."

"Anything else?" she replied quickly. "Don't even dare—" She paused, interrupted by the loud and robotic voice of the teller.

"Hello, how may I help you today?" the robotic voice began to greet. The teller requested identification, other soon-to-be-outdated access cards, and multiple signatures from her.

In her haste to fill out the forms, Alex was gone. *I can't believe him*, she thought. She assumed the situation meant he would wait with her quietly, not walk off back to his fiancée.

The ramifications of her capabilities being exposed seemed too much for her to fathom. Experimentation was what Cassandra feared. It was either that or she'd be the newest freak show. Having learned all about people like herself during her studies in biology, which no other student took as seriously as she did because they lacked the imagination and discernment to differentiate fiction from reality, she knew life would be horrible if discretion was not met.

She conducted lots of experiments but never on large living animals, only single-celled organisms and plants, conducting all other forms of dissections on computer simulations. Biology interested her more so than chemistry. Her reason for disliking chemistry did not have to do with its heavy demands on her intellect but the way it confined her imagination. However, biology allowed her to learn much about the outside world and understand its organized complexity. She knew nearly all the animals and plant species, foreign and domestic to the planet, inside and out. Most of the life on the planet was insectlike, reptilian, and fungal, which meant that few docile creatures lived in the Northern Hemisphere. The animal life that lived in the Northern Hemisphere consisted of carnivorous, snakelike, nitrogen-breathing marine and subterranean life-forms. The irony of the anticipated situation occurred to her.

She was again interrupted by the teller and was instructed to collect her access cards. Relief and brimming pride took her by surprise. She was now officially a certified chemist and biologist with access to more resources, funding, and perks. Her residence might soon be bigger than her parents' one day. Scanning both the cards, she was amused by the holographic designs and stylistic lettering. Her four years of learning complex theories and notation now seemed worthwhile.

Exiting the building and entering the bustling corridor, she looked around for her brother. As expected, he was standing by a teleportation device and kissing a very attractive woman. Cassandra's gaze intensified as she moved closer. The athletic woman was well dressed in a soft dark blue material held together by a dark blue button-down that gave shape to her curves, covered her arms, and collared her neck. Cargolike white pants completed her outfit and presented her as very smooth. Her skin was a lovely bronze and her eyes a very strange bright blue. Cassandra's pace increased as she reached them. "Hi," she said, awaiting the couple's passionate kisses to end. She stretched out her hand at the bright-eyed woman.

"Hi, Cassandra. It's nice to meet you. I'm Sky."

Alex interrupted, "Commander Sky. I can't pronounce her last name." A playful voice shouted and stopped as he was playfully nudged. "I can't be bothered now. That's changing."

"Call me Sky," the beauty insisted. The two women looked at each other as if sizing the other up without being externally provocative.

"Okay, well, I won't be a stranger. Should we hug?" Sky said, only to realize how awkward she sounded. Almost entirely unintentionally, thoughts were exchanged, and defenses went up. Sky shook her head as if to ask what just happened, but her military training had brought this feeling to her many times.

"I'm sorry. My hair is just terrible today," lied Cassandra.

"Don't worry about that. It smells fine," Sky insisted earnestly.

"You said you wanted me to go somewhere with you?" Cassandra said.

"No, I didn't . . . but I was going to ask you if you'd like to come on a trip outside these walls with me and thin lips here," she continued, realizing her mistake.

Cassandra's eyebrows tensed up for a split second. "Yes!" she shouted. She thought too fast that moment.

"I'd be delighted," Cassandra said slowly. "I can't believe you'd ask me." She was excited.

"That's awesome. It's going to be a great . . . fun . . . family . . . a family trip," Alex said, consciously sensing tension between the two women. "We're not going to be that weird family where no one understands or likes each other."

"Is he always like this now, or is it a facade?" asked Cassandra.

"Nope, that's him, authentically."

"I hope you can cure him."

"You're the scientist," Sky said, sounding friendly.

"Why don't we eat, kill an hour? What time is it now? It's 1400. A late lunch?" The women did not answer him. "So what do you think, ladies?"

"That won't work for me," said Sky.

"I can't either. I wish I could, but I have to move out of my dorm today to my new quarters."

"Sounds prestigious," jested Alex. "Any old electronics you want to throw out, just call me."

The sister and brother exchanged departing words, and Cassandra waved at her future sister-in-law with feelings of uncertainty. She knew that something terribly damaging had occurred during their first meeting but hoped in vain that time would lead to forgetfulness.

Tired and a little on edge, she arrived at her dorm to find a crowded hallway filled with anxious movers. She imagined that now would be a wonderful and appropriate time to use her abilities but couldn't lie to herself. She took the staircase, ascending fourteen floors, to her room and gathered her belongings. Calling out to her dorm mates, whom she had first believed to be in their rooms, she realized that they had all left and that her goodbyes had gone unheard.

Suddenly, her messaging device rang. It was not a friend. A prism complex operator forwarded her eagerly anticipated instructions on how to proceed to her new quarters and that the movers were arriving soon. She would also have an office. And as she awaited the message's end, another one arrived. It was a highly encrypted message from her father. The message had detailed instructions on her new training schedule that was to begin the following evening. Looking at the slight bruises on her left leg, she looked forward to beating her previous record.

CHAPTER II

FEUD

Deep within the jungles of the Southern Hemisphere, a circle gathered. They had spent much of the night discussing current events and gossiping under the large stars and other various constellations. The dawn flowers opened, and the sun rose above the horizon. One youth parted ways with the others.

A swift figure moved through the dense forest. Strange noises echoed as the shadow passed by. The shadow's path led to a whitely lit prism complex. The lights outside the prism dotted its walls. As if awaiting the entrance to the prism structure to open, the blur hid at the side of the darkened pavement entrance. The two large plain brass gates at the southernmost entrance opened with a sliding motion, and two steel-like aircraft landed on helipads closest to the entrance. Quickly, the blur entered the prism. As the invisible figure stood motionless as sentries scanned the area, its shadow vanished. The invisible man activated the transport device as burly, raptorlike sentries stomped out of his range. Entering the device, the figure was instantly transported upward to the living quarters of the prism.

Upon exiting the prism, the figure uncloaked, only to discover a man standing, staring up at him. He was first startled. "You're up quite early, young man." The man scanned him from top to bottom as peculiar expressions formed on his face.

"Yes," the dirty, mud-covered adolescent said. "I must be going. I had some landscaping classes this morning." He walked away swiftly.

Turning to his left, he noticed another transport device coming online. He moved around the first corner. He scrambled for the proper access card in his left pocket, which he retrieved as the sound of hard footsteps approached him. He opened the door and, with unbelievable speed, entered the apartment, closing the door with a loud clang. Using his quickness, he sped away to his chambers. Removing his mud-dried clothes and rinsing his face in the closest sink, he moved diligently to his hovering bed held by magnets.

As he did so, he heard the voice of his captor. He quickly threw himself under the sheets as the room's door opened rather harshly. "How was your rest, dear?" a strong elderly voice yelled rhetorically.

"I'm sleeping," an indignant voice said from underneath the sheets.

"Are you?" she screamed angrily. "You must think I'm a fool!" The woman's stern face crumpled even more. "Mr. Albright saw you in the hallway"—she paused to gather herself before completing her sentence—"a very strange muddy teen. But of course, it's not you."

"Fuck off," he said rudely, uttering curses silently at the distasteful humor.

The woman walked into the lavatory and returned with a handful of mud-flaked clothing. "You've been out of the facility again, and this time, I've had enough!" she screamed, pausing for a moment to inhale. "What is that? What's that smell?" She inhaled the fumes of a strong substance. "Timothy, have you been at it again?" She was uneasy in her anger.

"Just leave me alone. Lady, I don't have to listen to you. You know what?" he said in sequence, not giving her a chance to respond. "Two months from now, I'm an adult."

She screamed, outraged at his reaction. "You know, I warned you. I was serious with your parents, and I'll be serious with you.

I'm very serious," she carefully enunciated. "That was it. This was the last time. Get your stuff packed because you're leaving." The woman's tone was faltering, and she slammed the door upon leaving.

"Who are you?" he distastefully said, leaping out of the bed. His untidy dark brown hair hiding his full features still lay entangled in his sheets. The youth was angered, and his features made that evident. He realized that he did not have to obey her rules; after all, his parents had listened to her, and what happened to them was grim in his mind. He was an orphan. His mother and father had perished in the violent conflict that was waged on his planet.

He gathered his belongings and entered the washroom for a second time. Seeing his reflection in the mirror, he began to think about the past. His sole relative was his grandmother, his father's mother. The youth had lived with several adoptive families before he was reunited with his grandmother. The other families instantly chose him in the catalogs because of his high intelligence quotient and handsome appearance. They gladly gave him away after determining unsoundly that he was the cause of some costly fires and critically injured playmates. His grandmother loved him. She taught him how to meditate and focus, but he resisted her every positive action and tested her short limits, and in her old age, she began to become less patient. Over the years, she had witnessed him break every fragile object she had ever cared for and seen him with.

Looking in to the mirror, he viewed his muscular physique. His dark brown hair was manageable, and his darkened skin tone reminded him of his many adventures in the jungle. He glanced over his dark brown eyebrows, sharp nose, green eyes, and anchorlike budding, downward black mustache as he leaned to wash his face. His chin was solid and his lips a thin dark pink. His ears were unnoticeable beneath his overgrown hair.

The jungle was especially slick that morning and was the cause of his dusty appearance. Not that he fell. His fast pace was quick and lifted mud and debris from the ground. He had first ventured into the jungle after being dared to retrieve the tail end of a spacecraft rumored to be buried on the prism grounds. His first trip outside the facility was stressful and exhilarating. He remembered how his heart raced as he walked through the halls stealthily. He had mastered his art. He was invisible to all forms of detection when he wished to be. He had learned this years ago while being pursued by towering men with savage-looking weapons. He could not exactly remember how the event occurred, only that he was right beside the two fearfully indescribable creatures as they looked for him.

The weather was unpleasant during his first visit to the jungle. It was pitch black outdoors when he looked outside the gates of the prism. A mess he could not clean up distracted his grandmother as he crept into the halls of the corridor. The walls were a sky blue and the floors a pacific white. Evading the motion-sensing sentries that towered above him, which at the time reminded him of gigantic laser-tailed robotic dinosaurs, he arrived at two large black doors with brass outlines. The sentries' movements centered on his position. Their red laser-light-emitting lens and drooping, raptorlike metallic head terrified him, causing him to back against the walls. It was purely coincidence that the gates opened, and he bravely stumbled outside. The wind howled wildly. Yet he was unable to feel it. It could have been his first viewing of the opaque sky littered with bright stars that numbed his senses had he been a less curious child.

His schoolmates could not believe it when he showed them the rusted piece of what they believed to be a spacecraft. It wasn't the tail end of the buried spacecraft. He broke off a midsize piece from the first aircraft he could find with a powerful tug, and instantly, large spotlights beamed on him. There were rumors of a child's shadow being seen outside the prism complex that night, and they helped substantiate his story. His boldness and ability to leave the prism would have been a remarkable feat for anyone to accomplish. He became instantly popular in all social spheres, and even older youths remembered him.

Of course, he was questioned about the incident by two officials, but his late great-grandfather's reputation favored him greatly. A legendary warrior in the ranks of the military foreshadowed his destiny. Truly, his lineage was strong; but not understanding his ancestor's great accomplishments, he did not speak of it. The officials gave him a light warning about staying indoors, being careful to not accuse him of anything. As they left, his fearless defender transformed herself into his merciless accuser.

He was enrolled in a semicommunal school and given many extracurricular chores, such as martial arts, kickboxing, and sword mastery. After two years, he was quickly dropped from the programs, with the instructors stating his lack of obedience as the reason for his dismissal, which was true to some extent. Their real reasons, however, were that they feared his potential and lack of obedience. He was too strong for his age, and they felt angered being unable to truly defend themselves. After this incident, he was inwardly devastated and disinterested in pursuing postsecondary studies or anything related to the art of combat and advanced arts, which would have resulted in his graduation as a special operative or intelligence agent. Timothy hated the system bitterly for the remaining months and ended his tenure in school at his earliest opportunity, which led to his present stagnation and boredom.

Many of his childhood friends graduated from their various elementary and postsecondary studies, never breaking ties completely with their legendary friend. Among those who remembered him were outpost guardsmen, who gladly invited him to various events and even to accompany them to their posts at night. His trips into the dense dark jungle brought many revelations. There in the jungle, he got to hone his abilities. He sparred with his friends, who marveled at his strength and agility but more so at his ability to mysteriously form fire in his open hands. In the jungle, he was also exposed to various social herbs. He wasn't interested with the herbs themselves, only their effects and the satisfaction it gave him and his friends. The effects of the drugs were compulsive and liberating.

The dangers of the jungle would have stayed hidden from him had the group's pulse-emitting device not malfunctioned. "That night was crazy," he said to himself, remembering it vividly. Within less than a minute, huge insects descended on them. Luckily for his friends, who were then untrained in the art of combat, the youth was a quasi-expert in martial arts; and combined with his abilities, he was a lethal weapon. The insects were quickly crushed and dismembered. Walls of fire deterred the poisonous ones from coming out of their cool borrows. Nevertheless, the group fled back to the safety of the prism.

He left the lavatory cleansed by a needed shower. Entering his messy but orderly room, he sorted through his accoutrements. Upon placing his last and most prized possession in his green inner coat, he reflected briefly. After saving his friends from the large bugs, his courage received much gratitude over the following nights. Friends and acquaintances pitched in and used their welding and technological expertise to create a very professional-looking sword. Forged from rare silver metals, the vertically double-edged sword blurred with heat when activated. The point between the handle and the sword's blade glowed a flaming red.

Interrupted from his thoughts, he became uneasy. A serious voice greeted the heavy-stepping men at the entrance to the apartment. The footsteps of many loud feet approached him. *Do they have to send so many of them?* Timothy thought, thinking that his grandmother must have warned them that he was dangerous. His room opened slowly, and in walked several armed guards.

"Fri—" The guard stopped himself abruptly. "Timothy Ang, you have been ordered to leave these premises by the primary resident," said that guard closest to the door, stumbling in speech beneath the robotic tone of his black helmet.

Light steel-toed boots shone. The three guards were in full battle gear. Their reflective black suits displayed their serial ranks on the left of their breastplates: two sergeants and a second lieutenant. Their helmeted heads, awkwardly made uneven by their headsets, were complemented by the metal-satin material used to hold their utility belts, which blended nicely with the many devices they held. He had seen them before. Timothy thought for a second that the guard was about to call him by his nickname, but the initial panic of the situation had deafened him.

"Furthermore," the guard continued, "you have been accused of leaving the prism structure. You are aware that is a punishable offensive?" said the guard in a false tone.

"Yes," he said slowly, unafraid, his face visibly obscured upon realizing that the guard had a very fake tone. For a split second, he heard a stifled laugh and looked in the direction of the source but was distracted by the other guard.

"I'm going to have to ask you to please come with us."

Correct arrest procedures were followed. Timothy was now shackled. The guards led him outside the apartment, and as he was led away, Frior—Timothy's nickname—watched his grandmother with intelligent hatred. Her stature was bold. Standing in the near center of the room, her eyes shifted slightly, avoiding his stare, with her exercise equipment still on. Casually, she walked over to the center of the interior and then went to sit at a beautiful sun table, turning her back on him. She began to eat her oatmeal cereal.

The youth was ordered to stand on a boxy-wheeled platform outside the apartment. Restrained bearishly, his arms and legs went numb by the tap of a long flat-handled object. As he was transported through the corridor and around the corner to the transport devices, he noticed the many spectators in the hallway. He was quickly loaded onto the center of the transport device, which was the largest. As it was activated, it moved downward, descending over sixty levels. The device stopped, and he was wheeled into a military zone. It was surprisingly empty. It was much more spacious than he had first believed. It had many red and black seats and offices behind a semicomplete dark-wood-colored metallic wall that was behind a hall accessible by a broad gray-stepped staircase.

He looked up at the guards, puzzled, as his reflection stared back at him in their visors. Laughter ensued. One of the guards fell against the steel wall and began laughing. "What's so funny!" yelled the youth after uttering curses.

"Tim, we're sorry we had to do that." The guard closest to him chuckled as he wheeled him from the transport device.

"No, I don't believe it. Really? You guys," the youth said in dismay and swore again in excitement.

"You are so damn lucky that I was on duty this morning at the operation bay," the guard to the left said. "I got promoted to lieutenant last week."

"No way. Great news. Sweet, man. Lieutenant, eh? How come you don't look any different from the rest of them?"

"I get to choose my own uniform color from black, white, red, or blue. And yes, I still have better armor selections."

As they continued to talk, several other low-ranking soldiers entered the military zone, walking past them in similar orange-colored uniforms, unbothered.

"Yeah, buddy called us to help book you."

"You should have heard that bitch." The guard to the right laughed and continued, "She was all, like, 'I want this secondary resident removed from my residence because he's on drugs, and he's been out of the facility.'" He mimicked the elderly woman's voice. "And when I asked her if she could prove it, she got so mad and started mentioning how much credits she had access to and why she could destroy my life if I didn't take her complaint seriously. 'I was off doing my morning exercises at the senior facility, and I returned to find him covered in mud. There's no mud permitted in this prism. I've lived here for years.' And when she told us she thought you were under the influence, she just lost it." The guard laughed, followed by the other guards. "How do you make someone that mad at you?"

"That's not that funny," the youth said. "She seems 'serious,' the word she keeps using, very serious this time. It's never gone this far before. Okay, I still can't move, guys." The guard quickly neutralized the earlier effect by using the other side of the flat-handled object.

"All right, so what happens now?" inquired Timothy.

"Unfortunately, you're going to have to stay a few nights in confines," a guard said remorsefully.

"Really? No fucking way," Frior said, not asking a question. "Don't joke about that."

"No, of course not. I was thinking that, since you're almost an official adult, you should join the force," the lieutenant said.

"I don't understand. Won't you get into trouble?" asked Frior, rotating his arms and stretching madly.

"Nope, no one's going to know about this except us. And you're in luck because today we're going on our first unsupervised reconnaissance mission. There's a brood of bugs getting too close to the complex," explained the guard.

"Won't someone see me? I can't stay unseen for too long."

"Nah, you won't have to do that. I have a suit for you."

"Is it your old one? Tell me it's not."

"Maybe you'll learn something new about yourself," a friendly high-pitched voice said.

Turning around to identify the familiar voice, the group exhaled sighs of relief, and Frior saw his favorite person. Snow was suited up head to toe in ever-white battle gear. Even without army gear, it was tacit that she was a worthy lieutenant. The group greeted her with a smile, screams, and a few waves. "We're leaving soon, so stop playing around," she said, jumping down the flight of stairs and joining them. "I know all about it. I'm not objecting to anything. You scamps are in luck. We should have fun today. I'm always the kind and restless type."

"Thank you," Frior exulted. "Thank you so much."

"Snow, no way, white today? Very nice. It suits you."

"Thank you, Lieutenant, but it's my show today. I'm of equal ranking with you now, sexy. That should make you happy? Are we going to talk more or get to work anytime soon?" Snow questioned sassily.

Frior was roughly suited up. The young lieutenant was prideful when it came to time and did not object to or dissuade Frior's petition to join the excursion. After unsuccessfully trying to convince him that he should have stayed in confines or returned to his grandmother and rebuking many flirtations, she became outwardly indifferent about the issue.

As they got ready to leave, an urgent message came into the nearest console. The operator forwarded the message. The lieutenant received it from his headset. "It's your grandma," Snow said loudly, extending the syllables in her sentence. "She said to let you go tomorrow morning. She's looking out for you."

"I think I'll still be here next month. Forget tomorrow morning," he said ungratefully, hiding his relief. He knew she was a strict woman, but she cared for him.

Arriving by airship to the location of the hive, Frior realized how uncomfortable he was in the battle suit. It was not a perfect fit, but he wasn't going to complain about it. The group received their objectives to plant the subcharges five hundred feet or about fifty meters in the insect's hive and transmit its coordinates to the nearest satellite. They huddled together and chose their weapons carefully from the combat cases. Frior had a short lesson on how to use the weapons. The well-modeled gunlike weapons they selected were powered by solar energy and simply emitted highly concentrated light energy accompanied by metal bullets. Snow showed him how to target and amp his shields and reminded him to watch his footing.

As they ventured closer to the large opening at the center of the dry hill, the sun blazed down on visible details of the small mountainside. The heat waves moved across the dry plain as they reached their target. Insects swiftly moved toward the hill and descended into the opening. Frior was baffled at the sight.

Insects flew past them as they walked onward. At the bottom of what had appeared to be a hill was the flying anthill. Peering down into the opening, they saw thousands of deer-sized insects moving swiftly; and almost on cue, a multitude flew out of the cavern. The air was then filled with the sound of large agitated flying monsters. They were, at the most, five feet in diameter when in flight, which was big for their menial duties, but their structure was formidable. Their exoskeletons were dark brown and near black in appearance, and they were wasplike as they did have long sharp, protruding stingers. The insects had narrow foreheads, upon which were mounted red-tinted eyes, which communicated directly with the queen. These insects were weaponized by the invading alien forces during the war that raged on Darth. They seemed hardworking and docile at first glance, but their engineering was purposed to destroy, and given too much leeway, they would inhabit the entire planet.

Frior's focus drew away from their insidious appearances. Some of the bugs were more mature than the others. Collectively, they were great in number, far greater than the Darforian and Harforian population of Darth. Sunlight that flooded into the cavern was constantly interrupted by the movement of the bugs.

The silence of the troopers was broken by bellicosity. The white-suited woman jumped into the cavern, landing catlike in the outer ledge. Along the utmost ledge, the others soon followed. The long wasplike insects were riled. They slammed into the intruders. They were incited. The humming, buzzing, and scraping were deafening. The insects scraped their suits mercilessly with their stingers before being subdued by the powerful weaponry. Frior felt zero feelings of regret about defending himself. The troopers responded with powerful weapon fire. The bugs went to pieces at the impact, and the noise caused a surge of movement from the bottom of the cavern. They did not ooze blood as one would expect when blasted by high-powered weapons because of the intense heat the weapons emitted.

"Come on!" yelled a soldier.

"Let's move to the bottom of the cavern and set the charges," one of the troopers said.

They quickly extended their grappling devices, securely attaching them to the walls of the cavern and descending the ropes. Frior was completely unaware of how to perform that spectacle and was left to face the brood of wasplike creatures alone. They stung him repeatedly, and it took him almost forever to react as if he was anticipating pain.

"Forget about aiming! Just shoot and get down here!" a voice of ecstasy screamed. "And you better not hit us, newb!"

Frior did as he was instructed and attempted to descend the rope of one of the grapples his friends had used. Unfortunately, his vision was obscured by the flying terrors while in his haste, and he slipped off the ledge, landing on the ground rather softly in a mess of wet dirt and arthropods. His friends looked down on him and yelled praises. Having fallen ten stories to rocky and muddy dark depths, he slowly stood up feeling heavier than usual. Realizing that his abilities were the only reason he survived the fall uninjured, he was angry. His friends had not warned him of the danger, or so he thought.

The air was denser with angered insects. They scraped against the suit of the trooper by multiples of five and fell by threes. Frior was not used to this type of combat. The insects gathered around the junior on every side. A loud, explosive noise filled the cavern as sparks emitted from Frior's suit. The troopers on the upper level looked down at the source of the smoke. They descended to meet Frior as he swung heated fists in a flurry of movements, killing many of the insects.

"We're only ninety feet down," an urgent voice said.

"What's happening with you?" Snow said, looking around and immobilizing the insects that swarmed above her and then proceeding to help Frior.

"Oh, sorry," she said casually as her weapon misfired, hitting the rookie in the midsection, and her head turned to view her team descending another fifty feet.

The suit remained undamaged at the site of impact, but Frior felt the pain. She carefully approached him, mindful of the insects, and observed his molten hand gear. There was still much smoke in the air and a noxious, toxic smell. Frior's suit was literally melting. "Dude, how am I going to explain how your suit is that melted?"

Frior became anxious. His frustration was understandable. His suit was too tight, and his chest now stung like a real bug bit. Snow carefully came over, exchanging encouraging and reassuring glances with him. Frior's hands were now free of the armored gloves, which had melted away, and surrounded by a strange heat wave. He pointed his hands toward the locus of the hive, and two large reddish-white flames erupted from his palms. The cavern was instantly illuminated by the flaming insects, which flew for a moment and fell acidly to the ground. The team was perplexed by the sight of the uncountable flaming insects and, at the same time, by the realization that their young understudy—the rookie, Frior—would surpass them both in skill and ability eventually.

Dusk had almost fallen before the remaining four hundred or so feet were aberrantly achieved and the location of the hive transmitted to the satellites. They got the queen potentially. Instantly and with warning, the troopers disappeared and reappeared on the outskirts of the prism structure. Almost immediately, they removed their helmets, desperate for fresh, clean air. The most experienced warrior felt a strong feeling of familiarity and pointed his hands up at the sky, with his helmet returning to his head without palpable cause.

Incipiently, four circular balls of light entered the atmosphere. The paths of the objects in the sky led directly to the hive and heavily impacted the site, instantly causing a mild tremor that intensified. A bright, blinding blue light turned near dusk to dawn, and waves of radiation swept over the surrounding area nearest to the former anthill. The shadows of trees and all those outside fell on the western side of the windowless prism. Frior looked around at the three soldiers who cursed themselves for their momentary blindness. Having viewed the entire event, wide eyed with awe, he lowered his hands to reclaim his fallen helmet.

CHAPTER III

OUT OF OBSCURITY

During the past three months, Cassandra became very comfortable in performing the duties of her new job as a scientist, despite the arduous nightly trips to the subbasement. Her day began early and ended in the late afternoon, giving her plenty of time to train and rest adequately. Her workstation was only a three-minute stroll from her condominium suite.

She had never had such comfortable and fashionable living quarters. The layout of the condominium was open and very livable. The condo had three rooms, a gold-carpeted living room, light-brown-tiled kitchen, a bathroom, and a fully stocked office. Her office had a view of the east corridors and the low-gravity rink. The condo came with daily laundry maids and hourly chefs; she preferred her 1701 hours chef.

After weeks of dismissing glances and weak social skills, she finally mustered the courage to invite the chef to stay and eat with her. He wasn't the most handsome person, but the way he prepared her meals stood out among the rest. He was a young, twentysomething man with perfectly trimmed light red hair and eyebrows, expressive forehead, and midhigh cheekbones. His nose was curved from the side view and directly above a well-shaven triangular-like chin and large mouth. What really amused her about him was his angelic smile, which wrinkled his narrow eyes and revealed a row of straight white teeth and healthy gums.

He joined her with opposition as she had expected. He sat down charmingly to her right side, nearest to the kitchen. He spoke softly to her as she sipped her cold citrus drink and peered toward him. He congratulated her repeatedly on her academic achievements, which led to her present position. His name was West. He had a full neck with a very visible "Johnny's apple" or voice box. His voice was strong and entertaining as he spoke of his day unquestioned.

As the conversation grew more personal, he informed her that the vision in his left eye had recently been impaired because of a terrible workplace accident. He told his true story with utter acceptance. "And just as I sliced into the pepper, it exploded," he said. "A piece of the core hit me right in my left cornea." West's head nodded slowly.

Cassandra tried not to laugh. His white chef robe was still very clean, despite his workday starting early, and he still had other clients to see. Today he wore a green-and-white wool turtleneck underneath his chef robe, but overall, his style was acceptable. The way his brown eyes gleamed made her feel fulfilled.

"I've tried to book an appointment for months now, but I'm always preparing someone's meal, cleaning it up, or throwing it out," he continued.

"Those new synthetic peppers are very dangerous. Let me see your eye," she said, sounding empathic. Her left hand moved over, touching the side of his smooth face as she stared into his blue eyes, eventually focusing on this left eye. Her vision was beyond excellent. She could see his clear, veinless eyes. Directing her attention to his irritated cornea, surprise appeared on her expression.

"Wow," he said. Her gaze remained transfixed on his eye. "Your hands are cool and refreshing, and this place it pretty warm." It was a lie; he thought her hands were much too cold.

"Now, West, you shouldn't wait too long to get that looked at. I've been looking under microscopes so long my eyes have become one," she boasted, causing him to smile.

"You didn't even have to violate my personal space. You really know how to look after people," he said as her cool hand left his face. They chuckled at the rapport they shared.

"Put some ice on it tonight and see a doctor as soon as you can," she said, picking up her black messaging device from the white table. "Send this serial number before five tomorrow, okay?" The man transmitted the number to his own blue messaging device.

"Thank you. I will." He then realized the conflict. "I'll find the time to get it looked at. I just started working this job. It's too soon to be missing days," West said unselfishly.

"Yes, you can. It's not a problem for me if you miss a few days to sort yourself out with that eye. I won't be here tomorrow anyway, and my friend Dr. Aloe, we studied medicine together. She's a good eye specialist. She'll have your eye fixed in half an hour tops."

"Gee, thanks. I don't know many doctors that aren't booked. Where are you going?"

"I'll be off working overtime," she lied.

"You don't have any incentive to do that," he said, smiling. "Your apartment is as beautiful as you are."

"Thanks, West. That's so sweet of you. I love my work. I try decorating when I have time. The cleaners are thorough. I love my work. I'm not a scientist too because I want the fame or riches. I want to help other people. I'll be working for my personal development. You see, I'm trying to submit a new theory I and several colleagues have been working on. I've started the work on it three years ago."

"Ah, a three-year-old masterpiece. What's it about?" He got up to retrieve a new dish from the kitchen.

"Stress on biological beings," she said, stopping for a moment to think.

He returned with a huge bowl of colorful salad and a dessert plate with a soft, moist piece of chocolate cake. "Well, I'm all ears.

We have lots of time. Please tell me more," he said with a small grin.

"You are actually interested in my work. I didn't think you were at first because everything has been all about you for the past hour," she said, surprised at his genuine interest. She did not like moist cake and quickly solidified the dessert as she ate her salad.

"You're a biologist and a chemist. I can't help it if I want to listen to Ms. Forty-Four out of Seven Hundred in IQ among This Year's Scientists about her newest theory before it's presented to the scientific community."

"How did you know that? You must have read it somewhere."

"I take an interest in all my clients. I stay informed."

"Okay, let me continue then. My hypothesis is that when organisms are placed under a high level of stress, after trying to face the problem on the only level they know of, which of course is the physical level, and they fail to alleviate the stress, they have to retreat past their primal state to a deeper place within themselves."

Stunned by her intellect, he said slowly, "Whoa, that's an interesting concept. I'm impressed, but tell me more about this place."

"Okay, well, how I see it is more of an origin point of all life-forms. It is something that pertains to consciousness and what it means to be a living organism. And when considering our similar designs, it's obvious that this deeper place is common to all forms of life. After struggling to change their environment and behavior, they eventually decide to change themselves by altering their behavior, genetic makeup, or energy. They themselves are not the catalyst of the transformation but through a process I can only describe as an upgrade phenomenon."

"So basically, you think the change or changes happen to the present generation or single organism—the one that underwent the stressful encounters, not the previous generation—and in turn, the behavioral or genetic changes are passed via some unknown power to their descendants?"

"Yes, almost, exactly. I knew you were a smart guy. That's what my research team and I are setting out to prove."

"How would you support your theory?"

"That's the thing. I'm much more interested in the theory for its theoretical and philosophical values than how plausible it is, not that I think it's impossible to support it soundly. I know what you're thinking because I know the factual proof will be difficult to find and explore, but if I was focusing on factual proof, I'd start with the insects infesting the lands of the southern prisms. It's a highly complex theory. West, I take my research seriously. I wouldn't divulge too much."

"Fascinating. You have a rare mind. You have an exceptional mind." He smirked, and she couldn't help but smile too.

For the first time in years, she felt truly loved by a stranger. The conversation ended when West noticed the time, quickly gathered his culinary tools, and swiftly left the newly made home after promising to visit the eye specialist. Cassandra felt an emotion she had not felt in a long time for and from a stranger.

After finishing her frozen cake, she retired to her luxurious white bed. She felt male attention before but not quite like this. Cassandra was reminded by a direct audiovisual prompt on her messaging device that her newly engaged half brother promised to schedule a date for their excursion outside the northern prism. She knew Alex, but she didn't know everything about him. His mind was a chaotic place like most, full of wants and contradictions. She truly felt at ease not having to read West's mind, but her unwillingness to move the conversation to something more romantic or carnal scared her. Tomorrow she planned to train all afternoon, requesting an early dismissal for the day a week before in advance.

Her three months at work drained her emotionally. Her sleek black lab coat and usually matching flat shoes made her look stylish and drew much attention. She did not work alone. Seven coworkers arrived to work two hours after she left, and eight arrived when she came in the morning. Cassandra was gearing up to be the lead scientist in her unit. She conversed with her older coworkers easily. The coworkers who were closer to her age envied her. Years before, they heard all about her during their studies and after their graduation. They congratulated her half-heartedly at first, but after realizing her insight, they quickly stopped their attempts to belittle her and instead chose to avoid her work area. They were all persons well accomplished in their various fields.

Her individual tasks at the laboratories were simple: unifying vaccines for people, sequencing amino acids, and testing cosmetics on synthetic skin. Managing her schedule became very difficult with the intense training schedule. Her father was not only protective but also a hard-to-please coach. Her training regimen included lifting heavy weights, running for fifty minutes in a hyperbolic or gravity chamber, and sparring with unarmed outdated prototypes known as Gunner 8 robots. They shot blank, fast-moving projectiles at her that left her hurt but otherwise uninjured whenever she got careless.

One night her father met her in her condominium suite. He congratulated her on her ideal, picture-perfect condominium and her position of leadership in her workplace. The man was quite youthful for his old age. His hair was jet black like hers with lines of gray. He had narrow hazel eyes under large rectangular eyebrows and large boxy lips that were supported by a square recently shaped gray-bearded chin. He moved confidently and, combined with his military uniform, commanded respect. His unwrinkled skin, lightly tanned complexion, and dominant and perfectly centered nose challenged paper age. She greeted him with a hug upon closing her door. "Where's my 1200 chef?" she joked.

"You don't need strangers cooking for you. Next thing you know, they're talking to you and sleeping with you. You're all knocked up and paying them child support."

"Yeah, sounds romantic."

"I brought you something you'll like," he said, placing a blue box on the styled white table as he marched into the kitchen to retrieve some utensils. His voice was fatherly. "You'll like it. It's roasted onions with bright yellow chickpeas. Us military folks have it all the time." The man sat down to start the meal without waiting for her to be fully seated.

"I'm not a soldier. But I am hungry. I'll try some just because I'm curious," she said skeptically.

"That's a good girl," he said, not meaning anything belittling, but she still stared at him intently as she took her first bite of the surprisingly delicious meal. She could not help noticing his brown leather overcoat snug behind him and the light-brown sleeved shirt he wore under it. His status was pronounced by stars and symbols and read "High director of intelligence and operations" in short form. "Have you met anyone yet?"

"Dad?" she said, taken by surprise. "Please don't ask me that." He was one of the few people who could surprise her.

"With all the training you've been doing, you should be able to control yourself. I just want you to be happy and get something out of life."

"If you must know, no. No, I haven't. I'm focused on my work for now."

"Good. That's good to hear. Don't settle. I'm proud of you."

"I did make some new friends," she said, describing West to her father in detail; and after about four minutes of conversation about the chef, he interrupted her.

"You shouldn't be telling everyone your ideas," he told her with concern.

"I know, but I really trust him. He's candid and professional."

"Well, this topic is almost exactly what I came to discuss." He looked at her sternly. "I want you to change your command code for the subbasement to a nickname of some sort by next week. I know this may seem hard for you to understand, but not everyone in my position will value your uniqueness like I have and—" She stopped him from finishing by placing her hand on his hand.

"I know. I was thinking of changing it to something less traceable also, but I didn't know how to tell you over the transmission network."

"You don't have to show it to me. Your training is your responsibility now. You're a smart young woman. I also have to tell you something you don't already know and haven't thought about," he retorted.

31

"What?" she questioned with great concern.

"I'm leaving the planet in a few weeks."

"What? Leaving the planet?" she said, trying not to scream. "You're leaving the planet. Have you left Darth before?"

"Yes, I've been assigned a special mission."

"I'm coming with you. I'm strong enough. I've mastered all my abilities. I can do this," she said, looking at his sanctioning face. "You do want me to come along?"

"No. It's not appropriate for two family members to go on. Family members aren't allowed on these kinds of missions."

"No way. You can't leave now. Can't someone else go in your place? You've been in the force for over fifty years. You're indispensable. I don't see why they would send you on a dead-end mission."

"Cassandra, I'm not young. I'm gathering years, and no one in the force is indispensable. You know better than that."

"Yes, I do. I understand, but I don't understand entirely. You're the only one that can go, aren't you? When are you coming back?" she asked eagerly, but silence filled the room.

"A month from now," he said, sounding truthful.

"Have you told Alex you might miss his wedding? You know, he'll be devastated. He won't wear it on his sleeve, but he'll carry it like a red flag. You're the only one we really have. You're the only one I have. And I don't know if he could take losing you. I don't know if I could take losing you."

"I've raised you both well. You'll manage without me for a few weeks, a year, yes, even a lifetime. I'll be back sooner than you think. I don't have a choice. These things, they don't change. You'll make me proud."

"Tell me when you're leaving and the second you come back, okay?"

"Done. However, what I've told you is confidential, and don't tell Alex. I don't like too many people knowing where I am or where I'm about to go."

Their conversation ended soon after the meal did. When she was distracted putting away the utensils and setting aside her laboratory notes, he placed a small boxlike device underneath her table as he put on his coat. They exchanged goodbyes, and she encouraged him to talk to Alex before his departure.

"Don't forget to train. I've seen what you're capable of. You still need some refining, but you're a powerful force to be reckoned with. It's not a matter of trying to get better. It's actually more about being your best" were his last words that day.

She spent the evening developing a code name that would strengthen her and keep her identity a secret. "Psyy," she finally decided. The name was soft sounding and strong at the same time. It was not connected to her by any means, and few meddlers would take interest in viewing the training room while she was training and discover the deactivated sensor array.

The following day, she decided to find common ground with her coworkers. Biological mysteries were the most favored subjects to discuss in the office, and many calm arguments resulted from uncompromising viewpoints. Cassandra got into one such argument on her fourth week on the job. She couldn't believe that most of her colleagues did not believe in a singular Designer. She, at first, believed that sharing her faith at the workplace would help break the ice between her and a more experienced younger colleague she decided to mentor as they worked on a gigantic world-simulating container, and it did.

The world simulator was made up of several glass chambers against the wall at the farthest east corner of the laboratory. It had a chamber that condensation formed by mixing water and other gases together. It fed into an open chamber located beneath a bright, heated light source. The chamber was composed of soil samples and housed a few tiny living specimens never placed in the chamber. A chamber of water was below it, attached in three places to the soil chamber by one hole in the top center and two tubes at both sides of the upper chamber. The gas chamber was connected to a liquid chamber and had powerful hydraulic pumps on either side of it. When the pumps were activated, they pushed the air from the first chamber into the second, causing liquids to be pushed up into the soil chamber from all three entrances. The water was evaporated by the strong light source, and steam filled the sky of the soil chamber. The world simulator was over 105 years old, and the soil chamber was covered with small greenish microbes and single-celled organisms. The preliminary design confirmed, with a high degree of assurance, that it was airtight and did not contain any known living contaminants on its construction.

"Don't you see how everything looks similar on the cellular level? It's so ordered in its complexity." She had a soothing deep work voice. "I doubt life would exist on so few levels if it wasn't. Something enjoys focusing its attention on us, watching us, and the lives around us progress and evolve. We're obviously some form of great pride and amusement," she honestly said, and her colleague smiled, agreeing with undistracted interest.

"What?" The cheeriness was killed. "The nonsense is too much. Ms. Vyers, why are you filling that girl's head with bullshit?" one colleague said in the semicrowded laboratory.

"I'm just telling her about the possible existence of one powerful entity that created—"

"I'd stop that now if I was you," the dim-eyed scientist working in the back of the laboratory misspoke. "Some scientists lose their right to practice sharing those views."

"He's right, dear, you should have picked philosophy if you wanted to spend your day talking about fiction. It's just inappropriate to go on like that," said an elderly biochemist sitting a few chairs beside her.

"Don't spread your beliefs here. This is a place for fact and unquestionable reasoning," said a stern voice.

"Okay, maybe I shouldn't, but you just closed your mouths, and if you can invidiously close your mouths, how come you'd also assume that someone or something designed everything and controls the universe?" she said, unheated, stopping herself from quieting the room cognitively. She had only said it to make them ponder the thought and to dismiss them from her private discussion, but some were deeply offended.

She received a stern warning in the form of a message the following morning from the Department of Scientific Research's ethics commissioner, who warned her to end her harassment of her coworkers and to respect the beliefs of others. Responding professionally, she called her father and explained the incident to avoid him from hearing about it from secondary sources. Unknown to her, on the same day she received the complaint, while the chubby elderly man was at a distance, the ethics commissioner would visit her workplace unannounced.

Her research team moved frantically to complete the timely recreation of annual vaccines, and in walked the red-suited, gray-collared, black-shoed, white-haired commissioner. He halted their progress and apologized to her for what seemed to be half an hour for a regrettable very big misunderstanding. He offered her time off work and other bonuses, which she refused, but she told him what she really wanted: the deadline for the annual vaccines moved to the end of the following week. Their conversation was audible to everyone present, and her colleagues cheered her on endlessly because she gave them a valid excuse for completing the impractically scheduled vaccines at a comfortably workable pace. Her status was now unshakable, and this allowed her to share her views moderately. Cassandra reminded herself, as she considered to let down her guard, not to mistake praise for friendship and knew that it would take more testing to bestow that title.

Night fell on the prism complex, and the corridors dimmed. Psyy looked down from her suite at the quiet place and decided that she could wait no longer to continue her training. Gathering her various belongings and putting on her light-purple velvet top with matching dark blue skirt, she left her condo carrying a big dark green bag. She yawned tiredly. Her purplish-blue heels made no noise as she moved down toward the subbasement. The dark walls of the corridor were dimmed, and she looked at bluish-white lights mounted on the white doorways. She was in an upscale part of the prism as the white-potted greenery suggested. Her neighbors were athletes, actors, teachers, and nurses; but the occupants of these gold-handled units were defense lawyers, surgeons, inventors, mechanics, and technicians.

She finally reached the transport bay and set her destination. The subbasement took a while to reach, and slowly, she watched the levels go by in the transport device. She exited and walked down yet another light-blue flat-tiled corridor. Psyy saw several armed sentries move by her, undisturbed, as they detected her access cards. She was in a military zone heavily traveled.

Four squadrons of newly trained soldiers walked past her in plain clothes. She could see the sweat that glistened on their faces. She could tell them by their inability to contain their anxious thoughts, having passed a midnight assessment and being newly promoted. They noticed her, and she broke her longtime rule of not waving at strange men. Screams and whistles echoed behind her; she couldn't decide whether she completely hated the way she was treated.

She finally grew tired of the repeated scenery just as she came into view of the giant door to what was known as the battle complex. She walked toward the light-blue door and swiped her access card in the slot to its left. The door opened slowly, raising into the ceiling. She entered the large room, and the door closed slowly behind her. The room had dark blue carpeting and was enclosed by multiple windows that were held together by black bars. She peered down ten meters through the windows into a midsize empty, seatless stadium. Psyy scanned it with her mind to confirm that it was, in fact, unoccupied. She sensed something behind her, but when she looked, there was no one.

She walked toward the change rooms and returned five minutes later wearing a loose-fitting bright-blue-and-dark-green full-body military suit, her hair bundled up underneath a matching hood. Her comfortable athletic blue military boots barely suited the outfit. She held a tubelike inactivated weapon. Psyy quickly walked down the spiraling staircase and rapidly opened the doors of the stadium.

Entering the stadium, she walked over to the consoles and locked down the battle complex. She entered her password into the keyboard and changed her display name from CASS Y, a name no one called her, to Psyy. She stretched first and then activated her program. Instantly, the lights dimmed to a deep red. Psyy stepped in the glowing red circle in the middle of the room. The program was beginning.

The gravity of the room intensified by ninety pounds, and her body reacted with a sudden downward movement, from which she jerked and recoiled, collecting herself rapidly. Four walls to the side of the stadium opened, and in walked nine raptorlike red-eyed robots with hooked claws. "An upgrade," she said. "That's no surprise." Her father must have replaced the badly mangled robots with brand-new ones. She concentrated, preparing herself for an intense workout. It was always hard for her to gather her strength and suppress her fears.

A fierce sound filled the room as a light-blue corona surrounded her body and began to intensify. Her energy field was building. The robots galloped toward her on both sides. The black lustrous robots were six feet tall, leaning in, and their bladelike, movable claws pointed downward. The two that took her head-on were ferocious. Bright laser light left the robots' eye-shaped right structure, deflecting and de-energizing as they landed on the blue energy field that surrounded her body. Deep red laser lines originating from their eyes went over her chest and legs.

Psyy leaped into the air and spun around, her leg fully extended. She landed a critical blow to the robot nearest her, and its fragile head ripped off its shoulder, causing sparks. Her breathing increased. Having landed perfectly, she directed her left hand in the direction of the robot to the left that charged her and her right hand to the ground. The dark jaws of the robot were strong and led its charge. A powerful blue blast of liquidizing light left her hand and struck the robot in the face, fusing its jaws together with a thick layer of dry ice. The robot was still in full motion, and she ducked as it reached her. She moved her right hand up, grabbing the robot under its arm, securing its broad metallic neck in a viselike grip. She bent her knees in perfect form, pulling its upper body down with her and causing its legs to raise off the floor. She took only two seconds to prepare herself before she threw it across the room. It electrified as it scraped against the gravity-dense room.

Quickly, Psyy hit the robot behind her, and it broke to pieces as it slid into the wall. She then lifted the robot that began to target her as she was hit with an array of distracting laser fire. She was a telekinetic ice queen. The disco ball effect irritated and distracted her, causing the robot that her mind held to fall to the ground, uninjured, with a clang. She ducked and rolled across the ground to the robot in the corner of the stadium. The unending flash of red light suggested that a high level of danger existed. She exhaled.

Standing up, she uppercut the robot she was nearest to. The powerful light intensified around her fist, and her glowing fist traveled upward, impacting the midsection of the robot, ripping through its robotic components. Her hand exited just below its left shoulder and grazed the robot's neck in a curved motion. The robot fell, bursting into flames and exploding loudly as its battery exploded. Her heart pounded.

She felt a rush of fierce hot air emanating from another explosion. She had been blown to the side of the room by an exploding projectile that hit her from behind with great force. Her back ribs hurt slightly. After hitting the wall, she stood up, and the corona around her body strengthened. Two more rounded projectiles left the midsection of the raptor robot as its ribs contracted swiftly, and a spray of fast-moving metal spheres hit her, exploding with a sharp sound as they landed against her corona shield. Shaken but unscarred, she lifted her hands together, forming an X; swiped her overlapping arms forward into the air; and fell over from the pull of gravity. Her ankles burned from the heavy gravity and her unbalanced footing. A loud sonic boom filled the room as all the robots walking toward her and the projectiles they launched were pressed against the wall by a forceful blast of air. She hit the floor with a metallic thud. The projectiles exploded, damaging the robots, which were quickly pulled to the ground.

Psyy stood up nearly breathless. She called out to the voice-activated system, "Level 2!" She sounded out of breath. "Second command, lower the gravity by thirty units." The system did not respond verbally, but she knew her orders were obeyed because she could now stand up straighter. The heavy gravity was the only thing that made level 1 challenging.

She quickly moved over to the center of the room as it began to dim red. Level 2 commenced rather quickly. Four shifting floors opened in the floor, and two one-meter spiderlike metallic robots leaped twenty meters in total off the walls to the ceiling. The spiders were well built. They were designed for agility and precision. Psyy lifted herself into the air, defying gravity; formed a ball of blue nitrogenous liquid between her hands; and projected it forcefully at the nearest spider. The spider moved quickly, and the liquid ball mashed against the ceiling, making it spiked with a thick layer of ice.

The spider leaped at her, its front legs pointed. Anticipating a brutal impact, she responded by using telekinesis and spun it around with her mind, dashing it to the floor. It landed hard and awkwardly but quickly leaped to its feet. The two eyelike green structures on its robot head began to glow as a small light-gathering cannon on its back started to retract. Seconds before the cannon completely retracted, the robot was thoroughly frozen to the floor. Ice gleamed in the dim red room.

The second spider took her by surprise with a forceful energy blast. She was disoriented for a moment. Blue light radiated around the room as she stumbled to the ground. Psyy picked herself up higher into the air to gather her bearings and formed several ice spikes that she flung at the spider, shattering its hard exterior as it leaped toward her. She inhaled deeply. Having landed on her with a spark of light, it scraped against her light shield, and sparks flew as its metal exterior created friction against her corona-like energy shield. Her soft epidermis remained untouched as it was veiled with a highly charged subatomic energy. Psyy tried to fling it off, but it kept slicing away at her. It prevented her open hands from touching her face as she attempted to grip its pleated metal back exterior. Its claws were sharp and could have inflicted injuries worth weeks of recovery.

Out of desperation, she descended closer to the ground and was hit again by powerful light energy blasts. She expanded her corona-like force shield into a circular bubblelike sphere that sent the spider flying through the open air and clanging to the floor. She then focused her mind, trying to resist using her tangible strength. A familiar anger and frustration drove her. A bright sphere of gathering light formed in her right palm beneath the shield and quickly left it with a slicing sound, taking energy from the shield as it exited. The blue beam went directly through the spider and continued to travel into the metal floor. The robotic spider burst into pieces. Burnt and molten parts of the spider littered the floor, and a large bubbling crater was visible in the metal floor. The red light that dimmed the room flickered.

She remembered that she was not supposed to use her most primal power while in the battle complex. She felt guilt, and mild anxiety overtook her. It was too powerful. It was a highly concentrated plasma light energy blast capable of breaking molecular bonds on contact, and it injured her too; there was a recoil factor. The plasma energy was extremely hot and scorched her palms. Her ability to create ice was probably nurtured to offset the heat created by the plasma blasts. She formed blue nitrogen liquid in her hands to counter their effects. She tried to use her mental powers to defeat her obstacles, but it seemed only able to slow down the robots, and that tired her. Her unexplainable ability to create ice by liquefying the high concentration of nitrogen gas in the air amused her at times. She could build an entire fortress of ice if she wished.

The spiders were always elusive, and by now, there were seven in the room. She was unduly tired, probably from the unexpected robotic spider landing on her. Three of them pounced on her again after she had let down her energy field. She could not sense the mindless robotic life-forms but was prepared this time. She emitted a pulse of blue and blurred energy simultaneously that took effect a half meter around her chest. The pulse violently knocked the three spiders backward, and they were pulled to the floor before breaching her core perimeter of ineffectiveness. She dropped down, revengefully crushing one robotic spider's exposed belly beneath her feet. Her corona grew brighter and brighter by the moment.

Psyy propelled herself forward, cleaving the spider against the wall with her extended fist. She felt unsatisfied, feeling impressions of its crushed exterior in her fingers beneath her energy field. Then she noticed the ice that she had formed earlier, and it gave her ideas. Her hands emitted more liquid light, shaping it with her mind to a rectangular translucent liquid light as it moved toward the spider in the left half of the stadium. She bent the slowly solidifying liquid into chunks of ice as the spider leaped toward her with an electrified exterior. Abruptly, she stopped the ice in midair and sandwiched the spider between the rough chunks of ice. Holding it firmly with her mind, she emitted another layer of liquid light around the spider, bringing it back to her location. There in the middle of the stadium, she spun it around in her fast-moving orbit as two powerful blasts of light energy hit the strong energy field around her. She hurled the ice-encased spider at the first shooter. The makeshift comet shattered as it impacted the hard floor with a loud, high-pitched note, leaving a long scratch across its surface. She noticed that the spider did not know where to move. She distracted the spider's sensors just long enough to successfully bombard it with sharp-tipped, cometlike objects.

Her heart pounded quickly. The battle complex returned to its proper lighting. She did not complete the level in the allotted ten minutes. She decided to end the program. "End program and begin battle complex repair sequence." She felt somewhat pleased with her controlled performance that night.

She gathered her belongings and sighed, realizing that she never tested her newly designed tubelike weapon. She had been working on the device for about nine months and realized its lethal potentials. In the core of the weapon was a thin strip of powerful crystal-like magnesium that held light energy for long durations of time. It was an object capable of cutting through almost any surface, and she was anxious to test it out on the heavily armored, scorpionlike tank that was lowered from the ceiling when level 6 came. She had beaten level 6 once, and that was when she cheated. She blasted a two-palmed forbidden, concentrated blast of plasma light that ripped through the circuits of the mammoth scorpion robot and shut down the battle complex, alerting the prism and causing her father to make a great deal of explanation. Her disobedience had resulted in the mind occupying changes in gravity and even her hands being tied behind her back during her infant training sessions.

At nearly three in the morning, she reached her condo. She was so tired, and having been absent from the room, she easily identified the strange noises. It beeped slowly. She moved to the kitchen, baffled by the invisible origin of the increasing sound. She looked around frantically but logically. She dropped and placed her right ear to the floor to see if something had been planted in it. She swore out of desperation. As she lifted herself from the floor, she paused, noticing a faint light underneath the white table. She crawled on all fours toward the table and looked up at it cautiously. She exhaled faintly and then laughed. She smiled not from satisfaction but at his mysterious ways. At the bottom of the device, fine, flashing red letters read "Psyy, I've left." How did he know her new name so quickly?

CHAPTER IV

INTO FEAR

The end of another workweek had arrived, and the young lady was very anxious to spend her fixed monthly income. She woke up early in the afternoon after another intense midnight workout. In her black underwear, she left her white-sheeted bed and placed her feet on the lightly heated gold carpet. She walked to the front of her bedroom and opened the door to her walk-in closet. Her condo was plain in decor and spacious. Her bed was in the center of the bedroom. Her room had no windows and a door far to the side.

Admiring her several pairs of thin blue jeans in one corner of the closet and then retrieving a folded white T-shirt, she decided to be less conservative today. She styled her long curled black hair in front of the mirror. She focused on her light blue eyes intently. Her skin was pale and her nose plain, and without her naturally shiny, lustrous black hair in the foreground, she was simple. It would have taken all attention from her face had it not been for her light blue eyes and thin pink lips. She didn't know what to do with her hair this morning.

Reminded by the pores on her nose, she left the bathroom to attend to her face. She brushed her teeth, tongue, and inner cheeks for several minutes in front of the larger bathroom mirror before attending to her face. She washed her hands thoroughly. She rinsed, lathered, rerinsed, dried, and moisturized her smooth visage. Brushing her teeth was the easiest task of the morning because she didn't have to squeeze toothpaste from a tube. A small tubelike plastic packet was inserted in the space between the holding area of the red toothbrush and the base; all she needed to do was apply pressure at the bottom of the toothbrush.

Purse in hand, she left her bedroom. As she was about to leave her condo, a pleasant feeling from earlier entered her mind. She instantly knew he was expecting her to call him. She took off her laced white winter boots and walked back in her living room. Her white T-shirt with blue horizontal stripes matched her blue alligator-skinned jacket and made her fitting jeans pronounced. Her athletic physique was now visible. She was 5'9" and now strangely 170 pounds, a believable figure, which was composed mostly of muscle and an extremely high bone density.

Taking a seat on her red leather couch, she took out her messaging device and entered his ten-digit messaging sequence. She attached a long earpiece that extended from the black messaging device and placed it in her ear. Feeling the effects of a long workout, she threw her legs up into the chair and raised her feet lightly into the air, revealing bleached white socks. A dial tone became audible, and an answering machine forwarded her to an awaiting message. A strong, gruff voice entered her ear.

"Hi, I knew you would call me. I haven't gone to the doctor yet. I have a good reason though." His voice paused as if to yawn or think. "I've been sick for a couple days with the flu. It's hard to breathe. I hope I didn't give it to you," the voice said. Loud dry coughs were heard in the background. "I can't believe I got sick. I'll go get my eye checked after today though. I know I didn't get it from you. My daughter was sick last week. Ah, I know I didn't tell you about her yet. I was going to. I went to visit her and her mother yesterday to see how she was doing because she had the flu and . . . I'll talk to you tomorrow, maybe not tomorrow because I took the day off." His stifled flam cough trailed the last word. "And I can't remember which days. Talk to you soon, and thanks again."

Calmly, she ended the message as the answering machine relayed various options to repeat and save it. "I just wanted him to be a good friend," she reminded herself. She let out a sigh of fatigue. She remembered that she had told him that it was nothing serious. She liked West a lot. He was attractive, and rightfully so, other women would notice him. She assumed he was probably ten years older than her and visited many other locations in the prism complex daily, which gave him ample exposure.

She felt slightly betrayed. He had a daughter. Was she from a previous relationship or marriage? Was he married? She pondered these questions. She regretted not reading his mind entirely and realized that she was only a child to him, if in fact he willfully didn't mention his kid.

Reaching out her hands blindly, she retrieved her purse from the living room carpet and stood for a while. She walked to the door. A sudden sound hit her ear, and she realized her mistake of not turning off her messenger and removing the earpiece. She answered the device. "Hello—"

Her introduction was cut short by an impatient male voice. "Cassandra."

"Alex?"

"Did you know anything about Dad leaving the planet?"

"No. Um . . . yeah, about that . . . didn't he tell you?"

"No, I found out from Sky," he said, sounding upset.

"I told him to tell you."

"Well, he obviously didn't. I just can't understand why I'm always the very last to find out about anything important."

"Alex, stop. He had to go on a mission. It's not the first time he's done this."

"I know. Stop treating me like I'm a child. I'm a grown man. I know it is a dangerous mission, Cassandra. He's traveling to the home world of a barbarian and senile race of beings."

"How did you know that? I don't think we should talk about this right now."

"Yes, yes, we should. Unlike your scientific studies, mine actually reveal some meaningful secrets about the universe."

"Okay, so how much did Sky tell you exactly? Obviously more than enough for you to piece things together. I want to talk to her."

"She's at her office for the morning, getting us approved for the excursion you promised you'd come on. I hope you cancel or change your mind because there're enough liars in this family."

"Oh," she said, trying to brush off his insult. She had regretted not telling Sky to keep military things a secret, but then she remembered something awful.

"Oh no, I'm really sorry," she said remorsefully. "I totally forgot you were planning to ask Sky to marry you next month. I really hope he'll be back in time. I told him to tell you he was leaving, and he couldn't do that. I just don't understand him sometimes."

"It's okay," he replied expressionless. "I wanted a small wedding anyway. Hey, I told you to stop doing that. It's bad of you. I didn't give you a time line."

"Don't be like that. I'm sorry. He'll be back in time. That's what he told me. He's never missed anything that's this important to you. I . . . I think your wedding's very important too. That's why I told him to tell you—"

"So you couldn't tell me?"

"I wanted to." She paused.

The dial tone was heard, and Cassandra was left holding the phone. She listened intently, giving him a chance to rejoin the conversation. He had hung up on her three times so far in her life but not for reasons of this magnitude. Perplexed, she dialed his number, becoming somewhat irritated as the rings drew on. Right now, she had a sparking hatred for men in her mind and decided to confront the real instigator of the conflict. If her father did not want Alex to know he had been sent on a secret mission, his wishes should have been respected.

She grabbed her silver-zippered, blue leather jacket. Setting the door to lock and slamming it, she stormed out of the condo. She walked down the corridor, furious. Fellow pedestrians watched her visibly upset body language and stared intently at her. The society was very high fashioned, except for those in the military. Arms crossed and face reddened, she walked down the corridors. As she approached the transport bay and waited for the long near-rush-hour line to diminish, Cassandra leaned against the nearest woodlike wall and began to think, her eyes transfixed on the floor. The military zone became her destination. There, she hoped that she could access some files on the location of her father and the duration of his mission or perhaps get a hold of Sky and force her to reveal her inside scoop.

She entered the transport device and descended into the subbasement. The silver gates of the transport device opened, and out she walked into the crowded military zone. It was bright but dull with translucent lighting. Fully geared soldiers passed by, moving aimlessly up and down the pathways. She admired their sleek black uniforms and waved half friendly to the four men who watched her in a distempered mood.

She walked into the military zone and entered a room that seemed half empty. She was surprised by how easy it was to enter the soldiers' dressing rooms. She looked around to see if anyone noticed her. She walked toward the doorway surrounded by a dark steel wall. She sensed something faint. Her heart jumped as she was surprised by the mechanized yell of a guard dressed from head to toe in glamorous green military armor. Cassandra was stunned to see a cloaked guard. She didn't know they had them on the northern prism's base and was disappointed with herself for not detecting the female guard sooner.

"Civilian, state your purpose for being in these areas. Since you don't have a reason, I am going to have to ask you to come with me."

At that moment, Psyy felt the fear inside her flutter. She began to slowly move her left hand up into the air. Realizing her evil intentions, the guard responded, "Ah, you know it's me?"

"Sky?"

"You didn't. I can't believe you didn't notice me following you. I saw you move down the transport bay on sublevel 132, which was when I thought I'd follow you."

"You followed me?"

"Yeah, I was just leaving my office upstairs. I was in the singular changing room and decided to leave in stealth and get out of this place quickly. Don't tell anyone I did this, okay? I'll get sanctioned, probably demoted." She laughed loudly beneath the cool suit. "What were you looking for? Were you looking for me? What happened to not being strangers?" She noticed the angry expression on the well-dressed scientist's face. "You seem like you're in a pissy mood today. What's wrong?" Sky said, sounding puzzled behind the mask.

"Alex called me. You told him about the secret mission my father is on," said Cassandra with some hesitance. "And when you did that, you not only broke the strict codes of command within the military but you also destroyed any trust I had in you. I see you're used to that."

"What? Yes, I did. Oh, I did. I told Alex something that was top secret. Yes, I did, and I only told him what I was instructed to. By his father. The high director. I was just as confused as you are right now. If it makes you feel better, I told him not tell you. I knew you would overreact. I thought he understood me."

"This is so typical. I knew you knew my father. Well, Alex told me that you told him that. I guess I should be grateful Alex trusts me more than you. But you've screwed up, not him. He didn't know any better than to call me on a public line. And now every operator in this prism knows of a level 1, top secret military operation. I didn't come here to say hi to you. I came to find out everything you know about me and my father because, frankly, I don't buy your bullshit story about meeting and all the lame excuses. You know about the aliens on Pylon Six, and you know more about me and my family than you're willing to share. Remember the first time we met?"

"Yeah."

"It all makes sense now."

"Ms. Vyers, you're so smart, yet you fail at playing the fool. You're exactly right. I've been aware of your special gifts for quite some time now, before your brother told me how strange you were. But if you must know, I've been working with your father for several years. You see, nothing stays a secret for too long without help. I'm one of the few reasons you aren't in pieces in a dissection chamber, a big reason, if not the big reason. So before you get me any more agitated, I suggest you follow me using your 'secret power' of telepathy, which all Harforians possess," Sky mocked. "Alex is probably sick waiting for me in that land craft, wishing he could go beyond the walls of this prison—I mean, prism. Alex didn't hang up on you. He didn't hang up on you. I hung up."

"Bitch."

"We're going exploring today. And if you do show up, you better show up all happy and cheerful," the metallic-green-armored woman said as she turned around slowly and vanished into subspace as her right shoulder faced Cassandra.

You call me a bitch. I'm going to call you Psyy from now on. It sounds cool and mysterious, a voice echoed in her imagination.

Cassandra's heart was pounding. Her face was now an unhappy color. She should have pounded Sky, messed her up completely. Her light blue eyes moved up and down slowly in confusion. Did she really think that she could exposure Psyy the person? The nerve she had to come out to her so roughly. If she did in fact know of Psyy's powers, she must be a deadly spy and worthy adversary. Was it all innocent, if she was in league with her father, the high director? *A Harforian soldier most definitely*, Psyy concluded. *Probably a half-bred Harforian?*

A strong mental image entered her mind as she saw vividly the location of a light-green figure fainting in and out of light backgrounds. She began to walk in the directions stated. To the highest ground-level floor of the facility, she went by the transport bay. She was beautifully dressed but greatly distressed. Questions went through her mind about the number of people in the military who knew about her condition. She felt so vulnerable now and uneasy in herself. Psyy deeply regretted her confrontation with the armored Sky; her fists tightened. The woman had weapons on her person that could kill her in a split second, if given the right angle.

The perimeter bay is a wide-open dome within the prism complex. It was brightened by sunlight and was filled with many sophisticated land craft. There were about three hundred of them spaced out in a zone of safety throughout the complex. Only twenty of them were in motion at this moment because few were allowed to leave. She watched as the moving vehicles were guided on a track that led to wide tunnel-like exits to the left of the steel-walled structure and entered on the right. The floor was covered with intricate tracks that led to every parked land craft. The land craft were curved in a triangular shape, and the passenger compartment remained open, covered by a glasslike, see-through material. The structure of the land craft was supported by large black, gold, or silver metallic bands that looped around the vehicle twice vertically and once horizontally. They appeared to have little diversity; some appeared slightly clearer and opaque than others, but in terms of size, some were larger by a few meters.

As she moved closer, she noticed a clear and silver banded land craft as she walked over the first row of tracks. The ground was softer than the flooring of the interior of the prism and was well cushioned. She looked up, sensing someone familiar. A mental image entered her mind, leading her to a silver-banned land craft to her right. As she moved toward it, she noticed that the ground beneath her rose slightly. She was now on a track and was in the path of a moving land craft. It did not have on its forward lights. She walked down off the track and looked back as a slow-moving gray land craft slid along the track to an exit tunnel not far from her.

She looked up and noticed a brown-haired man slouched against the driver's seat of a silver-banded land craft, his head on the glass; he looked like he was reading. He turned around and recognized the woman who walked toward him. She waved half-heartedly. He nodded at her, and she looked up with a small smile. He wasn't a telepath, but he noticed her indifference and knew that whatever tension that existed between them was of his doing. He opened the door of the land craft and moved over to the passenger seat. "You actually came. I can't believe you hung up on me."

"Who's telling you this? Sky? Alex, I never hung up on you."

"Yeah? Okay, I'm sorry about this morning. I just don't like arguments and being hung up on. Had the line not been jammed, you would have been justified to end our conversation," he said, his light brown eyes glimmering from the reflection of the sun.

Anger surged through her, but she didn't respond to Alex. She took the time to respond and noticed what he was wearing. His gray, red-lined full-body exercising suit looked comfortable on him. It was zipped up to the top of his neck. She looked intently at the zipper. His features anticipating her next move, she quickly grabbed his zipper, reaching around with her left hand. She zipped it down below his neck.

"It's not that warm," Psyy said before becoming stunned. Her eyes looked questioningly on his exposed neck. Several darkened blemishes covered his lower chin and upper neck.

"Oh my goodness," she said, shaking her head in surprise and disgust.

"You weren't supposed to see those. See, we're not so different. I'm nosy, and you're blatantly intrusive!" shouted Alex as he zipped up his zipper a little less close to his chin than it had been.

"So wow, you must really like her. Ouch. I'm scared. Those things look like they've been on you for weeks."

"Well, I told you, I want to marry her. She's the best girlfriend I've ever had."

"I'm not so sure about that. She knows all about us, me, Dad. I think you should take another year to decide . . ." She couldn't finish her sentence.

"No, I know she told me everything today," he said. "Everything."

Having not finished her first sentence, she noticed and sensed the green figure approaching the car. Alex opened the door and moved over to the back of the land craft, his head nearly touching the ceiling of the vehicle. The woman was still in her best matching green but out of her stealth suit and armor. She wore a green protective bodysuit. Her hair was straight now and long, and goggles were mounted on her head. Her bright turquoise eyes enhanced her facial features. Her dark skin shone.

"Hey, babe," she said to Alex, "you look cold." She sat down in the passenger seat nearest him, her right hand reaching forward to adjust the heat. They kissed passionately and then softly. "Some of us are going to wish we dressed for the cold." She looked at Psyy's blue leather jacket, white T-shirt, and tight blue jeans.

"You know, I don't get cold."

"Darling, what took you so long?"

"I had to go visit my friends at the two communication centers," Sky said, looking quite stern.

"You know people there?" He paused, expecting an answer. "Who don't you know?"

The impatient driver interrupted them, "Alex, I was trying to tell you something important. Maybe we should step outside and talk."

"Why can't you stay here and talk with me?" the bright-eyed woman said, narrowing her eyes at Psyy. Psyy's features changed suddenly as well. She had lost her patience.

"What's happening? I feel dizzy, like . . ." Alex had already fainted as his words trailed off.

"You're going to knock your own brother unconscious. You're too careless to be so endowed."

"I've had enough of you and your attitude," Psyy said, taking off her expensive blue jacket. "Well, I have to say, didn't you mean us, Dad, and I before? 'Cause that's what you should have said."

Sky's head slanted as she stared at Psyy with no fear. As she started the car with a press of the button on Psyy's right, she laughed, and Psyy mimicked her laughter, having realized that she had been listened to earlier. "I'm trying to be nice to you, but you—"

"Shut up. I can't stand your dumb games anymore," Psyy said coldly, turning around to make sure that Alex was still knocked out. "I want to know everything about you right now. What do you know about me and my father, who you supposedly work for? Right now."

"Later."

"No, not later, now. Now!" The car began to move gently forward, turning, guided by the tracks.

"You don't really care about Alex? He could have brain damage from what you just did. You're the reason freaks aren't allowed to live in the prisms. Why else would you turn him off like a toy robot? You must think you're a god, pressing people's buttons on and off like that. I don't think you'd understand yourself either, if you were me."

"You're are an irritating son of a . . ." She recollected her thoughts. She calmly stated, "He's a normal, ordinary, not to say simple but, yes, simple person. He's like me. Alex really wants nothing to do with the limelight of our world, except I'm forced to. Why is he getting mixed up with you? I don't know, but I will find out what you're after."

"You had a choice."

"And I'm honestly tired of this. You have ten seconds to explain yourself before we find out who the stronger hitter is."

"You mean business. Fine, I'm taking us to the ancient ruins of *Patomos*—you know, the ship that is half buried at the summit of Mount Taptoon. I want to uncover a new ship with your help. I deserve to be famous before I go on maternity leave, don't you think? Yes, surprise. So where do I start?"

Fuming, she said, quieted down a little, "Congratulations on your pregnancy, if in fact you are pregnant with my nephew. Start with telling me who you are." She contained her intense anger. The land craft turned right along the track.

"I can do that, but give me a second. I'm not used to using my mouth that much like some girls. My real name is Sky Arvona Nixyeo. I'm not from the surface of this planet. I grew up in space—yes, on the floating palace in the sky."

"The ship of the Harfore."

"Don't interrupt me out loud, please. Thank you. Yes, I'm half Harforian and half Darcon. My father is . . . was your father's . . . um . . . how do you say . . . teacher or training master. I've known your father for a couple of years longer than you have. I'm not going to tell you my age, but I'm not thirty. Three—no, more like four years ago, I moved down to this prism, not by choice though. I was forced to leave. You see, my father had died, and he was the only member of my family that was of pure Harforian descent, and I was forced to leave the mansion ship along with my twin sister. We parted ways soon after coming down here. She has a personality problem. I chose to do my studies here, and she went elsewhere. I had my training in stealth warfare and telepathic control. And that is when I met your father. He's an excellent teacher, did you know?" Her question wasn't answered verbally. The land craft approached the tunnel.

"To make a long story short, we became good friends," Sky continued. "I was his second-best apprentice, second to only you, of course. He rewarded me with the stealth suit you saw earlier. It could have been yours." She paused, awaiting anger from Psyy that never came.

She continued, "He told me he needed a favor. In exchange for my final evaluation, I had to follow you around every night for the remainder of my course. It was hard. I had nine other courses at the time. Yeah, you guessed right. I completed my degree yesterday. Thanks for congratulating me. I do hope you come to my graduation." She scoffed. "Some of—most of the trainees are still waiting for him to return and evaluate them, so you see my dilemma. I told you already, I'm the girl that's been watching you, rewriting the battle complex logs, fetching new robots, mending the floors, and repairing the unreachable places of the battle complex that you damaged during your careless training. Don't take offense to that. When I first saw you training and fighting, I couldn't believe my eyes. You're an awesome fighter. Yes, you need more work on your balance and to stop depending on your telekinesis and force shield, but for the most part, you are very formidable and intelligent."

"Go on, please."

"Okay. I knew it was possible to be psychic and telekinetic as well. And ice powers, superstrength, and energy projection powers. Is there any more? Like, what else really? Whoever, whatever designed you sure knows how to overkill a character."

"You know about the experimentations? The Arcon? The wars? You cleaned up for me? That was you the whole time? I thought it was the robots."

"Yes but only for most of this year, last year and half of the year before that. The first year I spent trying to keep up with you. The suit is really heavy. Of course, I know about the Arcon, the experiments, the wars. I'm in the military."

"Okay. Yes, I know the suits are heavy. I had one very briefly."

"What happened with it?"

"I decided not to take the two-year course."

"Oh, you weren't up for it?"

"I had to set priorities, and stealth training wasn't one of them. Was it you the whole time?"

Sky paused to think and answered, "I didn't do it every day. I had a few breaks. Your father must have been doing it solo before he recruited me." The land craft approached the dark exit tunnel. "I had to keep telepathic contact with your father throughout the course of the night. Yes, I was tempted to tell your secret, but I respect your father, and I knew the other generals would not understand how you could benefit them . . . alive. I had these feelings way before I fell in love with Alex. It's almost like your father wanted me to fall in love with him. And of course, you might not realize it, but your father has unexplainable powers. It's like he can manipulate time and space. The telepathic theory doesn't quite explain his functioning. I can't explain it, but maybe he's at such an advanced stage in his telepathy that he can read beyond thoughts. I have evidence to say this. Please allow me to explain.

"I was thinking about reporting you to the Temple Mind. It's a secret wing of the Harfore-Darcon Forces, the military that hunts down strange life-forms all over the planet. Even before I fully knew what I was thinking, he gave the entire class of one hundred trainees brand-new messaging devices. He told us not to open it until the course ended. Of course, none of the passing students listened to him, and I opened mine two days later. On the device he gave me, the display showed, at the exact moment I opened it, every number I wished I had to report you. The date the file was uploaded was the day before I thought of contacting the Temple Mind. I had the device in my possession. It wasn't connected to any servers. I can't explain it. I wasn't really seriously pursuing the thought. I just really wanted my social life back. It's like he can see into the future." The land craft stopped for a moment, reversed a few inches, and entered the tunnel.

"That's an interesting story. Couldn't he have just assumed you were going to want to quit? Or placed some powerful thoughts in your mind?"

"I've been using my telepathy my entire life. No one could mind-control me with my knowledge of the event. I ran through those thoughts too, but then I remember what I wasn't thinking about, and that was the numbers in bold in the middle of the Temple Mind's number, 70 and 1400. They were the grade I received on my first hand-eye coordination assessment and the date and time. I called the number and hung up. The day after, I opened the device and saw the same info. I'm really sorry I did that now that I look back. But if you had failed a six-hour-long exam because you had fallen asleep from babysitting, I'm sure you would have complained to someone and wanted that head-hunting reward. I had no one to explain myself to, but your father gave me a passing mark on that exam."

"I'm confused. That's bizarre. You failed an exam because of me. No wonder you hate me. This explains a lot." The land craft moved straight through the dark tunnel lined up with green lights. "Did General Vyers, my father, know about you and Alex?"

"Yes. I met Alex . . . when did I know of him, or when did I meet him? I met him at a pub in the subbasement. It was his first time there and my first time too," she lied. "I had to delay my trip to his dorm room because of the urgent message on my device and in my head. It sounded just like him. 'Stop playing around,' it voiced and then reminded me of our agreement."

"You made me feel so fearful. I feel so guilty knocking him out like that."

"I apologize," she said sincerely. "Alex has a great spirit. He'll be okay. Don't you worry."

"You know what, you're not so bad. I accept your apology, and I'm sorry too for being such a burden. I didn't know anyone else was in this with me. I thought it was just my family."

"No, I'm really sorry," Sky said again with emphasis.

"Thank you. I could get used to you. Your friendship would mean a lot to me," she said genially.

"It's time to wake up, Alex. I know a mind trick," Sky said, extending her hand toward Psyy. The women joined hands and concentrated on Alex. Sky thought for a second. A force left their minds, and Alex's body jumped. In his mind, he had seen a beautiful picture, and he smiled. The two women he loved most of all had hugged and gone shopping hand in hand. They arrived at the land craft together very happily, giving him kisses, and allowed him to take the driver's seat. Into the tunnel, they traveled in the land craft.

Alex woke up in the driver's seat and looked around to find the two women fast asleep. Sky was in the passenger seat beside him, and Cassandra lay extended in both passenger seats in the back, facing upward to the sunroof covered by two heavy coats. The land craft moved through the tunnel, making an upward, winding right turn. It seemed to climb ever slowly.

Alex reached over his seat and woke up Sky. He questioned her inanely about when he fell asleep and settled for her simple excuse in the form of a tired frown. The land craft now was moving uphill. By the time it reached the top, Cassandra had awoken. The land craft stopped as it met the plateau and jerked back a bit before being propelled upward, shaking the passengers, and sped onto ground level. Inside the land craft, the friends looked up to view a large snow-covered mountain. The mountain was massive in length, and its peak reached into the clouds. The wind was harsh outdoors, and the glittering snow reflected the sunlight-covered ground.

Cassandra anxiously moved Alex's seat forward and jumped out of the land craft awkwardly. She picked up the snow in her gloveless hands. It was powdered snow. As she bent down, rubbing the snow together in her hands, she was amazed at its softness. By now, her brother and his fiancée moved and were looking at her, puzzled by her amusement. She had to explain to them why she had not left the prism complex, but they didn't believe her story. She could have left the prism complex with her father and brother many times but decided to allow them to bond without interference from her distractive spirit. She smiled coyly as she stood up.

The two lovers had on their heavy coats. Alex and Sky were fully suited in light-absorbing black coats, scarves, gloves, goggles, and boots. The mountain towered between them. The clouds concealing the peak were brighter than the other clouds in the sky. Cassandra inquired where her coat was and was responded to by laughter. Sky shared everything with Alex, including all of Cassandra's amazing abilities. He had only known of a few obvious ones before then. They knew she didn't need a thick coat. Her skin insulated heat at an inhuman rate.

Sky told her that she could use their trip up into the mountain as training. They walked toward the hill. The signs read "Dangerous icy cliffs, high winds, and beware of nochs. Nochs were wormlike dark-purple beings capable of drilling through the permafrost and dwelling deep below the base of the mountains for no determined reason. Few scientists had ever researched the nochs thoroughly because of its lethal speed and sharp, beaklike mouth, and their research conflicted. Some said that it came out of the ground to breathe fresh oxygen and others claimed they fed off the remains of those that failed to reach to the summit. There were mixed reports of violent attacks during blinding blizzards that swept over the mountains. Few claimed that the creatures were scavengers, but all concluded that they must be carnivorous. The creatures were foreign to the planet, first being sighted two years after the end of the war. Few were ever seen on Mount Taptoon.

The mountain was a small hill in comparison to the many other mountains located along the mountain range that covered the Northern Hemisphere. It was an archaeological gold mine. It had been the site of intense air warfare during the war. It was littered with buried ships at its base and with debris from destroyed spacecraft and airships. The mountain was winding, and it took at least four days to reach its summit in good weather, which rarely came.

Cassandra refused to continue onward as they approached the mountain. She simply could not spend four days out in the cold wilderness; she was a full-time scientist. Sky and Cassandra agreed on a strange compromise. Sky calculated that if Cassandra would help them reach the summit using her abilities for ten minutes during the beginning of every hour, it would take them about six hours to reach the top of the mountain. Cassandra knew that she must have been planning this excursion with her in mind and doubted she would have continued it without her.

Their trek up the mountain commenced. Alex was the foremost expert in mountain climbing. He knew how to tie all manner of knots: overhand, figure eight, double figure eight, water, double fisherman's, Prusik, sink stopper, and pile hitch, to name a few. He had prepared the ropes they would use to scale the mountain in less than fifteen minutes. It took him another half an hour to secure the ropes to the upper ledge using the grappling launcher.

The women waited patiently, talking about their morning experiences. Sky couldn't believe that any honest man would neglect to tell a woman he considered a friend about his martial history and whether he had children as West had. Cassandra agreed with her.

Sky was helped into her harness first. After Sky was secured, Alex went to help Cassandra. He noticed how strangely bloodless and bright her skin looked. It seemed almost angelic. They began to climb the side of the mountain. The wind began to howl, and snow gently fell. The wall of the mountain wasn't too cold for Cassandra. She quickly began to scale the mountain, ice pick in hand. She looked down after climbing halfway up the fifty-meter cliff. Having viewed the top of two black objects climbing, she felt fear. He also felt quite woozy. The cliff was so high. She had never been so high off the ground before. She could see the sleeping forest around her covered in snow. The land craft to the left of the mountain remained parked on the tracks that led to the exit tunnel, which was now sealed by a silver metallic door. The exit tunnel remained aboveground for about eight meters before it leaned into the ground and leveled out with the ground.

She moved her head directly upward. The top of the mountain was so high up. She stared into the clouds, and snow fell into her goggles and on her face, causing her to shake her hair out. She looked up again, slowly overcoming the fear. She noticed large chunks of snow falling and reacted quickly. The falling ice was moved to the right of her. She removed her hook from the ice-covered rock and waited as her fellow climbers caught up with her.

As they reached her, they exchanged a few words regarding the importance of sticking together. Cassandra blamed her quick ascent to the fact that she was somewhat unaffected by the cold temperatures. They continued to climb together. They spoke, breathing deeply in between their sentences. They admired the view of the landscape surrounding the mountain and the height of the mountain itself. Climbing fast, they arrived at the next cliff about an hour later. Cassandra reminded Sky of her agreement, and Alex urged her to uphold her side of the bargain. Anxiously, he awaited Cassandra to act, remembering the novelty of viewing her use of powers for the first time. She waited for them to gather the equipment and huddle around her.

"You're going to levitate us up the mountain? I think you should let Alex secure a rope around us first."

"No, I'm fine. I got this. Trust me, okay, guys? You'll both be surprised, and don't read my mind. It could distract me," said Cassandra. She looked up, focusing on the location of the mountain. She closed her eyes and focused. The passengers waited. Cassandra's skin became surrounded by the strange corona again.

Alex couldn't control his excitement. "Awesome!"

"Be quiet," Sky quietly whispered. The ground around them glowed with a heated bright-blue light. The outside of the glowing circle became blurred. They could feel the ground beneath them move slightly to the left. The action suddenly stopped, and the ground beneath them shifted to the right.

"What happened?"

"It's not working."

"I can only do . . . hold on. If I fail the first time, it's like I won't be able to do it again for a bit."

"What are you trying to do anyway?"

"Ah, don't worry about it. Forget about it. Let's just do this the old-fashioned way," Alex said, his voice frustrated and manly. He secured the climbing rope again and told Cassandra they were ready for liftoff.

"Fine, let's just climb for now," Cassandra said, beginning to start her climb. Sky followed, kicking spiked boots on the side of the icy mountain.

They began to climb. It was almost four in the afternoon when they reached the top of the next plateau. The two ordinary beings were tired and hungry, and they all entertained the idea of an early dinner, having missed lunch, except for one climber. "Yeah, let's have a snack, but that's it. I want to meet the halfway point before dark. We're at too low of an altitude to stop for too long."

"Why?" said Cassandra.

"The nochs."

"What about them?"

"They'll eat us alive, if we stay here and leave food exposed for too long."

"Really, Sky? They aren't that bold," said Alex.

"I'm not taking any chances. We can finish these light rations, and then we'll start back climbing at 1630."

"No way. We missed lunch a couple of hours ago. I'm hungry. I could faint telling you this. You ladies can keep climbing if you want to. I'd have an early dinner any day rather than die of starvation."

The look on her face said outrage. "Come on, Alex, man up!" shouted Sky as her scarf slid off her face and displayed more of her dark skin tone as the rays of the sun illuminated her.

"You didn't let me finish forming the energy I needed to teleport us, and now you're going to complain about us not stopping to have dinner? It's only forty meters. Oh, man up," a jocular Cassandra said as the two women walked to the end of the cliff to pull up the ropes.

After finishing the small fruit-filled snack. They started to climb again. Up into the mountains, they went on an unintentional slant. The wind was strong and picked up the snow and ice on the utmost cliffs. A huge block of ice had almost hit Alex as he moved ahead of the women, who paced themselves. He was obviously trying to surpass them. He was successful and reached the next cliff two minutes before his female climbers did; his experience showed. They were deep in discussion about the nochs. Cassandra thought about conducting some independent research about the creatures and finding some way to present it in her thesis. As the two women reached the plateau, they could see the exhausted expressions on Alex's face.

"You beat us. Hail Alex, king of Mount Taptoon," she said mockingly.

"Look what you're wearing up here," he said, huffing.

"It's only cold for you. I can exhale colder air than this. At least I look good."

"Yes, you fashionable freak," he said as he fell in the snow.

Cassandra walked over to Sky to ask her more questions about the nochs. She wanted to know how they could reach so high up into the mountain. Sky explained that, unlike most mountains, this one was mostly made of permafrost, frozen soil, and snow. She was also puzzled by how the nochs could reach so high into the mountains. "I suppose they can dig through rocks or stretch or something," Cassandra said, not understanding her own logic.

"Maybe they can fly when they're younger," Sky hypothesized. Cassandra had not thought of that possibility.

"But how would they fly in these temperatures?"

"That's a mystery. I'm betting that they ooze an acid strong enough to erode sedimentary rock," said a booming voice in the distant background.

"That's smart. I couldn't believe that." Cassandra smiled, amused by her brother's intelligence.

"I'm doubtful," Sky said. "And this is a mountain covered in snow. Keep your voice down. Alex, we don't want any avalanches starting today. Please watch your temper."

They talked about a variety of topics. Their conversation was interrupted by Alex's manly voice that called them to a warm fire. They sat and ate a protein-rich soup mix that was steamed in a silver pot above the small fire. The ladies were impressed. Alex had managed to make a fire in fridge temperature. They neglected to inform him that they knew he had used a laser lighter. But the delicious taste of the mix he made truly impressed them. He had mixed a few cans of sauce and protein together randomly.

After the longer dinner, they continued up the mountain. The two lovers moved up tiredly. Psyy felt embarrassment returning to her. She had been unable to perform the teleportation technique she had perfectly mastered months ago. It was a surreal ability, and she knew it would shock Sky, who thought she had her figured out. Finally, around the approach of sunset, they reached the third and last ledge before the summit, and she knew she had to finish the trip before sundown. "I'm going to try again."

"Try what?"

"The thing that's going to get us up the hill."

"The teleportation?"

"Alex? You knew? Yes, you did hear me say it once or twice."

"Yes, I read a lot of books."

"Cassandra, you don't have to read minds to know something you've said ten times."

They agreed to form a close circle again. The ground began to glow, and the air outside the circle blurred. The light blizzard outside the circle was no longer visible. Even the light entering the circle became obscured, and the friends were in grayish darkness. No objects could be made out outside the circle. Alex was afraid, and Psyy could sense that Sky was becoming apprehensive.

The glowing sphere moved upward through the secondary level of the subspace. Psyy struggled to maintain the image of the second last ledge before the summit of the mountain. The outside of the now invisible half sphere from an exterior view became visible as the half sphere began to move. It was still extremely cold for the lovers. The three stood on the inner face of the half sphere.

Alex and Sky peered out through the sphere and saw black-and-white objects. Everything they looked at was black and white or in a kind of sepia. They ascended toward the second summit, and suddenly, the sphere spun on its only axis and entered the mountain. Half the sphere was now in the mountain. Psyy was separated from the two lovers by a faint outline of the crooked, snow-covered cliff. The equipment bags were on the energy floor of the half sphere. Sky moved her hand through the outline and marveled at the phenomenon. Alex remained speechless as he leaned against the half sphere's barrier and could only watch.

They had arrived on the second cliff, and Psyy opened her eyes and looked outside the half sphere. The outline of a midsize rock fell through the top of the sphere, going through Alex's forehead like it was a ghost. She had a similar gray outline surrounding her body and looked around, amazed that the sphere had not disappeared as they reached the second ledge. Sky motioned that they should continue to the summit. Psyy looked up and noticed the distance between them and the top. Psyy felt ridiculous for having kept her eyes closed through their ascent. She felt all-powerful and moved the half sphere up further into the air. Her teleportation also made her use her telekinesis.

She couldn't believe the view from inside the half-circular sphere. It was like she was standing on a see-through glass floor with gray sunglasses on. She would have shown more concern had she not seen Alex trembling against the side of the sphere. They all watched in amazement as the outline of several small snowflakes moved through the sphere. They glittered in a grayish light and quickly exited the side of the sphere. Sky stood leaning against nothing and was inwardly frozen in fear, but Psyy, unable to read her mind, freely mistook her fear for coldness. The inside of the celestial half sphere remained under the influence of temperature, gravity, and time. The possibility of the outside world moving slower frightened Sky. The exterior of the half sphere was not subject to light, gravity, most of time, and the other obvious laws of reality. Actually, the half sphere was invisible to nearly all forms of detection. For now, it moved at a rate of about 2.5 meter per second.

Psyy wanted to know something interesting. Was it possible for her to travel through the mountain range and rise above on the summit? She would try. She moved the sphere completely into the mountain. She looked up, dismayed by the outlines of rocks and metallic figures that went through the sphere like the light from a projection. She moved farther into the mountain, and the half sphere went pitch black. The outline of the conductor and her celestial half sphere were still a visible brightened gray.

The scrambling of feet and hands could be heard. Sky crouched to the floor, multitasking, and stood back up quickly with a flashlight in her hand. She shone it around the half sphere. Only the objects in the path of the light were visible inside and outside. Sky laughed lightly as she watched Alex stand up and look around frantically. He could not believe that the glowing gray person in the center of the half sphere was his sister.

Psyy opened her eyes as she moved the half sphere upward to the summit. None of them expected what would happen next. A lengthy dark-gray-beaked head peaked through the top of the moving half sphere. Shock and awe moved through the passengers and the conductor much faster than the large anaconda-like body of the creature could pass through the floor of the half sphere. The massive body took almost ten seconds to move through. The flashlight fell, and Sky screamed for almost as long as it took the creature to pass.

The half sphere suddenly reached ground level with the summit. The outside of the sphere was visible now. Sky, Alex, and Psyy looked through the outside of the half sphere in horror. Several large wormlike purple beings were sliding across the snow-covered surface of the summit. The creatures dived into the ground and whipped their tails against the sides of the tunnels. There were six of them. They were gigantic. Again, all of them screamed as one came sliding across the snow in their direction.

The half sphere began to glow and change to a strange blue light. The outside became blurred. Fresher oxygen entered their lungs. A loud sound of scurrying creatures leaping into their burrows ensued. They had reintegrated with reality smoothly. Psyy fell to her knee, feeling extremely exhausted. The nochs had fled in terror at the sight of the strange blue light. Alex was helped up from the ground by Sky. They all felt the tremors below them.

Sky opened her climbing bag and reached into her green suit beneath her heavy black coat. Her hands were cold beneath her gloves, which she removed. She opened the cover of the messaging device, dialed a number, and then looked up into the cloudy dark sky. Alex began to breathe deeply.

Again, the ground shook. Five meters away from the three adventurers, the ground burst open, sending dirt in every direction. Psyy quickly leaped, and her forceful corona shield formed around her body. The noch towered fifteen feet above them. It had six tiny black eyes on the side of its head. Dark purple shaded its underbelly and colored it more darkly as it reached around its exterior covering. It had a long sharp, pointed, birdlike beak.

With lightning speed, the noch struck forward at the three unarmed adventurers. A monstrous hiss left its vocal organs. It snipped at Psyy's protected legs and was blown back by a force so strong that it lifted the creature from its entry hole. It slid off the side of the rocky mountain, and its shrieks died down. Two more nochs, twice as big as the first, emerged from their burrows. Sky reached into her pocket and received a loaded, silencer-like green-levered weapon. She shot blindly into the air. She struggled to breathe for a moment and reloaded her weapon slowly. Sky fired a single red pellet at the head of the nearest noch. The creature's purple head burst on impact.

Alex had fallen over to the ground seconds before, yet another noch had surfaced and was again relieved by Sky. Sky's red suit attracted the eyes of the worms. A powerful blue light left Psyy's hand and severed the violent creatures from their parts below the surface. Dark purple blood stained the ground as headless, snakelike bodies continued to slide along the ground. The remaining nochs shrieked a deafening cry. Alex stood up and again fell over but was caught by Sky this time. He was light headed and stumbled under the weight of the black winter coat.

Another much stronger tremor shook them. Quickly, Psyy pushed Alex and Sky apart with her mind. Just as she did, a large noch parted the icy ground and surged to the surface, right where the lovers had stood, spraying a bright pinkish-purple liquid at Psyy. Luckily, it never touched her skin. The acid steamed as it landed on her forceful plasma shield. The alpha noch turned its attention to Alex and opened its beaklike dark purple mouth, revealing nine rows of uncountable daggerlike teeth on its upper jaw. The alpha noch motioned upward as if to spray. Its corrosive spit was lethal. Hard liquid bounced to the ground with a loud clash. Alex lay motionless on the ground, uninjured; his eyes flinched. Sky looked up to see the thoroughly frozen noch. Psyy leaped into the air and delivered a snapping high kick, bouncing backward and landing on the icy ground, sliding intentionally.

The wind doubled in speed, and snow began to fall. The towering noch broke slowly at its base. A blistering wind flew over the summit. Psyy looked up, saw clouds very close to her, and realized that they had reached the summit. A large aircraft parted the clouds and hovered at the edge of the summit. It was shaped like a helicopter without a propeller. It was gray and covered with frozen water droplets; bright yellow light left its forward lights, blue its back; and a red Darcon-Harfore Defense Forces (D-HDF) symbol was on the sliding door that opened. Two men in gray coats that displayed similar crosses on their white suits motioned for them to enter the aircraft. The tremors became stronger, and Sky grabbed Alex and ran with him to the aircraft. The curly-haired adventurer was last to enter the aircraft as the sliding door closed.

"No! We'll never get to see the crash site now!" screamed Sky, her cry evolving into an unfulfilled sigh.

"You called them," Psyy reminded her.

"I realize that. I wasn't letting you take us back down that mountain. At least we have our lives."

"I can't believe that anyone would think they were scavengers. Those are vicious overgrown monsters."

"I've never seen them at such heights on the mountain before. Actually, I've never seen them that up close before. It must be mating season."

"Next time, we'll see the crash site."

"Next time?" interjected Alex. "Maybe after I complete a ten-year defense training course."

"That's okay, you'll be babysitting," she said and winked at Psyy.

"What are you talking about?" said a tired and sarcastic voice.

"Maybe after you learn to tie and untie knots," said Alex. "Where's the other supply bag?"

"I got it," said Psyy tiredly as she coughed, resting her head against the side of the seat.

"Next time, wear a coat," said the other woman, which made Psyy's eyes roll as she yawned.

Cassandra looked out the window of the aircraft. The mountain was now in the distance of the dark sky. She had felt natural snow for the first time in many years and climbed a mountain. She replayed the adventure in her mind and determined that she had never been so intrepid and on point in her life. She had used her powers to protect her loved ones. She would cherish the unplanned experience greatly and yearned for greater but less responsible excitement.

CHAPTER V

PAPER TIGERS

F our months had passed since Psyy had missed another day of work, except for her scheduled days off, which she spent with her expecting sister-in-law. She had stayed home for a few days to rest after her first trip up the mountain, and thoughts of another adventure prevented her from fully resting. Sky shared with her how she had disposed of the operators' tapes that recorded the conversation between Alex and Psyy and that she was having a baby. Psyy stopped herself from asking what methods of retrieval she used but knew it involved some type of illegal brainwashing, and instead, she went ecstatic over the confirmed rumors of Sky's pregnancy.

Sky was interested in dramatizing West. West hadn't gone to see Psyy's eye specialist, but Psyy wasn't insulted. She and West were platonic friends; their relationship was based purely on employee-customer commitment. Their conversation touched on West vaguely afterward.

Sky also gave Psyy her freedom to train unwatched, but Psyy decided to suspend her training for a few weeks, forgetting her promise to her father. Psyy and Sky also discussed how their adventure in the mountain had become big news. The official investigative unit could not determine who or what was responsible for the slaying of the nochs. The public did not know the details of the incident, but the military would have investigated Psyy had Sky not relieved them of their interest. The two women's friendship blossomed and flourished. Their trust for each other became unquestionable, and they exchanged thoughts often during the daytime because, at night, Psyy busied herself with starting future research projects.

With Psyy well on top of her work, they decided to go back to the mountain; and after their second visit, they finally were finally able to uncover the half-buried ship that lay behind the rocky bend of the summit. Sky had used her military rank to reserve a small jet-shaped black aircraft for a quicker trip up the mountain.

The sky was a bright clear blue with few clouds in the sky. Psyy and Sky left early in the morning to take advantage of the calm weather without Alex. He was completing his last term of postsecondary education and welcomed few distractions. They had been suited for discovery that day. Photographic devices, archaeological tools, and scanning devices in hand, they took many pictures of the crash site that had been inaccessible to the other climbers because of the nochs and the harsh weather.

As a result of the attack, an extermination team had poisoned the remaining creatures about a month after their first visit. There were now few nochs on the mountain. Psyy wasn't sad about not seeing the nochs again; their extermination was necessary. The creatures were too dangerous to be allowed to traverse the open summit. Psyy helped her morning-sick friend open the door to the ancient spacecraft, but by law, they were not permitted to enter it. It was an offense punishable by jail terms and heavy fines. Sky wasn't going to stand in her way. She turned a blind eye to Psyy and went to eat another breakfast in the aircraft; she was eating for two.

In the dark spacecraft, Psyy found the frozen remains of a shredded black spacesuit. She kept herself suspended between the top and the bottom of the dark spacecraft and took a while to determine the true floor. Dressed in a black bodysuit, her mobility was made somewhat clumsy, and she bumped into the sides several times. The inside of the buried spacecraft was dark. She shone the six flashlights attached to the knuckles of her gloves over the large ridged gashes that were in the walls and floors of the spaceship. She could see the burnt trails that imprinted the metallic floor. She put two and two together and knew that the nochs must have killed any survivors of the crash.

She knew what she was looking for when she reached the helm of the spacecraft. The walls were dark green, and she moved aside the obstacles that kept her from venturing into the pitch-black ship. She examined the markings on the various control panels and knew that it was not Harforian or Darcon. The tales of two truly alien armies invading the planet Darth were now substantiated. The markings were not Darforian, the language and culture of the Darcon, or Harforian, the complex written language of quickly glowing lights, which she only recently began to grasp. She had only learned of the war from her studies. Her teachers and professors presented the war as a conflict between the Harfore rebel forces and the loyal Harfore. The Darcon had been caught in the crossfire. Her professors told her what they knew, but they had only told her and their classes half-truths.

Her father revealed the truth to her several years ago, but she was a scientist and needed substantial evidence. And now she had it. The Pylon and the Harfore had been at war for centuries. The Pylonites controlled the outer rim of the galaxy known as the nebula of Pyl. The insectlike creatures occupied seven planets and eight moons, according to her father, named successively Pyl 1 through 7.

The ancestors of the Pylonites were much like the Darcon, except they were much more grotesque. They had colorful eyes at first, were capable of altering their genetic makeup almost overnight, and manipulated their genes to maintain their dominance and power. They were not the strongest force in the universe, but they were the most cunning. They were known as shape-shifters capable of taking on many forms. On the palms of their hands were retractile points that could absorb small storable amounts of genetic material. They could grow the wings of insects on their backs with the right genetic potion or manual retrieval of genetic material via retractile needle organs. They were skinless in their true form, and this made them feel incomplete. They covered themselves with thin layers of armor and the genetic exterior of their compatible lenders.

At the first stages of their civilization, they were chaotic and chose to take the compatible traits of any life-form they could feed on. Order and enlightenment entered their gene pool when a careless error resulted in the crash of a royal Harforian spacecraft. The life essence of the gods on board was sampled by thousands of Pylonites. The extraction of these gods and Harforians made them stronger and wiser. It allowed them to survive the changing temperature of the planet. They grew rapidly and became stronger in appearance, now capable of achieving a limited flight. Combined with their long life span of over five hundred years, they were formidable. Collectively, they worked, and their colonies thrived, reaching the different requirements of the ages.

They no longer existed in small hives. A grand hive developed to house their chosen leaders and civilize the race. Their leaders were immortalized beings capable of being destroyed by nothing less than intentional murder. They became highly telepathic beings capable of transferring the most innate thoughts of their most powerful leaders into the empty vessel of another member of their kind. It still was unknown to the Harfore which of the seven planets fostered their Pylon leadership, who now possessed the strongest telepathic powers in the universe collectively.

The Pylonites were weak in comparison to the gods, who frowned on the death of the other gods and expendable Harforian royalty. Protocol compelled them to reclaim the technology on the crashed ship, which resulted in a war. They had not expected the demise of their kin but had prepared them for it. Within all the minor members of the royal Harforian lineage was a genetic trap. It would disrupt any organism that fed on the remains until the contaminant was decayed for several centuries. The trap concealed within the gods' genes caused an incomplete integration of traits and made any of their further evolutions temporary.

Many Pylonites died as they failed to adapt to the contaminant. The surviving Pylonites found themselves stuck in their present insectlike evolutionary form, no longer capable of changing back to their true skinless shape. Although they looked grotesque to outsiders, they did not consider that form to be hideous. The Pylonites now had rough, scaly, and brittle exteriors that took almost all remnant of color from their neutral eyes. Cursed, they became abhorrent of their own unpleasing forms and vowed revenge on the gods, who ruled over the Harfore and Darcon.

However, as evolution sometimes goes, there were, of course, Pylonites who were unaffected by the contaminant and achieved great power. When Harforian rescue ships arrived to retrieve the technology on the crashed ship, they mistook these interlopers as wounded survivors of the crash because of their bright colorful eyes and undistinguishable pigmentations in the darkness of the night. This new race became known as the Arcon. They were either extremely dark or extremely pale in complexion, and their palms were stripped of the gene-stealing organs. They lost the use of expressing their telepathic abilities on the others.

After the mistake was realized, it was already too late; they had orchestrated a near complete and total integrated annihilation of the Harfore and the gods on their home world, now known as Arcon. The remaining Harforians fled to the Darth with the few remaining gods to live with the nontelepathic Darforians. The technology on the annexed home world was, by far, too sophisticated for the Arconians to fully understand, and the games they created to master the technology became an important element of their civilization. They possessed highly reconstructive forms and were capable of great feats of physical strength. With all the acquired energy from the gods' technology, some Arconians could now fly and manipulate body temperature. They were indeed now a race of supermen. Their minds were also capable of evading and neutralizing the mental powers of the Harfore and Pylon races. The Arcon eventually annexed the surrounding planets of the Harfore with the aid of their former kin, the Pylonites, whom they placed in servitude.

The Arconians' only physical weakness was that they required conflict to grow strong, and their civilization filtered out the weak from the strong in a cannibalistic determinism. The Arconians became ruthless even to their own kind, and a system of power was established whereby only the ruthlessly strong and wise would survive to lead the lesser broods. The four champions of the game ruled the Arconian Empire with an iron fist, allowing no other winners to compete or be crowned. They now ruled the known universe in acceptable peace, only because they cannot determine the exact location of the planet Darth, but were very well in search of the remaining gods of the Harfore-Darcon dynasty and their technology.

Psyy realized that the time had expired quickly. She looked around the ship uneasily. She began to collect samples of various objects, including a small piece of the wall. She returned to the awaiting aircraft to reunite with Sky. Sky started the black aircraft almost intuitively minutes before she exited the massive crater in the ground, which was the only entrance to the vessel. She boarded the aircraft and was quieted as she attempted to share with Sky an intense zeal to examine her samples.

Sky received a rich sum for her discovery. She became the 9,993rd archaeologist to uncover an alien spacecraft. Her silver medallion and invitation to an honoring ceremony gave her a sense of job security as she took her maternity leave. Psyy refused her share of the bursary and told Sky that she had done enough for her already. Had Sky not noticed the foreign signature that marked the check, Psyy would not have. The sharp, crooked signature of another high director now replaced the perfectly signed signature of her father. Psyy knew immediately that she would not see her father again for years, and it caused her to weep inconsolably.

For the remainder of the four months, she buried herself in her work and decided to intensify her training in the subbasement as she had promised. She allowed herself to be distracted by happiness and sorrow for a moment when she attended the small gathering that recognized Alex and his new wife, Sky Arvona Vyers. Not once during the ceremony did she scan the audience, expecting to see her father. The most emotional part of the evening was when Alex made a toast to his late mother, who passed away exactly eighteen years ago.

The five troopers entered the jungle. It was designed to be dense and humid. Frior (pronounced as "fire") took out his military sword and sliced through the jungle. In their mud-splattered black battle suits, they walked through the muddy floor. The sunlight was barely visible beneath the dense trees, and every so often, large brown leaves fell to the mud with a thud. The branches of the long leafy trees brushed against their upper armor. He had gained a greater standing in the force and couldn't understand why he did not receive his promotion.

A loud, buzzing sound of dragonfly-like insects filled the air as shadows flew over them. He was the leader and commanded his infantry to increase their repellent devices or face failure. They moved forward through the muddy jungle floor, which leveled at their ankles. The trees were burdened with heavy, thick green leaves at their base. The trunks of the tree were painted green with an algaelike green mold. Small branches broke in the upper trees as a camouflaged, sticklike insect scrambled up the tree they were under. This mission marked the new adult's twenty-second training mission, his thirteenth in the muddy jungle.

"Save your ammo!" shouted the leader. He breathed deeply in the hot suit. "Now remember, people, we have only one objective, and that's to locate the enemy and rescue the hostages. So think twice before you fire anything."

"Affirmative."

"Yes, sir."

"Acknowledged."

"Okay, guys."

They advanced toward a dry-branch-covered burrow eight meters to their right. They approached cautiously. The trainees could see the arachnid's front tarsal claws and eyes lurch forward for a moment and then reverse back into the burrow. It was a beautiful red spider integrated by robotic technology for military training.

"Permission to shoot."

"No. Don't shoot unless you have a clear shot," said the educated leader.

"We need to split up. Three of us there," commanded Frior as he pointed to the dull tree four meters across from them. "Brock, you're with me. We're the bait. On my order. Five, four, three, two . . ."

They quickly crawled to their positions. Frior was the first to shoot the spider's exposed leg. It reacted as expected and crept back into its burrow. Unwilling to accept failure, Frior ran forward toward its burrow, anxious to end the skirmish. The spider pounced on him in a lightning motion and pulled him into the burrow. Forcing the spider off, he leaped out of the burrow and into the branches of the nearest hollow tree. He dropped to the ground, breathing hard.

The red-haired spider was 2.6 meters in circumference. Its chelicerae flared up, revealing ten-inch fangs. It left the cluttered burrow to retrieve its prey. It leaped forward, following the ninjalike soldier. Frior kicked the spider in its abdomen with tremendous force that hurled the spider into the metallic trunk of the tree he had fallen from. Frior shouted orders at his entranced teammates. They responded shaken and headed toward the hostages.

Stemum refacing the ground, the spider flipped back over. It swiped at Frior with its tarsal claws, leaving a deep scratch on the chest plate of his battle suit. Frior rained down punches on the red-haired spider, stunning it. He grabbed its exposed leg at its tibia and severed it from its coxa in an attempt to throw it. But its fangs sank into his armor, and he felt no pain. The spider intensified its grip and attempted to shake him violently. He resisted it, countered its motion, and grabbed the base of the black fang, irritating its rostellum.

His fellow troopers, having taken the large pretend hostage bags back to the platform, became fearful. They pointed their weapons toward the spider. Frior's suit sparked loudly, and flames erupted from his hands. The enraged spider rolled around the muddy jungle floor covered in flames, and a barrage of bullets impacted its hard exterior as it was lethally subdued. Smoke lifted into the air as Frior stamped out the flames. The junglelike lights in the room dimmed to a cooling blue.

"How'd you do that?"

"Mission accomplished. Good work, team."

"You make this seem so easy."

"Sorry, guys, I got carried away."

"It's cool. I couldn't stand this heat anymore."

"You glory hog," complained a weary voice.

"Did you see the spider grab him?"

"Yeah. I thought you were a goner when that spider pulled you in."

"Well, I almost pressed the panic button."

"There's no way I'm going through that whole mission again. Getting around those spiderwebs was hard enough."

"You're like," the man in charge continued, "some ninja slash ultimate warrior."

The soldiers walked toward the exit of the simulation room, leaving him and his new buddy Brock standing in the artificial mud. "You really need to control yourself."

"Yeah, I know."

"No, seriously, I've heard a lot of people talking about you. The voices are getting louder. You know what I mean?"

"I'm not afraid of anything or anyone, you got that? Good. But thanks for your concern," Frior said as he started to walk toward the simulation room's exit.

"Frior?"

"Yes?"

"You forget your 9-0-2," he said, referring to the riflelike weapon. He handed him the heavy weapon.

"Thank you," he said, not meaning it, and left the facility.

The soldier did not leave. He started to examine the remains of the burnt arachnid. He inspected them like an expert. He moved closer, examining the creature and looking for matches. He noticed that the tips of its fangs were shattered; he sampled a fang to help substantiate the grand story he would tell anyone willing to listen.

Frior returned home late in the evening and waltzed into his apartment. He was surprised that his grandmother was still sleeping and hadn't pestered him about his whereabouts. The humiliation she dealt him more than six months ago had strengthened their relationship. He no longer left the prism without sending a message or leaving a note. He was now a corporal, moving up the ranks of the military quickly for his age.

His grandmother gave him more space now that he was an adult and a military man. They now spoke regularly at breakfast and when he flippantly answered his messaging device. She woke up every morning for her exercises, and he had to leave an hour before her for combat training. She adjusted her schedule to accommodate his new status. She didn't ask for forgiveness because she knew he understood her duty. Their conversations usually occurred in the morning because he trained at ten; he worked out in the afternoon and went out with his friends nightly.

"Timothy, how are you this morning?" inquired the elderly woman.

"I'm great, Grandma. I slept well," he said, sitting down at the glass breakfast table. His green eyes watched her, and he smiled authentically. "How are you?"

"I'm fine, thank you. I made you breakfast."

"Oh, it looks good. What is it?" he asked as he began to eat.

"Spinach, garlic, chives, onions, black pepper, salt, and scrambled eggs."

"You know I don't eat this stuff. I can't eat certain things. But this tastes pretty good."

"There's nothing wrong with genetically modified foods. I know you do, but this is good for you. You have to eat healthy. You're a soldier."

"Yes, thank you. You're right. Where are you going this morning?"

"To the bio-dome just north of the prism. My jet comes for me in the mornings, remember?"

"I'll come with you one day."

"Oh, you never expressed such interest in me before."

"No, really, I want to."

"Are you sure? It might be too boring for you," she insisted.

"Yes, I want to see where you go," he said with real interest, his mouth closing to chew the spinach.

She smiled and looked at him to make sure he was being honest and then continued, "Next week, the class is learning the basics of self-defense. You can invite a friend. There are lots of space for visitors. Few of us are regulars these days."

"Sweet, I know who I'm bringing. That sounds interesting. I always wanted to know how to do that surf-and-turf thing," he said, imitating the martial arts movement.

"No, you won't learn that there. We're way past that. I'll show you that 'surf and turf' some other time." She continued her about the class.

"Those techniques sound intense," he said, somewhat embellishing his statement.

"Okay, you'll really have to come to find out for yourself. Who are you bringing?"

They finished the nutritious breakfast together with great discussion. Timothy's training and duties intensified. He completed five combat simulations a week and daily logs. His performance was a mediocre AA but was mostly a factor of him not listening to orders and failing to familiarize himself with the details of the weaponry. He had been promoted twice but did not understand why he wasn't a commander yet. He worked out often, which he found hard to do because it drew much attention to him. He could lift heavy weights, and all those who witnessed his strength were in a state of disbelief. From then on, he had done all his training in the subbasement's private wing, getting special authorization from his lieutenant colonel, a close friend.

He was beginning to become tired of his routine. His social life had stayed the same, except now he could say he was a corporal. It became the most important aspect of his life. He was handsome, and this drew lots of attention to him. His green eyes and dark brown, almost black hair made him enviable. His angular face was strong and caring at the same time, and his military status had given peace to his features; he smiled and laughed more. He was more talkative and never went to any particular event without cancelling on another. Timothy always had somewhere to go. He was not surprised when an invitation appeared on his messaging device. He was invited to the military gala where the elite members of the D-HDF met annually. His attendance was not optional.

The night would have been unproductive had he not met Alice. She was the most beautiful girl he had ever seen. He did not love her because of her long flowing blond hair, blue eyes, curvy figure, and beautiful face but for her fun personality. She could easily switch from being the most proper lady to the most flamboyant flirt. A back-exposing white dress covered the woman standing in the corner of the ballroom, and her eyes leered at him. The bright chandelier in the middle of the room was above him for a moment as he looked around to make sure he was her focal point. The ballroom was crowded with high officials and military commanders. Her glance changed to embarrassment as he eyed her, and she drifted to the corner of the dimly lit room. She was obviously avoiding him the entire night, and he made no attempt to follow her.

Many other women sought his attention, but he moved through the room in his contemporary black tux. He looked around casually for the woman. Finally, as the formal night when on, the festivities drew to an end early in the night, and he saw her exiting the ballroom. He had already decided not to pursue her further. Exiting the grand ballroom, he entered the busy and bright white-walled and brown-tiled corridor. He walked toward the transport bay. As he saw the crowded transport device begin to move down, an angered gentleman cornered him against the white wall. "You've been eyeing my girlfriend!"

"No, I haven't. Please let go of me."

"No, I haven't," mocked the tall formally dressed brown-haired man. "Then how come I saw you following her and looking all around the room when I stood in front of her?"

"Stop it, Junior. Don't you see he's just a kid?"

"Who's a kid?"

"Stay out of this." He could no longer contain his frustration. A loud tear could be heard as half of a tuxedo flung against the walls of the corridor and unto the floor, and the other half remained attached to its outraged owner. "You ripped my coat! I'm going to kill you!"

"Stop it now, Junior!"

"Get out of my way, Alice!"

The sound of spraying aerosol filled the empty section of the transport bay. An incondensable scream filled the echoing corridor as the brown-haired man clutched his eyes and fell to the floor in horrendous pain.

"I told you to leave him alone, and you're not my boyfriend, not anymore. Tim, we better get out of here."

"We? Weren't you avoiding me?"

The blond woman ran for the staircase, and he followed her as onlookers were drawn to the man on the floor. They descended nine flights of a bright, gray-walled, and concrete-stepped stairway and exited into the lower corridor.

From that first encounter, they were inseparable; and ostensibly, Alice was his guest later that month to his grandmother's morning exercise lessons. As they exercised with the elderly people, Frior could not prevent himself from being distracted by the bright stars in the sky of the open-air complex. He wished he had visited the facility sooner as he followed the instructor's directions to breathe deeper. Once again, he looked into the sky; and this time, he noticed a strange blue-and-green glare that seemed to flicker above them. He pointed it out to his girlfriend, but she was too engrossed in the exercise to acknowledge his concerns.

In the orbit of the planet, a large spacecraft drifted. It was shaped like an X. The exterior of the spacecraft that faced the planet was constructed from a reflective dark brown, visibly black material. Small tinted black windows appeared every so often on the exterior embedded below the near overlapping exterior. The side of the spacecraft that faced the planet pulsated a greenish metallic blue, and in the center of the spacecraft was a disclike formation covered with inverted metallic rods that linked together like a web. This structure emitted an eerie dysfunctional greenish-blue light.

Inside the facility, a panic ensued. Fully armed infantry units patrolled the white hallways and grayish floors as a high-pitched silent alarm cascaded throughout the facility. The guards were suited in black suits with white stripes on their left breastplate. The infantry unit separated into two groups of eight, and one moved left to the winding hallways while one continued onward to the command center of the ship. Large white metallic doors opened, revealing a sophisticated circular command bay. Technicians were at their posts, clicking buttons frantically and peering at ceramic view screens, and in the center of the room was a gray-cushioned command chair facing away from them as they approached. At the unoccupied space below the thronelike seat, they stopped and knelt, awaiting commands.

The chair swirled around slowly, and the acting commander of the spacecraft began to speak. His hair was a bright platinum blond and flowed down to his shoulders, and his eyes were a glaring blue. He had the face of a leader, focused yet at ease. A military cape was draped over the sides of his shoulders and hung under the sides of his chair. He was suited in an overlapping, reflective white fabric that was held together by circular gold buttons. "Have you found the source of the interference?" said a conserved voice.

"No. We were unable to access the grid platforms."

"You've been scanning for psionic interference for the past three hours and haven't found any. What we need are visuals. I know we're dealing with a psychic force, and that's exactly why I've ordered these technicians to review the visual recordings of every facility on this platform," said the arrogant blond-haired man as he turned off his earpiece and again faced the infantry.

"Shall we alert the—"

"No," he snapped, his eyes glaring down on the infantryman who spoke to the floor. "They are not to be disturbed in their communion. I want you to keep patrolling the halls until I say otherwise."

"You are aware of the urgency of the matter—"

"Of course, I am! What, you think I don't know that underlings in the Northern Hemisphere can see the station? So what? The people in those prisms can't see the sky unless they go out into the blizzard."

"Yes, Commander. The prism in the south will soon be able to see the station clearly, and they'll wonder about it."

"Who doesn't already?" he muttered. "How long till then?"

"Roughly eight hours."

"Until then, I don't want any more interruptions from you. The power grid explodes, or we've lost the visibility screens completely."

"Yes, Commander."

The infantry continued to scour the station, looking for anything remotely suspicious. The hallways were a bright white, and the lights within them made the interior of the station blinding. The eight infantry units approached a room that was yet to be searched, and almost instantly, their heads fell to their chest as they lost consciousness. As they mindlessly walked past the room, they jolted back to consciousness, having left the creature's vicinity.

Within the unchecked room, a creature stood on a platform surrounded by translucent light. A magnetized helmet on his large forehead was connected to many wires that fed into the floor of the electrified room. The creature's wings were visible. It had a grayish tinge in the bluely lit room. The creature had planned its entry onto the station for years. It took much planning to steal the form of a commander and gain access to the station. It had gotten rid of the only psychic capable of detecting the unique frequency of control it emitted by sending him on a one-way mission to its long-awaited home world. Anticipating the gods' timely communion, the creature knew it was time to set in motion its collectively planned actions. It would leave the accursed planet. Darth's harsh landscape stranded the creature for over a century.

The psychic capabilities it wielded were far more advanced than the man it feared, but it experienced much distress evading him. His purple eyes could see its obvious imperfections. Its deadly face was ridged and flat, and slitlike holes where nostrils should appear were above a broad lower jaw from which sharp, jagged red teeth overlapped the upper jaw. Small moist greenish-black eyes gleamed as the room electrified. Large bonelike projectiles were mounted on its shoulders, elbows, and occipital lobe and descended below its long neck. Its wings were spiny and raggedly wasplike and reached down to its lower knee. It had a springlike, bony stance, which made the creature more lethal in appearance. It walked on its sharp-clawed toes, and its stance was perpetually bent as if ready to strike.

It leaped across the room to the control panel, pulling all the cords that were connected to the device on top of its forehead and caused high-voltage sparks. Leaping back onto the platform, its thin eyelids retracted over its black eyes as they began to glow a translucent green below the thin covering. Its hands clenched wires that were connected to the ceiling of the room, causing a loud explosion. Its mental powers had now increased geometrically, and it focused using the extra energy received from the device on the most academically inclined prism and found several worthy candidates. They had more in common than high intelligence; they were unsatisfied with themselves, and this would make them easier to manipulate. It adapted to their various pains and identified the seven key scientific minds and then froze for a moment in delight.

The Pylon's eyes narrowed on an angle; it had found the untamed potential of a vulnerable mind. Unable to see the physical exterior of his victims, it sensed great power. The creature placed a tangling mental blind over her mind as the powerful creature had done to the six others, and instantly, it felt a strong futile resistance incomparable to the resistance of the others it had ensnared. The female was no ordinary being, and the creature was able to sense it with alarming clarity. Her entire life flickered before the creature's collective mind. The creature was all too weary of trusting unconscious images and doubted the realness of the thoughts when it watched beams of light shoot from her hands, and for a moment, the creature was baffled at how easily it eluded her consciousness.

The female was truly imaginative, and the creature pondered whether to conquer her vulnerable mind that very moment.

Suddenly, it was pulled back to its physical form as a large explosion filled the room. Shards of glass and metal fragments from the door wiped against the creature's bony frame as it sprang to the ceiling, discarding the helmet. The tailless creature dropped from the ceiling and leaped out of the doorway as a slew of bright weapon fire bombarded the room. It flew over the black-suited guards who entered the room and landed with a sharp-clawed skid around the curve of the silver-walled hallway. It stood motionless as fully suited soldiers ran by it, unable to sense it. It raced down the metal-floored hallways to the teleportation bay, only to sense a barricade of armed guards blocking its escape.

The lights within the hallways brightened to a nearly blinding white, and the creature reacted with a quick shriek. It was followed by a pulse of dark blue energy that caused the lights in the hallway to flicker to a dim blue. Unable to see, it sensed another group of infantrymen approaching its position and became a passive object in their mind. As the infantry passed, heading to its previous location around the curve of the hallway, it snatched the passing guard closest to it and sampled his genetic material, throwing his infected form to the floor. The infantry looked on helplessly, unable to see the creature standing around the fallen soldier; and by then, its transformation was complete.

Its flexible form had changed to that of the soldier, and it stood naked in the hallway as it replicated acceptable coverings. Its eyes were a bright blue, and it looked down its hair, wavy and black. The soldier's accoutrements formed from its skin and covered its new form. The troopers saw it for a moment before it made them unresponsive and snatched one of their helmets and gunlike weaponry. The infantry walked mindlessly as the creature commanded them to enter the teleportation bay.

As the door opened, weapons could be heard powering up. Within the teleportation bay, fourteen soldiers fully suited in black striped-shoulder wear had taken up positions to the sides and front of the doorway. Their advanced gray-toned weaponry was pointed toward the doorway and then locked unto the soldiers who dazedly walked toward them. They powered their weapons again and took aim. The barricading unit ordered the mindless soldiers to leave the area, but they were powerless to respond. Less than a moment passed after their orders appeared to be disobeyed, and the unit immobilized their zombielike counterparts with several clicks of gunfire.

The creature entered the room as the teleportation bay doors closed, and it threw an explosive device at the ceiling, causing a bright flash of light to confuse the unit. It joined their ranks for a moment. Half a moment passed before the infantry noticed an addition to their barricade. Loud, ricocheting gunfire ensued, and the impostor avoided the barrage of heavy artillery. It leaped against the walls, activated the teleportation bay, and caused the weak-minded member of the barricade unit to fire blindly. Bright yellow weapon fire filled the room. The creature fired at the infantry that detected it and hacked the minds of the novice infantrymen, causing them to fire madly around the room. A strong-minded infantryman successfully damaged its form with an unaimed attack, and a large gray burn was left on the creature's right arm, and it distinguished the interloper from the real infantry.

For a moment, it lost control over the weak minded and regained a small feature of its true form. Gliding inches off the metallic tile floor, it charged the infantry, knocking them to the floor, and threw itself against another infantryman, causing them to tumble to the floor as its control was reestablished. The teleportation device was fully powered, and the winged infantry evaded the friendly weapon fire to set the coordinates of the device. The doors to the teleportation bay did not open as a bolt of lightning entered the room and paralyzed the warring infantry.

The light rearranged itself into a blond-haired, white-cloaked figure as dark smoke filled the room. The teleportation device was now fully functioning and the subground energy dampeners activated. The blond man motioned his hands to strike the creature with a lethal amount of energy particles. A powerful blue light beamed down on them as the teleportation device became usable.

Two circles of electricity formed in the hands of the blond man and were discharged. The electricity did not affect the creature's heat-sensitive frame; instead, it was sucked through the man's body and into the floor, causing him much discomfort. The electricity damaged the weapons hidden in his suit, and he threw them aside as he propelled himself toward the creature. He reacted swiftly, causing sharp, cold currents of visibly blurred wind to leave his hand and trash the creature against the metallic wall of the teleportation device. It reacted by emitting a confusing burst of psychic energy that caused the man to stumble and misdirect his attack toward the teleportation device controls. Shards of ice formed over the colorful and metallic console.

The creature slid to the ground, clutching its arms. The superior warrior was light headed and disoriented, but his attack intensified. Whirls of arctic air lifted his long hair, and his eyes became brightened. A powerful, blurred gust of wind left his electrified hands, and the temperature in the room plummeted to the minuses. The room was now filled with a cold, airy draft that dried out the air.

The insectlike creature screamed as it threw off the helmet, revealing a blackened face, and thick steam left its broadening jaws and nostrils. It gasped at the sudden change in temperature, and its lungs could not endure. The atmospheric disturbances did not break its strong focus. The creature slowly reverted to its true lanky form, and its sharp toes scraped against the icy teleportation tiles as it was blown by fast-moving, visible air current against the cold walls.

The blue-eyed being was horrified at the creature's inchoate transformation. He was familiar with the manner of the creature that evaded his forces and infiltrated the station but had never a viewed a living one. A wave of blue light consumed the mass of the creature in a complete sphere of blue energy, and it vanished. Powerful bolts of lightning struck the teleportation device, and it was damaged beyond repair. The unconscious infantry started reawakening as injurious electricity traveled through them and exited through the metallic flooring. He regretted underestimating the creature and knew he would bear the burden of disrupting his superior's communion to inform them of the free-roaming Pylon.

She awoke in a cold sweat. The black-haired woman sensed a dark presence in her mind as she woke. A hideously cold feeling came over her when it attempted to touch her. She could not convince herself of a nightmare and threw her dark sheets off. She headed to the kitchen to get a glass of water. She shook her head as she walked toward the window overlooking the corridor, feeling numb.

Reaching into her right pocket on her one-piece midnight-blue pajamas, she retrieved the small device. It still said the same three words she had read every night that week. Her father had left her to pursue the greatest enemy of the fallen empire, the Pylon. Was he still alive? What force could have kept him away from attending her brother's wedding? And if he was such a powerful psychic, why didn't he teach her more? Why didn't he communicate with her telepathically? The questions haunted and shamed her ego. Pragmatically, she doubted he would return unscarred but remained hopeful that he would return.

Determined in her heart that the insinuations of his death would not destroy her sense of self and security, she placed the glowing device back in her pocket. She stared upward, beyond her window, and outside the prism sunroof. She viewed the beautiful northern lights that fluttered in the sky and realized her innermost desire to leave the hollow shell of the prism and find substance in the real worlds.

Teleported to the surface of the planet, the creature appeared in the westernmost prism complex. It was severely weakened and needed to feed on the biochemical energy within the attendants who welcomed the flash of light that teleported the unsightly form. Afterward, it evaded the novice guards in an inconspicuous form, avoided the outdated robotic guards that patrolled the interior of the military zone, and walked by stealth-suited sentries that fell against the walls of the corridor as they began to dream.

The creature found itself encircled by five robotic, raptorlike guards that had detected its light footsteps and spotted its figure on the ceiling. Their laserlike red eyes beamed on the deviant form and began to record the images. It was forced to take the only course of action it could. A burst of chaotic energy covered the creature with visible dark blue electricity and radiated into bright blue light as it left its body, striking the raptorlike robots. All electrical devices in the impacted space were disabled temporarily. The creature could hear the silent alarms as the living sentry detected the power outage.

The old man walked past the unpowered defenses of the military zone and entered the heart of the prism command system. He entered the office of a high-ranking official using the codes he had obtained on the orbiting station. He operated the most secure computer console and began the process of enlisting his army. He intended it to consist of an additional three hundred soldiers of varying classes and strengths and seven scientists he had discovered using the highly advanced technology on the station. These seven scientists would enable him to access and alter top secret biological, chemical, and technological weaponry. They would be an excellent addition to the seventy-three scientists the unit employed. Under the leadership of the form he awaited, his army would be untouchable.

The new orders he awaited to instate required the genetic and psionic code of a host of officials who interacted once annually. The knowledge the creature possessed and the hive mind's calculations had been an asset. It had taken the creature years to break through the powerful barrier that surrounded the planet and gain contact with the hive that had forgotten its warriors. Its meeting took place when it was unconscious, and erratic messages entered unsorted. An untrained telepath would have interpreted the information as babbling imagery and not realize its incredible realness. The mandatory addition of the recruits meant that they would be transported to the southern prism within the next two days. He reviewed his first targets and prepared his true form for his generous lenders.

Early that morning before dawn, his prey walked toward the office, unaware of the intruder. The bald gray-bearded man tripped over a solid object as he walked into his office, intending to reschedule his hectic day, before he impacted the ground; he was instead pulled to the ceiling as he observed that his computer console had been accessed by stained hands. A momentary predator-prey struggle ensued, but the wiser mind overwhelmed him. With psionic frequencies duplicated and genes fully extracted, his lifeless body was lowered to the ground. Having gained a new identity, the high director transported himself to the southern prism, where the secret wing of the military gathered.

The military headquarters of the secret organization known as Harfore-Darcon Off-World Intelligence (HDOI) were located deep below the station's subbasement. It entered the large blue-walled room as other high-ranking military official joined it at the circular dark blue table. The creature remained undetected by the stealth soldiers and the unanticipated Harfore security who guarded the room.

The creature sat through the majority of the meeting smiling slightly as it was informed of the major breaches in security that occurred that night on the floating station and in the western prism. It stared at the large blue squares that tiled the floor, waited for the remaining ten officials to take their seat, and glanced at one empty black-cushioned chair. As the other official's suspicions entered its realm of thought, the creature glared at them, subduing their instinct to run, until one by one they were telepathically paralyzed. Their bright eyes infuriated it. Its crucial workings leading up to this moment were revived in its twisted mind, and it knew its escape from the battlefield was soon at hand. By the time the last two gentlemen around the circular dark blue table began to notice the silence of their colleagues and its sputtering laughter, it was too late; their minds were prepared to be its willing victims.

CHAPTER VI

ALL ROADS LEAD

Wicked cold air poured into the triangular horizontal black aircraft as the passengers boarded. The pilot positioned the aircraft on the launchpad, and smoothly, the aircraft sped down the runway and lifted into the cloudy sky. She was dressed for the warm destination in a conservative green hoodie and military-like beige-and-dark-green pants. She didn't have any choice in her dress; it was the uniform of the forty-two scientists who were being transported to the southern prism.

At first, she didn't want to go, but Sky convinced her that leaving the northern prism was something that she needed to do. Sky explained that her stagnation in the prism weakened her emotionally and that she needed something to distract her from thinking about her missing father. Her decision to stay was not entirely selfless; she had wanted to finish her proposal on "purposed evolution," as she coined it, and regarded the transfer to the southern prism as a temporary excursion. She felt very privileged to be transported to the southern prism as it was rumored that only the brightest scientists of the three fields were transferred there, and she was the only one in her small but gifted research team to be selected. Her achievement was diminished by her colleagues who eagerly reminded her that she was haphazardly selected at the final moments for an excursion that had been in the planning stages for nearly two years.

Her newly cut hair was still brittle from exposure to the cold, and she knew that some humidity in the jungles of the south would be of some benefit to her. She now had straight black bangs just above her light blue eyes, which covered her small ears and flowed down just past her shoulders. Cassandra had made the wise decision to cut her locks the following morning, and much attention was drawn to her exterior because the hairstyle suited her head shape. That morning, Alex joked about her getting a tan, and she did not admonish his suggestions. West was glad to hear she was leaving because he was running out of meals to prepare, and with his open 1700 shift, he would be able to research sweet new recipes, but she promised to return by the end of the month, and he was grateful for that too supposedly.

She had begun to use a medical lip balm lately that had an awful taste to it; her doctor had prescribed it to her after her semiannual checkup. Her female doctor was very visual and informed her of any imperfections that graced her body. No longer would she have to concern herself with dry skin and lips, and perhaps her vitamin D levels would rise to par.

The aircraft was comfortably crowded with eight rows of five, and she was in the center of the third row, unable to see outside the window. The view from the exterior camera of the aircraft was choppy, and the images on the monitor she viewed from the ceiling of the aircraft were clear for a few minutes. The interference of the magnetic fields that surrounded the mountain range that the aircraft flew over was the cause of the choppy visuals. She acted on a thought to tap her light-brown steel-toe boots against the floor to counter the interference but was unsuccessful and only irritated the sleeping and studying scientists around her. Fed up with trying to decipher the fuzzy outside images, she retrieved her messaging device and continued perfecting her thesis.

The flight lasted for four hours and thirty-three minutes, and Psyy could not contain her excitement as she began to exit the aircraft. She looked up into the air and all around the dense jungle as she descended the stairs. The air transport platform was busy with action. She noticed the many other aircraft in the sky that flew over the southern prism. When her eyes finally glimpsed the magnitude of the jungle, she was again reminded of her childhood.

Her first visit to the tropical environment of the southern prism was very memorable. She had visited another prism a little farther from the equator of the planet with her father, and many memories surfaced in her mind. She had not remembered being outside the prism, but the exotic plant species and insects interested her. The dense green jungle encompassed the entire prism, and she peered down as she boarded an elevated transport craft that took the scientists on a route around the paved perimeter of the prism. Cassandra could see the fast-moving insects that flew through just beyond the reach of normal vision. They looked like small dots to her, but she could make out their swarm.

Cassandra was educated in the devices used to control the insects in the southern prism. The insects were too lethal to be kept unchecked. She remembered a dark tale her father told her when she pleaded with him to take the real jungle tour, and he instead distracted her with the simulations. "This place isn't just known for its beauty. It's also very deadly. You see, if ever the prism's repelling emitters were to simultaneously malfunction, thousands of insects would descend on the prism within minutes and feed on anything and anyone they could find."

His reference to a real event both surprised and scared her. The high director discussed how difficult it was to build the southern prism. It took the most resources to construct and maintain, but the sunlight absorbed by the massive solar panels on the roof of the prism made supplying energy for military purposes an asset. Most intergalactic spacecraft and satellites launched into space were conducted at this location. Upon the realization of this truth, Cassandra suppressed her instincts that screamed signs of a conspiracy at the prism. She again retrieved a small thin clip and grasped her shortly cut hair in her palms, making a small ponytail.

The transport craft entered a dark tunnel and, soon after, descended into a paved lighter-gray tunnel with bright, evenly spaced lights on the side. The scientist off-loaded and boarded six large circular metallic transport pads that lowered them for nearly ten minutes to the prism's subbasement. The scientists were taken to their various quarters to unpack their belongings and then went on a tour of the laboratories in the subbasement.

During her tour, Cassandra decided to take a detour to the botany facilities, and that was when she felt a pressing sensation in the middle of her forehead. She quickly faked a fainting against the gray-paved walls, and instantly, without her face toward them, two cloaked guards appeared to help her. Sky had been training with her, playfully showing her how to manipulate frequencies and shield against telepathic espionage. Creativity was the key to mastering her telepathic powers, and she was beginning to apply hers better every day.

Using a combination of dramatic flair and mental manipulation, she persuaded them to escort her to the small quarters. She entered the cramped space and closed the door. She had never felt so claustrophobic. The black walls and paved white floors of the room added to this effect. The design of her quarters was slick and sophisticated, but it lacked any sense of purposed comfort. It had a small kitchen, shower, sink, toilet-only bathroom, and boxlike bedroom. In the small bedroom, there was a coverless bed in the center, and it took her a quarter of an hour to fit the beige sheets on the empty bed.

Lying on the bed, she looked up at steel pipes that traveled through the ceiling. Her messaging device was strangely unable to access the wireless network and couldn't respond to the messages she received on the passenger plane. Alex had messaged her five times, a few of her colleagues also messaged her, and there were some messages from the curious friends too. This would be a challenging experience, and she regretted missing the tour. Having lost touch with her physical needs, her eyes closed, and she fell asleep suddenly.

When she awoke, it was 0105 hours, and she was furious with herself because the doors to all civilian quarters locked at 1215 hours. Cassandra was unwilling to damage the door or contact the security forces using the comm system mounted on the black wall nearest her bed. After shaking the door handle a couple of times, she walked toward the tiny black-walled washroom. After brushing her teeth quickly, she returned to bed and wished herself a quick, dreamless sleep.

The next morning, she was awoken by the sound of her messaging device; without it, she would not have known when day came. On the device's glowing blue monitor, she was instructed to report to genetic sequencing laboratories in the next hour. She dressed herself in her white lab coat and wore comfortable flat black shoes.

When she finally did report to the facility five minutes late, she saw forty other scientists hard at work determining the amino acid arrangement of three large biological molecules. The laboratory was like any other scientific laboratory she had entered, except larger and triangular. The entrance to the lab was elevated, and the other half of the room was evenly lower, accessible by a small descending staircase. Two of its sides were walled with glass, through which one could view the exterior gray-paved and white-walled hallway. The facility was state of the art and better than she could have imagined.

As she often did, Cassandra attempted to use her telepathy to quickly determine how best to start the process and direct her efforts. She felt a strong pressing on the side of her right temple, and after looking more closely at the other scientists, she noticed that at the side of their right ears was a small rectangular white metallic stripe. It was the cause of her inability to probe their preoccupied minds with ease, and again, she detected cloaked guards passing by the laboratory entrance.

Unable to determine precisely how much attention she had attracted, she assumed that all eyes were on her. Fear rising in her heart, she nearly panicked overtly. She quickly calmed herself, anticipating an attack that never came, and exhaled inconspicuously. After reaching for some facial tissue to falsely swipe her nose, she decided to be professional and ask questions directly.

After abruptly severing ties with his other less intimate relationships, Tim focused all his attention on Alice. She had practically become a member of his small family over the past week, and he felt threatened at first but gradually became comfortable with her endless desire to visit him. His widowed grandmother got along well with Alice but was, every so often, momentarily fatigued by her unannounced visits. Their relationship as boyfriend and girlfriend had been two months in the making, and his grandmother thought that perhaps she would be the one he married; why else would he introduce the two women?

Alice was so different from Timothy, and as his grandmother concluded, opposites attract and hold, so she decided to endorse their relationship. Alice was shy and talkative at the same time, and Timothy could go for days without speaking and was still very outgoing. They interacted eighteen hours a day verbally and seven hours a day physically and knew almost everything about each other.

The night he had attended his grandmother's early exercise classes was still fresh in his mind as an urgent message appeared on his desktop messaging device. He would find it hard to break the news to his girlfriend. Alice grew quite upset with him when he told her he would be deployed in the second southern prism just 120 miles from their location. "Can I come?"

"No, I'm not so sure what it is I'm partaking in. I'll be gone for a couple of weeks."

"I can sneak over there with you," she said and responded to his shaking head, "Yes, I can, and you can help me."

"I couldn't hide you forever," he answered, entertaining her suggestion. "They'll find you. Tell me you'll miss me."

"No, I won't miss you. I'm going. You can't just leave me here. Who will I talk to? What will I fucking do? Baby . . . I'll miss you," she said, bursting into tears.

"Don't make it seem so bad. I'm coming back," explained Tim as he embraced Alice.

"You'll be in wonderland without me." She sobbed as tears rolled down her eye.

"I'll call you every chance I get."

"Promise me?"

"I promise on my life I'll call you every chance I get."

The hours passed quickly, and Frior said his goodbyes to his grandmother and Alice as they stood by the underground tunnel way that led to the other southern prism. He stood cool in his reflective black-armored suit, his arm around Alice while waiting for the train. A green cap held her hair as eyeliner poured below her sunglasses and down her cold cheeks. Alice was dressed in a gray-and-white striped turtleneck with matching skirt and knee-high black boots. His helmet was on as procedure demanded, and he released Alice as seven other armored soldiers greeted him. The tunnel was lit with yellow lights at the top of the circular tunnel. His grandmother wore a long conservative blue velvet overcoat, a roundabout matching head covering that tied loosely beneath her chin, black gloves, and barely visible thin-heeled boots. One hundred soldiers and their loved ones stood on the paved platform waiting for the horizontal, obelisk-like steel train to arrive.

As he moved back to the two women, his grandmother spoke to him gently. "I'm not sure what they've called you to do." She paused. "I'm proud of you, despite the past we've had."

"I know," he said slowly. He meant to say more to her, but the train had arrived so quickly and so loudly. It shook the ground as it pulled to an abrupt stop but remained loud because of the electromagnetic energy that held it off the ground. As Tim boarded the train, he motioned a loving wave, and the train sped into the yellow-lit tunnel.

The train ride was quick, and it took Tim a few minutes to disembark the gray interior of the train. He stood on a paved metallic platform while other soldiers pushed past him. It took him several minutes to reach his barracks. Heavy footsteps marched through the military wing of the prism as soldiers headed to the military auditorium. It was a circular area, and the benchlike, padded red seats accommodated 4,300 easily. The flooring of the auditorium was a black rubberlike material. The room was lit with bright whitish-blue light that shone evenly around the room.

In the center of the auditorium was a smaller circular stage, and on the stage, there sat three men on three black chairs. Tim recognized them easily even in the dark—Commander General Amar Khan, Gen. Will Safino, and High Director Zarvo Leaht. Tim did not know much about Khan and Safino because they were rarely heard from. However, High Director Leaht had become famous for substituting for High Director Richard Vyers, who was since missing in action. His mission to Pylon was top secret, but Tim had connections deep within the military and knew a little about everything.

The three hundred soldiers took their seats around the stage. Tim had seated himself far left from where the three-men faced. High Director Leaht's microphone became operable, and he took the podium at the center of the stage. The creature's spell on the mind began to resonate throughout the room. It took ten seconds for the thick steel doors of the auditorium to slam shut.

"Hello, men and women of the armed forces. Today is a new beginning," the sharp and resounding voice said. "Unfortunately, I must break harsh news. It may not alarm some of you to know that a remnant of the Harforian god system is still intact." Monitors from the ceiling to the right side of the stage lowered, aiding his description.

"You have all been recruited for your skill and impartiality. What I am about to discuss with you is classified and of the utmost level of secrecy. Less than forty years ago, a war broke out on this planet. Seven million Darforians and four million Harforians lost their lives defending this planet—blindly. They died defending a race of less than ten, a race that considers themselves superior based on birth alone. Their time in existence has passed. They wish to feed off the labor of our two strong races and then dispose of us. Their success will not be ours.

"During the last month, you may have heard about the disappearance of a high-ranking commander, the man I now replace, Richard Vyers. He devoted his life protecting our institutions, and make no mistake, he was purposely disposed of. I have reason to believe that he uncovered a secret so shocking some of you may not understand its magnitude.

"We are still enslaved to these gods, and they are slowly becoming stronger, gathering their strength to once again descend to the surface of our world to rule us in bloodshed once more. 'Service, not servitude.' That is the founding principle of our union with the Harforians. My mother is Darforian, and my father is Harforian. I'm a mix of both worlds, you could say. These gods are neither Darforian nor Harforian. They simply want to enslave us, and we cannot allow it!" shouted the creature, intensifying its control.

Within seconds of his last sentence appearing from the folds of the subspace around the seated soldiers, fifty-seven cloaked commandos appeared against the shadowed walls of the auditorium. Their guns were pointed around the room. Red dots scanned those who might have caused trouble. "Don't be alarmed. These are our brethren, Harfore warriors with a conscience, and you must join them."

A slide image of a cloudy bright-blue planet appeared on the giant monitor. "This planet was our home. This is where we must return, if we are to survive. These prisons—sorry, prisms—are no place for us. Oh yes, yes, they are comfortable and slick in design. But, people, listen to me. Listen to your hearts. This is nothing . . . nothing but vanity." He snarled. "We need progress. We need true knowledge. I am tired of being trapped in this box, prodded and pulled by beings that don't have our interests at heart." He slammed the podium and continued his brilliantly deceitful speech.

The creature manipulated the inner desires of all who listened. The images of the planet went into a close-up. One-third of the planet was made of land, and upon closer inspection of the dusty plains, small square and rectangular structures could be seen clearly. Tim's green eyes remained transfixed on the stage. He tried to turn his neck away but felt as if he was half awake and half asleep at the same time. Permanent stains of conquest, power, and emulation consumed him. He tried to make himself invulnerable, but his mind was far too gone in a state of paralyzing shock.

"They have stolen our destiny, suppressed our populations, and now we must strike back. Stand now and take your place in progression," said the powerfully hypnotic voice.

No seat remained unoccupied after the creature's seductive and charismatic speech. Successfully, no heart in the room remained unstirred to their core. The rebellion of the colonies would lead to the ruin of the planet and the creature's long-anticipated freedom.

Cassandra had returned to her quarters after a long day of sequencing the three large biological molecules. They were much more complex than she had first believed. The team of twenty-five biologists had only completed 5 percent of the total work that needed to be done. She lay on her white-sheeted bedding, waiting for the call to dinner. She looked at her small reflection, visible only to her eyes easily, in the steel pipes above her bed. Her body looked bloated and her face obscured. Instantly, she was reminded of her failure in sequencing the genetic material she had sampled from the buried spaceship on Mount Taptoon. The material was far too worn to get a complete sequence.

The call to dinner came at 1900 hours, and she sat at one of the eight brown tables in the white-walled cafeteria. She scooped her fork into her cold cereal-like meal and looked around at the seven other scientists who sat at the table.

"You look sad."

"Oh, yeah, I'm just homesick," Cassandra said, startled, noticing the thin metallic device located on the scientist's right ears.

"Me too. I hope we finish this soon so we can get outside and enjoy the warm weather. I don't even know what we're working on."

"I thought I was the only one," said Cassandra, unable to piece together her thoughts before they became words.

"I think it's a weapon."

"Duh, we're in the military zone," another scientist said. "Why else would they need brilliant scientists?"

The other scientists conversed about various issues as they ate their warm meals. Finally, Cassandra decided to interrupt them. "What's that thing on everyone's ear? Guys?" she said, not managing to get their attention. Her telepathy had always made people so attentive to her. She read the name tag of the eccentric glass-wearing scientist seated in front of her. "Mr. Dean?"

"Yes, Ms. Vyers?"

"Could you explain to me why everyone has this blinking thing by their ear?"

"Oh, well, yes, that's simple," he said, showing her his ear. "This is a telepathic focusing device. It amplifies our thoughts—"

"And it guards against telepathic espionage," a dark-skinned, gray-haired female scientist said.

"I don't see why. I haven't seen any Harforian mind readers since we landed."

"Remember, we're civilians working with highly sensitive military technology. You should be wearing yours."

"Yeah, well, research has proved that some Darforians can read minds too."

"Maybe a few thoughts, but to steal and erase someone's entire active memories, that's doubtful."

"Then how come they're the only ones ever convicted for it?"

"You're referring to two incidents."

"True, true."

"I went to school with five of them, all beautiful, but I'll tell you," a large man said, pausing to swallow his meal, "always, always reading my mind."

"Those shiny-eyed people, they're so freakish. They shouldn't be allowed around us."

"They should all just stay up in that spaceship and leave the rest of us alone."

"You don't have any right to say that!" Cassandra screamed, angered by what she was hearing.

"I can say what I feel."

"Hey, you don't have on the tele-guard," Dr. Dean said, referring to the thin metallic device.

"She's bare meat for the enemy," the female scientist said as a roar of laughter filled the table.

"Nah, she'll be fine. The way you look, no one would even suspect you're a scientist."

"I think they've more than guarded your minds. They've made you all paranoid," she said quietly as she got up and left the table, exiting the cafeteria and walking to her quarters in a fit of passive rage.

Is this how people would feel about me, if they only knew? And by extension, I am Harforian, she thought.

The sunroof over the central corridor closed, leaving the large buildings in darkness. Orders to remain indoors echoed through the dim red corridor. Groups of fifty soldiers moved quickly through the prism, securing all teleportation bays and communication stations. Only their primary objective remained. A large fortified structure in the middle of the prism complex that secretly housed the faction of the Harforian overlord agency was their target.

Bright light shone from the many windows of the structure. The black-stoned structure was ninety meters high and cylindrically shaped. Fast-moving soldiers waited on the dark red marble floors a block from the structure, awaiting an obvious signal to move in. The agency overlooked all agencies and services in the prisms and was responsible for reporting all actions of the Darforian leadership to the overseers on their massive Harforian station that orbited the planet. Three soldiers moved in closer.

The signal arrived when sensors detected that the force-shield-like pulse that traveled through the walls of the structure had fallen, and the lights in the building no longer shone. Soldiers opened fire on the building in broad daylight. Blasts of hot laser energy melted the metallic-stone-covered doors. First, the cloaked guards entered the building; then unexpectedly, from the center of the building, parachuting figures descended, never gaining consciousness as they hit the hard ground. A group of twelve black-suited soldiers entered the building. Through the facility, they searched for Harforians who remained in the structure.

The creature was angered when he was informed that an emergency one-way teleportation device was located somewhere in the structure and that all the occupants of the building had escaped. He knew that his goals were still achievable. He ordered the soldier-technicians to arm the weapons of the prism and launch a powerful heated assault on two randomly selected prism complexes. The creature gave the technicians the access codes they needed, and they carried out the creature's orders without hesitation or reasoning.

The creature's powerful ally descended from the surface of the planet in the only functioning transport device. The new high director and his eleven generals had reached the site of the most devastating weapon. They armed the circular catapult-like black device that was located deep within the subbasement.

The eighteen green metallic silos on the edge of the dense jungle began to open slowly. As the ball-like black devices began to reach the surface, nine red dots appeared in the bright midday sky. They came into view as glowing balls of light held together in white-capped capsules appeared over the prism. Fifty meters of greenery around the silos became flames as they impacted the site of the silos and ripped into the ground, causing waves of burnt branches, roots, leaves, dry mud, and burrowed insects to lift high into the air. A lavalike canyon now burned alongside the prism structure that had been shaken violently. The large arrowlike missiles screeched through the sky and, minutes later, reached their targets, causing much destruction to the exterior of the northern prism and a glowing crater in the eastern side of the southern prism.

On a cloaked vessel orbiting alongside the massive station, a silver-handed being in the highest chair of command addressed an alert command center on the station. "There's nothing I could have done. We've been blinded up here. He's locked us out of our defense control grid."

"I hear you, and the failure remain yours."

"Yes, I have no further excuses."

"This situation is completely of your doing. My brethren and I are starting to doubt your ability to lead our kinsmen."

"This isn't your kingdom."

"What's that? You stand in my judgment," said the silver-faced god, pausing for a second. "Nonetheless, I have power capable of correcting any incompetence."

"I beg your forgiveness," the commander said falsely.

"Without action to correct your faults, you shall beg it no more. You shall take with you a hundred vessels and the resources required and descend to the surface of the planet. Find this alien interloper and bring his mind back to me intact, and mind you, do not harm the populace," commanded the dourer purple-eyed god. The visual link between the two massive vessels ended, and the blond prince vented his frustration on those around with shrieking curses.

"What weapons are available?"

"We have no weapons for the remaining hour."

"Technician?"

"Near god Thunder, I suggest we create an electromagnetic storm above the offending prism complex."

"What did you call me?"

"Sir?"

"I am no god. There are no gods. Never refer to me again as such."

"Master, I must warn you that even you cannot blaspheme a god."

The blue-eyed, white-cloaked warrior could find no reason to rebuke the technician before the crowded command center that listened to him in disbelief.

"Stop standing around. Prepare the vessels and coordinate the commandos your god requested. That prism is damaged enough. Create five storms over the remaining prisms."

"Commander?"

"If he has command codes to the southern prism, he'll transport himself to the weakened southern prism and arm its warhead. Create the magnetic storm and make them unusable."

"The warhead on those prisms cannot harm the station?" the high-ranking technician said as he was swiftly interrupted.

"Just do it," Thunder said as he left the command center.

Returning from the laboratory in her cheap white lab coat, Psyy walked down the hallway of the subbasement as she felt a small tremor become stronger. Opening the metallic black door to her quarters, she stopped for a moment as cries of unbelief entered her mind. Reacting quickly, she reached for her black suitcase and ran to the small bedroom, throwing her suitcase underneath her bed before sliding there herself.

The pipes that traveled through her quarters burst, and sprays of gray liquid and water soaked the room. Several cracks formed near the edges of the walls, and more water dripped unto the floor. She could hear the many sounds of unending alarms. The ceiling above her quaked and creaked. Sensing that the large earthquake had ended, she crawled out from underneath the bed. Standing up, she pulled her suitcase out and ran to the exit.

The door was locked, and she opened it with a blast of motioned air that left her hands. She nearly slipped as she walked out into the wet corridor. Water gushed out of cracks in the ceiling. Fearing the corridors would flood, she froze the large leak with her open right palm. She lifted herself from the ground and flew through the hallway, sensing no conscious minds around her. Quickly, she tried to assess the transportation platform; but as she reckoned, they didn't work.

Seeing the doorways that led to the transportation platforms in the wall, she opened them forcefully with her mind, bending a meter-long oval entrance in the doorway. She threw her bag through the entrance and then her body, realizing that the opening led to a floorless dark drop. Capturing her bag, she allowed herself to fall for a few seconds and levitated her light body high in the transport shaft. She could sense rescue workers running down the stairs to rescue those who need rescuing and felt somewhat guilty for abandoning them. But she was focused on one task: returning to the laboratory near the surface and stealing the biological samples she had been sequencing. Psyy suspected they must be the reason behind the "earthquake." She had felt the energy source of the earthquake and knew it had resulted from a massive impact of something militaristic.

She elevated her body higher and higher at a rate of two meters per second and let out an unwelcome scream. The items in her unlocked suitcase clanged against the metal walls of the dark shaft, and she did not see them fall. She swore loudly as she paused in the dark space, conflicted on whether to descend to the bottom and retrieve her smashed devices and stylish clothing. Anger and regret were her primary emotions. Overwhelmed, Psyy flew onward, ascending to the level she believed the scientists were on, only because she sensed the presence of many cloaked guards. Why had these people practically abducted her and placed her in a genius camp where she slaved away on some type of weapon?

The bright blue light surrounded her body in a strong shield of light energy. Anticipating conflict, she propelled herself to the rectangular visible landing spot, waiting for a moment as her shield intensified. She could sense the movements of cloaked guards passing the doorway. Sparks ensued as the large black metallic doors of the transport device slammed against the white metal walls of the laboratory zone as they scratched the walls. Psyy flew with great speed through the hallways, having abandoned her near empty suitcase. She scattered the already cracked glass wall that led to the laboratory and landed on the white metal floor.

Cloaked guards descended on her position. She gathered one of the samples that remained in a large black microscope in the middle of the room, which were hidden behind the ledge of the solid lab desks. Five cloaked guards entered the laboratory and saw a glowing woman in a pink lab coat standing beside a large green microscope. They pointed their weapons set to kill and pulled the trigger. Metallic bullets impacted the form they imagined. The guards had become aware of the illusion but had little time to prepare for a blast of cold that encased all the invisible guards entirely, except for one whose head was unfrozen.

"Tell me how to get out of here. Now!"

""I don't know! I'm so cold!" the artificial voice cried.

"Whose orders have us here?"

"I can't remember."

"You assholes tried to kill me!"

"I did—yes, I did. You're stealing, looting in a time of disaster."

"I'm not. I'm securing the samples. I know it's what they're after. I've been concerned about this from the beginning. What have we been working on here?"

"Arcon . . . the new high director, Zarvo, is a god in disguise. You were working on the sequence of three gods. We're trying to create compatible Arconian cells on Darth to eventually fight back against the Arconian Empire."

"And? Where are the other two samples? Just think loudly, and I'll hear you. Hurry up, please."

Can't breathe, the guard thought before fainting.

Psyy waved her hot hand in the direction of the five red-suited guards, and they fell to the floor as the ice became water in an instant. She ripped the access card off the guard closest to her and flew into the air again as she entered the hallway through the shattered opening. Cloaked guards followed her as she evaded them and entered the transport shaft, ascending to the surface.

Sixteen helicopter-like black aircraft hovered over the southern prism. The commandos on the helicopters looked down at the flaming jungle from the open door of the helicopter. A large canyon of lava flowed alongside the prism. Halfway from the jungle horizon and the prism complex, a swarm of flesh-eating green-tinged insects could be seen amassing. The sky was filled with thick black smoke that blocked out the sun from their perspective. Forty dark-blue-suited commandos landed on the roof of the prism and, using their powerful laserlike weapons, carved a large circular opening. They descended on ropes into its dark corridors. They landed successfully, and the attack began.

Cloaked warriors were quickly subdued by the telepathic commandos, who detected them easily. Their swords of force dismantled the cloaked guards' armor faster than thoughts could react. They walked the shattered halls of the prism after the detection of untrained soldiers and descended into the transport shafts that led to the underground train station.

A squadron of fifty soldiers waited for the second train that had left the station to transport their eighty comrades to the northern prism as directed. The telepathic commandos approached the soldiers who stood, unable to see them. The sounds of slicing bones, cartilage, and armors filled that station, and wild panic took over the ranks. Bright red blood flew against the steel walls of the station.

Frior turned around to see what caused the vile sounds, and after blinking for a third time, he saw an awful sight. Dark-blue-suited men with long bloodied steel-like swords slashed away at his fellow black-suited soldiers. His heart pounded stronger. Rage overtook his panic, and his inner strengths were forever unleashed. With lightning speed, he charged at the seven commandos with missing punches and tackled four of the commandos to the metallic floor. He rose to his feet, pushing himself off the ground with his hands. White flames erupted from his hands again, causing sparks, blowing the three stumbling telepathic commandos against the doorway they had entered. Their armor had caught fire, and they ran around helplessly. He reached for their swords, and a wave of psychic energy pushed Frior for a moment.

You're infected. You must be purged. Stand down, Soldier. These thoughts entered his mind for what seemed like a few seconds before he resisted, and his adrenaline kicked in overdrive. A black vial of energy adorned and darkened his black-suited armor as three small javelin-like objects impacted his helmet, bending and snapping as they broke against his armor. No longer could he feel the wave of psychic energy propelling him to the ground. He felt lighter and more destructive. A ball of dark water-like energy amassed in his hands and radiated in the form of waves toward the two commandos who opposed him. The sound of brittle bones breaking from under the weight of the force of energy that consumed them filled the chamber, and the forty soldiers directed their weapon fire at the commandos who were now visible. An even louder sound than the breaking bones filled the station.

A flaming train pulled into the station louder than it had arrived. Half melted by lava, the doors to the train did not open; and behind the train, a wave of lava entered the tunnel, melting the metallic floors of the chamber as it flowed beside it. "Move back to the surface and wait for reinforcements," Frior commanded.

"I'm in charge of this mission, Corporal. I'll give the orders—"

"No, you won't, not anymore. I'm the strongest. I'm in charge. Let's move," Frior said as he started to leave, and others followed.

"Those were elite commandos hunting us. We'd better stick together."

"He's strong. I'm following him."

"I understand, General."

"Fine."

"That means we're enemies of the overlords."

"They said we were infected. I could hear them in my head."

"Follow me to the surface," Frior repeated himself.

"Why?"

"You four, follow me. Don't listen to him," said the commanding colonel.

The squadron split in half; twenty soldiers marched toward the surface, headed for the air bay, while twenty were drawn to secure the entrance to the transport device for the subbasement.

The doors to the transport device opened, and one man stepped out; a creature stepped out too—Gen. Amar Khan, the creature in disguise. General Khan addressed the soldiers. "There is a female scientist scurrying through the facility in the western side of the prism. She has something of great value to me. What she has is the map for our very existence. Don't even try to reason with her. Secure the sample in her possession and bring it to me. And be mindful of the telepaths. They are quite formidable. Use these devices," he said, directing the soldiers to a large black briefcase that contained hundreds of small lidlike devices capable of drowning out and countering the telepathic attacks of the enemy Harforians. "Have they secured my vessel?"

"Yes, sir," the soldiers said in unison.

"Now take leave, quickly." The seventeen soldiers sprinted toward the western staircase and vanished. "You three will remain at my side until the appointed time. Corporal Ang, for your most valiant display of courage, I shall demand your immediate promotion to brigadier general and a notable place in history when our new world commences. For now, you are at my right hand. And there, you shall take the reins of our destiny. Lead me to my vessel."

CHAPTER VII

CLASH OF THE PERFECT

Wasplike red insects flew over the prism complex, yet pockets of space remained between them and the helicopter-like black aircraft. They tore into the uncovered air and land craft that remained on the prism pavement, scraping against their metallic exteriors with their gleaming black stingers. The sun beamed down on them, casting their shadows hauntingly.

Within the white lead interior of the helicopter, a message was received. From the circular opening on the helicopter's back compartment, fifty-one and a half feet in circumference, silver balls fell from the opening and unto the pavement. The balls bounced off the tarmac with a bouncing clang and landed again on feetlike legs. They appeared to be docile small, half-a-meter-long spiders. Unseeingly, the design of the robots was to confuse and destroy. The fifty shiny robots climbed up the wall of the prism and entered through the large damaged sunroof. The large swarm of red insects flew past the prism, and the sky was again clear of biotic noises, until the sharp screams of real-life raptors echoed through the forest.

Arriving on the main floor of the subbasement, the doors to the transport device blew open and fell against the hallway;

the scientist landed on the ground, exhausted from her longest levitation. Cassandra leaned against the wall of the transport shaft, unable to stop the itchiness of her cool clothes. Her shape still beautiful, she looked at the faintly glowing outline around her body as it vanished. She again became alert to the sounds of quick movements.

She started to run through the dark corridors and realized that she had no sense of direction. Anxiety took over, and she decided to try leaving the prism the easy way. She stopped in the middle of the dark corridor as emergency lights began to flicker, sensing her movement. A circle of blue light surrounded her, and her teleportation half sphere successfully formed. Cassandra lifted her energy vessel into the air and entered through the ceiling of the corridor. She moved slowly at first but then sensed the fear of occupants huddled together in the rooms she passed through, and her guilt of not aiding them caused her to ascend faster. She passed through many floors in the subbasement with her eyes closed. It was clear the civilians were in distress.

"What's happening?"

"It's a lockdown."

"I'm going to go try to see if the doors are unlocked."

"I'm scared."

"The power's not working."

"I can't even call the rescue workers."

"Why do they always lock the doors?"

"Remember, we stay inside until we get the all clear."

"The wireless system is down."

"This sucks. I can't take waiting."

"I'm missing my programs."

"Is someone coming to help us?"

"Was that ever an earthquake?"

"Who's coming to help us?"

"I hope this is just an earthquake . . . and the Arconians aren't back."

Finally, Psyy reached a level where some form of assistance was being given to the occupants. White-suited rescue workers were moving through the corridor, requesting information on injured occupants and counting numbers. She felt light headed and realized for a moment that she might be running out of oxygen. In her desperation to move the sphere faster toward the surface, the half sphere gained volume and accelerated.

The group of seventeen soldiers had reached the surface of the prism and waited within the gray-walled stairwell leading to the corridor. They were evenly spaced between the upper and lower staircases of the floor, their large riflelike weapons loaded and drawn. Suddenly, a knock came at the small greenish-blue door leading to the corridor. Their scanners within their suits showed nothing. There was a small knock again on the door. The soldiers pointed their weapons. Large bullet holes appeared in the door and blew it from the exit as the soldiers moved out into the red marble corridor. The brightness of the corridor, which they had left in darkness, alarmed them, and the cracked sunroof became visible.

They looked up at the stone building they had recently raided and formed a defensive formation. From their breastplates, they retrieved small compactible, handleless, scissors-held, fanlike black objects that unfurled into shields two meters in circumference made of durable but thin black material. They quickly formed their defensive stance known as the beetle. The men formed a circle where the soldier on the outside overlapped their circular shields, leaving small gaps from which weapons protruded from all sides, while the soldier in the middle held their shields above their heads. The formation looked more like a moving table with evenly projecting rifles on both sides as they walked through the corridor and waited at the doors of the transport devices.

The soft sounds of movement caused unaimed gunfire to fill the corridor. From the sunroof of the prism, three bright steel balls fell on the soldiers in defensive formation. The balls exploded upon impact with the shell of the beetle. The shoulders were pushed to their knees, but their shields remained strong and intact. Aimed gunfire filled the corridor, and burn marks from the gunfire stained the walls.

Six steel spiders ran across the red marble floor and were blown to pieces by the gunfire. Twenty steel spiders ran down the high structures within the prism. Mounted on their backs were small rocket launchers that fired conelike missiles down toward the soldiers, exploding into thick balls of fire as they reflected off their shields. The soldiers fired at the boxlike structures, damaging their exteriors, which caused more glass and building material to crash to the ground. The soldiers began to move away from the transport doors, shooting as they walked on glass and other debris. One awkward motion in their formation was all it took to create a small opening, and the spiders were ready. Three dashed for the opening, one was damaged as it leaped into the air, and the other missed the space completely, bouncing off the electrified shield of the beetle. However, one breached the exterior of the beetle and exploded, sending the soldiers flying into the air against the transport doors and corridor walls and into the middle of the corridor. The soldiers scrambled to their feet, only to be tackled by spiders that attached themselves to the soldiers, electrifying them into surrender.

The general had made it to his poly-craft regardless of the helicopter-like aircraft that hovered above him in plain view. The bright sun healed his wounds quickly, and the clear sky tempted him to fly. He reached the tarmac with his new brigadier general and expendable meal covered by a clear screen of imageless light. He didn't have to hold hands with Frior to remain invisible, the wave of airlike energy encompassed him before setting foot unto the tarmac. The half-a-meter-long metallic spiders passed him swiftly, and even as larger, four-meter folded spiders descended to the tarmac from large parachutes only meters away from them, his speed did not increase. The creature enjoyed his ability to conquer minds and admired the powers of his newest follower. He had no respect for styling and had not duplicated the general's declarations as well as he should have. Instead of his armor appearing bright silver, it was an unpolished light gray.

They had reached the location they needed to on the tarmac and waited for a moment. The ground beneath them began to move, and they started to rise. The large platform beneath them moved six meters aboveground. A large metallic spider ran past them, headed for the prism. The ground magnified beneath them, and the platform flipped. Six helicopter-like aircraft scrambled to their location, hovering aside from the now steel circle in the middle of the tarmac. Nothing resurfaced from the tarmac as the pilots of the aircraft had expected.

High in orbit around the planet on the Harforian station, communication channels between High Director Zarvo Leaht of the Harfore-Darcon Forces (HDF) and his technicians opened. "Have you reached the surface of the prism yet, sir?"

"No, I'm gathering airships and ammunition in the first southern prism."

"Is that really necessary?"

"Yes, my studies have shown that this Pylon is capable of controlling massive amounts of psychic energy. He'll want to convert as many followers as he can. And I'll need the right equipment to stop it."

"Pylonite," said the technician, correcting the commander. "Hold on, sir, I'm monitoring something. I suggest you get to the southern prism and survey the damage."

"For what? He's already left."

"Well, sir, I don't think it has."

"What? You think I don't know the urgency of my mission!"

"No, of course, you do. It's just we haven't confirmed that . . . hold on, sir. You may be right. Our sensors have detected a vibration that matches that of an underground vessel. And its movements seem to be leaving the prism."

"I knew it."

"Is it any longer detectable?" the high technician asked his staff. "No, it has left the detection zone. It's unbelievably large for an underground vessel."

"Ah, just great," said the angered acting high director. "In what direction? And when?"

"Northwest at . . . 0940 hours, our time, southern zone time 1304 hours. However, there are still more fighters on the surface battling the MEs. You should—"

"That's hardly worth my time," he said, his voice pausing. An unexpected snap of anger occurred in his voice. "Technician, listen to my orders and stop giving me suggestions. Order the prisms to close, reseal all gas lines, and start the subterranean scans around a two-hundred-meter circumference of all prisms. I don't have to tell you to arm the ground mines on all prisms, except the southern ones."

"Yes, sir." The communication link closed. "I already have," the technician said mockingly.

The six large metallic spiders sprang into action, scaling the white exterior of the prism and entering through the scattered sunroof. Dropping like bricks unto the red marble floors through the bright waterfall of light that entered the prism ceiling, they landed on their eight legs. They scrambled down the corridors toward the living soldiers, quickly slaying them with the large scythelike claws on their front legs. The spiders were four meters in diameter. Their steel-colored frame defined their lethal purpose. Three laser turrets were mounted where its eight eyes should be, and it had various hidden visual, temperature-monitoring, and audio-monitoring devices. The T-19 Arcane was a weapon of Harforian military invention and capable of fast destruction. Thousands of its previous prototypes lay in ruin on the planet Arcon.

A ball of blue light formed instantly in the corridor and fell into the floor. The ball exploded just as quickly as it had formed, leaving a large shallow crater in the marble floor. Dust and particles of the floor flew up into the air as a woman with a blue glow stepped out of the crater. Psyy coughed as she gasped for fresh air. Her teleportation had worked, and she now felt more secure with her potential.

Looking around at the bloodied bodies that littered the floor, she gasped. The light that poured in from the cracked sunroof hurt her eyes for a moment. The blood on the walls and floor of the corridor was enough to make her heart pound with fear. Her strength and logic took charge, and she looked around for an exit.

She picked up on the sounds of walking black-suited soldiers who appeared at the far end of the hallway. Her eyes peered at them as a large metallic spider fell on top of them, pinning them to the ground. Many images of bravery filled her strong light-blue eyes, and her tiredness left her. A blast of blue light left her hands and burned through the top of the spider. Now airborne, she reached the soldiers, kneeling to assess their condition.

"Don't move. You could be injured. Are you okay?"

"Are you a medic? You're glowing."

"No, it's just the lights. You're alive."

"What happened?"

"They attacked the compound," said a faint soldier.

"Who?"

"The Harforians."

"They've attacked all the compounds," repeated the other soldier.

"We all work together. Are you serious? Are you sure? Why would they do that?"

"They want the surface of the planet."

"That doesn't make sense. I don't believe it."

Her conversation was interrupted by a powerful blast of orange light that bounced off her glowing body as she knelt. Blood sprayed on her shield of light, causing it to sizzle and buzz. She felt the piercing pain in her back and investigated with her hand. Her epidermis bled. Her clothes were ripped. The thought of the dead soldiers passed her mind quickly as she feared for her own life.

She spun around quickly, seeing the four-meter spider that walked toward her as it began to spray more bullets of orange light. The blue light around her body intensified. A powerful blue liquid light left her hand, freezing the spider to the ground as her kicking foot shattered the dry ice that covered it and its two front legs.

What the hell is that? she thought as she looked around to see the dark-blue-suited commandos.

"It's not a soldier."

"Who cares? We better destroy it."

"It's a glowing woman, maybe one of the jungle people."

"Who cares? She's damaging the equipment and obviously resisting us."

"And she's a telepath."

"Yeah, she can hear us."

Her heart pounded fiercely. "I'm a civilian. Help me. You guys did this? Why?" she questioned as her mind slammed the commandos against the edge of the intersecting corridors, knocking their weapons from their hands and overcoming them completely.

She looked at the light that shone through the sunroof and realized her foolishness. She ascended to the opening, and silver balls descended from the ceiling, causing her to be puzzled as she climbed into the air. Looking down, she again saw the ripped armor of the dead soldiers, and she felt a shock go through her body. Small steel hands were wrapped around her body, constricting her hands. Instantly, her mind tore them off her body. Another steel spider landed on her head and fell off in a spray of sparks. She needed to leave. She grew desperate.

In a swift, upward, divelike motion, she exited the prism and entered the bright, open air of the rooftop. Just as she thought her ordeal was over, she looked up into the sky. The sky was filled. Helicopter-like black aircraft hovered around her on every side, and she began panicking. She watched the helicopters for a moment, admiring their shiny exteriors. The sun took her focus, and she looked down into the dense green jungle. A shiny metallic circle on the ground took her attention as it reflected the sun. A large spider came through the crack in the sunroof as she turned around. It would have made her tumble down the rooftop had she not grabbed it instinctively and thrown it off the prism exterior, causing it to fall to a shattering end. A helicopter-like aircraft moved in on her position. She waved her hands madly in the air for help. "I'm a scientist! Help me, please!" she yelled, waving her hands madly. She listened with her mind.

"Okay that's the target?"

"That is the target."

"Looks harmless."

"She's the one we saw shooting that cannon of light."

"All right, we'll help you. Arming weapons."

"Targeting."

Cassandra's heart raced; a million different thoughts flipped through her head. She heard the laser cannons arming on the helicopter. She reacted unconsciously to several movements. She forcefully pushed the chopper to her left on its side, causing other helicopters to shake in the sky. A straight blast of cold air left her hand, covering the heated surface of the chopper in ice. She spun around in a full circle, kicking the large spider that tried to scale the prism wall back down to the interior. Rockets were launched. She jumped off the rooftop, and her white lab coat was left floating in the air behind her. A loud explosion turned the prism rooftop into hot red flames, scorched her coat, and made her sweat. She landed weakly on the tarmac.

Psyy was exhausted. Now she was dressed in a sleeveless purple top and black shirt with her black pantyhose underneath. She formed a great ball of liquid light. The wind blew her black hair. She hesitated and then hurled the ball up into the air with an unnecessary motion of her hands. It smashed into the chopper like a snowball of dry ice, and the chopper fell on its side for a moment as she slowed down its descent, causing it to slide across the tarmac instead of exploding. This feat of mercy would come back to haunt her. The blue light around her body had started to dim as she saved the chopper.

A sharp bullet impacted her right arm, causing her to flinch. Her injuries were apparent but not deadly. It wasn't just her clothes that wore the scars of the bullets; now her arm did also. Psyy grimaced and touched her right arm with her left hand to check what damage had been inflicted. A slight but painful scar had formed crookedly on her bicep between her shoulder and her elbow. Shock was her first emotion. But before she could shake her head and run into the jungle, another large bullet whipped by her. A deep, unexplainable sadness took over her. And combined with the third emotion, utter rage, she was no longer holding back.

The list of upsetting events overtook her mind: the sad disappearance of her father, anger at her father for leaving her and her brother behind, anger with her colleagues for complaining about her ideologies and theories, anger from being imprisoned in the prism complex most of her life, and anger at herself for allowing her high-fashioned clothes and accessories to be lost in the transport shaft. Her messaging device was backed up several times, but how would she get a hold of a new device now that this war had started? The anger consumed her. It combined into one highly charged thought.

Her body stood still, but her mind moved around the prism complex rapidly, assessing the situation. The five functioning helicopters moved closer to her, arming their deadly weapons. Ten commandos turned skilled snipers on the rooftop pointed large black guns at the back of her turned head. Nineteen small metallic spiders scurried down the exterior of the prism and leaped onto the tarmac. High in the clear blue sky, seven large metallic spiders were parachuting down to the surface of the prism. The loud screech of raptors from within the dense jungle around her didn't shake her. First, she put on what seemed to be a smile, but it quickly faded, and then intense anger appeared on her face. Subatomic particles of force surrounded her body, and a full circle of forceful blue light that projected from her locus of energy came into her effect, and her offensive was now prepared.

The blond and fair-skinned man walked leisurely down the dark-gray-tiled aisles of his vessel and into the blue carpet of his office. He had an alert walk. His open white trench coat displayed a black jumpsuit that held tightly to his body and collectively made him look larger than his actual size. He stood just over six feet, looked through dark-blue eyes, and had a face that seemed unendingly angered. His sharp nose and specifically pronounced canine teeth vilified him. The large zeppelin-like light-blue vessel he now commanded floated just above the mesosphere of the planet.

He waited in his office, watching down on the surface of the planet through the windows that were really just images sent to a gigantic wall by the exterior cameras. Watching the panel of computers that decorated his wall, he felt tired. His only time to truly relax was now, and he took advantage of his latest moment of peace. He turned off his computer monitors as he dropped himself in the black armchair in a spacious sitting area, which was well adorned and designed by him for him. A glass table was in between the two armchairs. A loud beep was heard from his monitors, and the intercom in his room requested his presence at the helm.

"Disturb me now," he said as he pressed the button on his messaging device to turn it off.

"System offline 334," he commanded, and his office became a faraway island.

He fell into a shallow sleep. Thunder was merely the name given to him by his adoptive mother. She loved him as any mother would, but he felt fully disconnected from her inner world of power, which was why she demanded he be made a ruler of the Harforians before her banishment. The power she had seen in him was enormously focused, it scarred her twice, and she took the proper steps to rid him of them but not entirely. At first, the heavy woman envied his cuteness but gradually grew so attached to him that his success became her own. She had already had a child of her own, but he was already past the age of babying.

"What is that you're holding?" the bald-headed youth said, waiting for an immediate answer. "Mother? Don't hide things from me. Tell me."

"It's a child I rescued from the surface."

"Is he dead?"

"No, he's sleeping."

"Does Father know?"

"Yes."

"What does he think?"

"He loves the child as he does you."

"As much as me? You barely know him."

The monotone voice of the woman hushed him. "Don't raise you voice. You'll wake him."

"Tell me."

"Of course, we don't love him as much as you, but we will soon, and so will you."

"Why is it he has blond hair and I have none?"

"I told you he's not my child. You're not related, dear. He has different parents."

"Oh, so we'll look different forever?"

"Yes, but you'll all carry the same things I've taught you deep inside your hearts."

"I know this already. She's far too big to be a baby you could carry."

"He's a boy, like you."

"I know that. I just said the wrong word."

"That's what happens when you speak without thinking."

"Mother?"

"Yes?"

"What happened to your face?"

"Nothing's happened to my face. It's just a blemish. It's the light from the sun. I'll be fine."

"It looks really burned. And you seem scared. You should stop going down to Darth."

"Child, you ask far too many questions. I'm sure your father wants you now."

Thunder's power to command the temperature and light made him an asset to her. She brought him to many places, including the planet Arcon. There, she was welcomed, for no one knew her true face, and her powers mimicked that of the inhabitants. Sadly, the day came when her deceitful ways were discovered. "You hid the weapon from me all this time."

"He's not a weapon. Who told you?"

"He is what he is."

"I shall determine that."

"I'm the one that's done everything."

"Speak no more."

"Leave her alone."

"The child is brave. Perhaps I will allow him to live. I shall return his power."

"You, however, Athor, shall not be so lucky. For your betrayal of the gods and this empire—"

"Stop! She's not yours to control!" The blond boy wept.

"Remove him. Restore the power to this room."

"I never revealed our location. I just thought I could join them and defeat them from within. They think I'm an Arconian. Imagine what we could do if I entered the leadership."

"Lies. I have read your heart. You're in love with one of them. You've defied me, humiliated me. Thank you, my son, Salientian. I would have never determined her true motives without your assistance. Today you are no longer a woman's apprentice but a god. Your communion will start tomorrow." He touched the shoulder of the then newly bald child. "For in truth, I have spent more resources creating you than I ever did on any other possession."

"No. He's not ready. This is the child that should take the covenant and the title. He is salient," said Athor, her mouth closing underneath her mask.

"I shall wait for the brightest star to face our direction before I execute my judgment, for I have already decided."

The moment came when the sun did face her direction, and she still lived. Salientian betrayed the ruling god and took control of the planet Darth. The overheated and aged body was powerless to summon help as he fought his own kin. Three thousand servants were sacrificed with their former master that day, placed in a room that was unprotected from the intense heat of the nearby sun.

The god Athor, who should have been at their side honoring her master, was spared, forever exiled on Arcon by Salientian, her mind swept clean of the location of Darth and Hier. He would not kill Athor, but he would make her suffer by giving her the wish that she so wanted. Salientian sent her away with nothing, but her memories and powers to Arcon to live as a slave. Naked and bare, Athor was marooned on the planet Arcon, supposedly left to die or achieve her possible mission—infiltrating the Arconian leadership and providing intel to the HDF or Salientian because of their psychic link. Salientian, the silver one, claimed his right to rule the planet Darth and continued his reign for generations. Athor's adopted child, the blond one, would be kept in check under the watchful eye of the few remaining gods as the weapon they needed to create an army that would one day conquer Arcon.

Jeremiah Newnham believed he had a happy childhood but grew into a cold, unhappy man. The silver one had altered his memory, changed his childhood, and made him a near god—good but not good enough for the communion. Fatherless and motherless yet very wealthy, Jeremiah had slaves to serve him, protect him, and keep him from abusing the surface dwellers or perhaps from saving them. He was the most powerful weapon on the planet Darth as the gods had planned.

A jolt brought Jeremiah back to the waking world as he wiped his mouth that had obviously drooled. He sat upright in the chair. The large window in his room began to scramble. A challenge appeared to him, one too worthy to pass. On the wide screen, he could make out the image of trees from the jungle scattered all over the tarmac of the southern prism. The chaos amused him; four molten T-19 Arcane spider robots lay broken, two choppers were split in half on the tarmac, and another was covered in uncommon ice, but the sight that alarmed him the most was the large silver circle that lay in the side of the prism. The thrown object left a sizable gash that revealed the inside of the prism to the burning sun above the jungle. The flaming cases of T-19s that the zeppelin-like spaceship had dropped earlier that day were still falling to the ground. The three choppers engaged her in combat and were respectively frozen, crumpled, and melted by her might. Ten more choppers closed in on her position, firing missiles, which were deflected by her telepathy into the jungle, frozen, and exploded by the faint blue light that shot from her hands. What shocked him the most was that she seemed to enjoy and was unreserved in the damage and chaos she caused.

He nearly laughed when he saw the frozen commandos unable to remove the ice that covered their hands and feet, gluing them to the ground. Jeremy did not hesitate to call for his servants, who came into his office quickly, carrying his mental guard, war gear, magnetic gloves, and several heavy riflelike black weapons. A worthy challenger awaited him, one with no willingness to run.

Gathering his full-body armor suit of gray, he threw off his white trench coat. Placing his silver metallic facial mask over his face, his dark blue eyes, and thick blond hair that fell over on forehead, he prepared himself to defeat the most entertaining performer he had ever seen. The woman was magnificent and powerful. The breathing holes for his nose made the mask look reptilelike, six for breathing, two for seeing. He attached his large black rifles to the sides of his arms and concealed the six red explosive devices under his left wrist. The swordless knight ordered the zeppelin to open for him.

"Order the alpha group to disengage the enemy and leave the prism area."

"Sir."

"Are we directly above the prism?"

"Yes, Commander."

"Open the hatch and begin to lower the *ZF*," he said, referring to the zeppelin. "And don't come too close to surface until I say."

"Yes, sir. Commander, will you need a parachute?" said his aide.

"No," he said, irritated.

"The teleportation devices are still functioning."

"I am aware of that. Only when I say are the commandos, the choppers, the spiders, and anything else to return to the prism. I want nothing disrupting my concentration."

"Yes, sir."

"I work alone. Got it? Regardless of what you see happening, do not interfere to help me," Jeremiah said. "It may be a hindrance."

"Yes, Commander."

"I'll be back soon."

He leaped down the dark hatch, and his whole body became static. His eyes glowed a light gray, and rapidly, as he slid through the hatch, electricity surrounded his body. On the exterior of the light-blue zeppelin, he was ejected from a small opening. He fell through the air headfirst. The electric field around his body became stronger as he descended at speeds of over six hundred miles an hour. The bright sun did not daze him. His background was the clear blue sky. His platinum blond hair fluttered behind him, illuminated by the sun. His arms, which carried his guns, parted from his body, and he shaped them as a diver would. The wind rushed past his body, causing much fiction; his body sped up as he saw the faint clouds forming in the sky and transforming into a flash of lightning. The lightning branched into the tall trees as it struck the jungle.

Her mind was distracted from viewing the damage she had inflicted in her reckless offensive. A bolt of lightning on a clear day was a rare sight. The sun had faded a little but still shone strong. She froze the last of the commandos in the damaged helicopter; she chose to keep the bunch of them in. Psyy felt fearful of the power she unleashed and the limits of her output. Hearing the loud sound of helicopters retreating away from her, she felt puzzled at what to do next. The six large buildings in the prism were now in plain view of the sun, and the small insects flew by her closer than ever.

Her clothes were badly torn, but generally, she still looked conserved. Her exposed arms had light red bruises all over them. The sleeveless purple top she wore looked burnt. The black shirt had not ripped except at the edges. Her silly black pantyhose was utterly hole filled, and the part below her knees had been stripped off her body and now lay in a million little pieces, blowing all over the cratered tarmac.

She would have lowered her guard had she not seen the bolt of lightning strike the jungle in plain view of the prism complex. Could people inside the prism see her? Had they seen her fighting? Fighting to protect herself instead of helping them? She hoped not. An anxious bolt of lightning struck her, and she fell to the tarmac. Rising quickly and glowing ever brighter, she looked around and saw the masked blond-haired warrior.

His gray eyes stood out to her, but his appearance did not distract her from throwing shards of ice and concrete in his direction. He disappeared and reappeared beside her, pushing her to the tarmac with a gust of air. Her mind locked onto him for a second and threw him. Again, lightning moved to the tarmac, recollecting into a rifled warrior. His blond hair whipped around wildly as she propelled herself toward him, her powerful shield glowing a brilliant blue as gunfire bounced off her natural body armor. Her hair was dry, and her hands were heating up. A sharp blast of plasma energy left her palms and melted the weapon in his hand and on his shoulder. He reacted by striking her with a powerful lightning bolt. She barely felt the current that flowed down her energy shield.

Psyy grabbed him with her mind, binding his hand. Thunder transformed to light and leaped at her. She felt a firm hand grab her left hand; they were energy field sparking. She was flung for moment into the collapsed wall of the prism. The metallic circle was beneath her. She turned around, sensing him in the sky above her, and blasted him with an ice beam. An ice figure crashed to the ground as lightning burst from the frozen statue. He felt anger at himself for being so clumsy.

Psyy's exhaustion wore on every part of her body, yet she still fought the greatly helped warrior. A powerful ball of plasma energy left her hand and shattered what remained of the statue. A lightning drop kicked her from above, and she was pushed backward. She punched, but he was gone. Her heart had been pounding so hard for very long. Her mind had been attentive for so long, and this threat was overwhelming her alertness. Her shield began to fade.

Lightning struck her again, and she felt it. Her arm burned like a beesting. With plasma energy, she sliced the large metallic circle into half as she jumped over the burning line. She flipped the large half of the metallic coin upright and shielded herself from powerful strikes of lightning. Thunder could not understand why the woman hadn't collapsed yet. She was a terrible fighter by his standards, and he allowed her to keep up. He was puzzled by her ability to handle the cold temperatures that resulted from the use of his powers.

Sparks flew into the air. A thunderstorm of lightning fell on her, and she tripped backward. She looked up and saw several small red objects falling in the sky. She couldn't think fast enough to move them, and they exploded above her. She was thrown inside the darkened prism. She picked herself up quickly, thinking she might die. Psyy looked at the reflective buildings of the prism. She screamed as felt the full force of lightning strike her. Her arms electrified. A reactive, unchanneled wave of forceful energy shook the buildings around her and threw the armored knight to the ground.

He, at first, thought she exploded but stood up in time to see her running toward him. He decided to test her combat skills. She punched him; he blocked her. She kicked him in his shin and was shocked by electricity, which seemed not to faze her. Her hands were hot, and the punch she landed on his chest melted his armor slightly. Even with the very noticeable scar on her arm, she looked pretty. Their eyes met. His were a darkened gray.

He tripped her. She tripped him. He regained his footing with a whirlwind-like gust that sent her high into the air and crashing to the corridor floor. A surge of icy energy left her body as she hit the ground. The corridors, the bottom half of the buildings, and his feet were covered in a thick layer of ice. And by the time he looked up to see where she was, he had already been kicked by the ball of light that exploded in front of him. He was ripped from the frozen floor and would have flown into a building within the prism complex had he not converted his body to subatomic particles and slowed his impact into the building.

He returned to his feet and struck her with two strong volts of electricity that she could not deflect or dodge. She fell instantly and lay still. He walked toward her, the ice melting in his path. Thunder exhaled deeply and commanded his vessel. He looked at her, almost feeling sorry before remembering the damage she caused. She had battered purple botches all over her skin. Her clothes were ripped to pieces by his electric strikes. He bent his knees, about to turn her over, assuming she might be dead.

He was frozen in place as she rose into the air, her near naked body a blinding radiant-blue light. He tried to look up. Never had he felt so powerless. He could feel a crushing sensation around his entire body. Slowly, his body converted to particles of light energy; and still, he was confined. Thunder was lifted from the corridor floor and into the air. The woman violently motioned her arms in the direction of the building, hurling the mass of flesh and light at the building he had nearly impacted earlier. The ball of yarn-like white energy wrapped him tightly, and the warrior went through the exterior of the building smoothly, but the second Psyy fell to the ground, truly unconscious, his motion stopped inside the building. Unconscious her healing processes accelerated, she would live.

The energy ball unraveled, releasing Thunder, and a shockwave of light energy caused the structure to collapse. Images of a life unknown to him entered his mind and became as real as the thoughts he believed were true. The large woman he called a servant appeared to be a close friend and mother. The god he served and called brother appeared to be his enemy. His power appeared more narrow than crooked.

A bright bolt of lightning left the collapsed building and entered the dust-filled air. Thunder appeared above the naked woman and withdrew his concealed weapon from his holder. He pointed the weapon and pulled the trigger. He didn't want to be wrong twice. The gun had not fired because it had short-circuited. His armor looked less shiny, and his hair appeared a plain yellow blond. He tried to strike lightning, but his hands only sputtered. His legs felt so heavy. He slipped on the wet marble floor as he reached for his messaging device. This small battle could not have taxed his power to this extent; the residue of temporal energy that lingered lessened more than just the fiction in the room. The masked warrior could not contain his thoughts anymore and collapsed.

Cassandra would not awake from her sleep for some time. Her unconscious form was taken to an underground holding cell deep beneath the first southern prism. There, she lay strapped to a narrow upright dark blue bed in a metallic chamber. A large mask over her face fed her pure oxygen and other life-giving gases and also assisted in keeping her unconscious. She was held in a great blue-tiled hall with several other people. Six soldiers were suspended in chambers above her.

A silver being and several commandos walked down the hallway and stopped as they reached her. "This is the woman, Salientian."

"Leave us," he said as the commandos filed out and left the hall. "So the ruling god was successful in designing more of you creatures. I have envisioned you for nearly all my life. How did your father, the high director, hide you from me for all these years? I want you to draw the creature to me so I can kill it." He paused to laugh as her eyes fluttered.

"You can hear me? Aha, but I know you can. Don't worry about the genetic molecule you risked your life to obtain. I've destroyed it. No one will create beings more powerful than me. I will find out who assisted this alien Pylonite scum and have them destroyed. The acting high director is who? Why would a fellow god betray me? Don't they know what I'll take from them? Back to you, Ms. Vyers, this next phase of your metamorphosis, it will give you such character." He snarled. His mind was great; it surpassed his physical strength. A pulse of grayish-purple energy, only visible to the telekinetically gifted, filled the room.

Miles away, the creature's eyes opened. The weak but cunning silver god, Salientian, was too close to his current position to be ignored, and the powerful mind he had tasted earlier was also there. Gen. Amar Khan's flesh spoke for him; the course of the underground vessel shifted away from the northern prism. Deep within the earth, a jagged, egg-shaped steel-colored vessel spun. Its partially teleporting outer shell spun rapidly in the new direction of travel.

CHAPTER VIII

IN CAPTIVITY

Cassandra had begun to drift into the serenity of her past as the silver one's blurred screams echoed through her off-center mind. Sky, the pregnant woman; Alex, her brother; Richard, her father—they all appeared in the glimpse of bright light. *Where was she?* questioned her logic. How come she felt awake yet asleep at brief moments and then drifted back to true sleep, unable to reach consciousness? Her mind was in a tug-of-war with an unknown substance that fed through her breathing tube. Her thesis, her job, her love life, her imprisonment in the southern prism, her clothes, her scars, her fight with the beautiful warrior, her missing father—these problems consumed her.

Tired of condemning herself for her failure and inability to act, she fell into a much deeper sleep. The flash of pure white light was blinding, but she steadied herself on her throne of flesh for a second time. In the darkness of her mind, she found comfort. She had always loved the cold.

The warrior nursed his wounds and felt very confused. In the infirmary of the southern prism, he remembered his pains. He sat on the thin rectangular hospital bed, his dark blue pants his only clothing. He waited patiently, his thoughts on eternity. The medical examiner's prognosis would eventually come.

He looked around the small office—the cupboards and the sink across from him, the terrible bright yellow lighting grid above him. It made him sick. Jeremiah's hair needed to be reconstructed after the battle; the shift in time had affected all the dead cells in his body. He looked down at his freshly fallen cheese-colored hair as it lay in the black bowl beside his feet. Every muscle in his body had tensed up upon contact with the building. His bones ached, and he was visibly weak. His ocean-blue eyes were dry and blinked constantly. He had never felt so mortal in his life. His power had returned, but he still felt very feeble.

The blue-robed medical doctor entered the room. His black beard and brown eyes reached eye level with his patient as he sat down on the light-blue swivel chair. "Commander, good day."

"Practitioner, what have you found?"

"Well, your blood cells are stable. You won't be passing out anytime soon. But you were exposed to highly charged radioactive particles."

"What do you mean?"

"We haven't determined what the particles are, but they are radioactive."

"Have they altered my genetic material?"

"No, it just looks like they've aged a bit."

"Aged?"

"Your nonliving cells. I'll need you to take these orange pills with a glass of water daily . . ." The doctor's voice trailed off in his inattentive mind.

"So I've aged?"

"Parts of you by about eighty years. The microscopic X-rays revealed particles binding to your cells, and they may be lessening. I can't be sure. The last scans I took seemed to be better than the first."

"Worst. Better. Make up your mind. Why haven't my bones broken then?"

"I'm not sure. And I couldn't investigate any further. Your unique abilities may have accounted for that."

"Any other advice, Doctor?" inquired Jeremiah.

"Yes. Try to avoid another conflict like the last, until you determine the cause of the radiation."

"I know the cause," he said under his breath.

"What's that?"

"What else? What about the strange dreams I'm having."

"I'm not really a psychiatrist, Commander. I don't know what to do about that problem, but I'll try to determine the half-life of the particles. Take the medication twice daily with water."

"Will they affect me?"

"No, no, but you might experience some light-headedness. That's all I can tell you."

"Is it?"

"Yes," the doctor said hesitantly.

"No," he said, his false mind-set returning. "That's not it."

"Commander?"

"Doctor, I've decided to relieve you of your other duties. You'll be joining a team of six radiologists, subatomic experts, and armor designers," he said seriously and reached for his white vest on the bed. "I want you to determine the subatomic matter around my cells in the next week and oversee the construction of a suit capable of deflecting this unknown radiation."

"The week? I told you! I couldn't! I . . . I tried!" cried the doctor. "It's not my field! It would take years for me to determine it alone! I'm sorry, Commander, but what you've asked, it . . . it seems too far fetched." The doctor was unable to contain his unwillingness to change his profession. "I won't do it. I can't."

His sharp teeth clenched. The doctor began to push the chair backward in fear. Stunned by the boisterous opposition of the doctor, the feeble warrior struggled to summon a strong enough electric current to prevent a scream and lost his nerve when he heard many footsteps approaching the open doorway to the doctor's office.

"Indeed, it does."

"Brother. Salientian?" he said, sounding surprised.

"What are you doing here!" shouted the dying voice.

At the doorway of the doctor's office, a large chain-robed silver-faced man stood before him. His purple eyes stared into the blue eyes of his brother. He knew the thought barrier he had placed in the warrior's mind had been damaged by the woman's hidden power.

"Doctor, leave us. And disregard his last orders," he said. "However, you are relieved of all your duties here in the southern prism. The northern prism is in greater need of your skills." The doctor quickly left through the second entrance.

"What? This is an outrage. Come back here," Jeremiah said, sounding delirious. "You don't care about learning how to guard ourselves from this effect." He was nearly in tears. "Brother, I'm in so much pain."

"You've survived worse."

"No, I haven't!" cried Jeremiah, making a cringeworthy face.

"You have too much on your mind," said the silver one as electricity flashed around Thunder's weak body. His blond eyebrows and gray eyes narrowed.

"What are you doing? It feels like my heart is in my head. I can't think."

"Typical." Salientian laughed a deeply and meanly as the warrior's teeth clenched. "Don't be angered. I am concerned. Believe me, I am the only god that has your interests at heart. Would you fight me for my good intentions?" he said, not needing an answer. Light, whirlpool-like purple markings could be seen over his exposed hands. His bald head shone. "Do you mind? Assist your lord."

Thunder raised his hands reluctantly to dim the lights and barely performed the task, and the lighting in the room was now dimmed significantly. Thunder's arms and hands struggled to balance his heavy body on the edge of the bed.

"You were far more affected by the woman's power than I had first believed."

"No. Her power? She is weak. I could have eliminated her on several occasions, but you said not to kill her."

"You follow all my orders? She appears stronger than you as she sleeps."

"I don't care. For what reason have you graced me with your presence?" he said, off base.

"I've come to make sure you stay among the living and return you to your best state of mind. His eyes began to glow a bright purple. He stopped speaking. "Listen to me. Listen . . . to . . . me. That woman is your servant." The red-eyed god's face flashed before his mind. "You are my faithful servant." His duty to the silver god was reinforced. "You are also my brother." A long childhood appeared in his mind; his bond to his brother was strengthened. "You lived a perfect childhood." False thoughts of training and study flickered past his brain cells. "Your powers are weak in comparison to mine. You shall only strike unfocused light. You shall not surpass me," chanted the silver being with an echoing effect before ending his powerful gaze and transferring the images of crooked lightning.

Hypnotically, Thunder personalized the thoughts of the silver being, his eyes returning blue. The god returned to speech. "Do you understand?"

"Yes, brother."

"Take note of your condition. Take the proper precautions and return to your command post on the station. You can't stay here too long, or you shall die. And you won't see the woman again, until I purpose your meeting," said the god. The light and size 12 footsteps of the ancient hybrid and god, who controlled the planet Darth, and a host of invisible footsteps can be heard exiting into the hall.

Jeremiah was left dwelling on his false past, strengthening the growing hypnotism and curses. "I'm not afraid of anything," said Jeremiah as he picked up his white overcoat from the floor.

"I'm not weak," he whispered, and a cruel smile crossed his face.

The exterior of the subterranean vehicle spun wildly toward the surface of the southern prism. Timothy (Frior) remained strapped into one of the twelve black seats in the front row, still in his black suit. The subterranean vehicle was designed to be used in extreme emergencies, and he believed the attack on the prism constituted its use. His heart was fully engaged in the trick of the creature. A gray-haired woman entered his mind. He could smell warm perfume but didn't make a mental connection.

Khan's form had remained on the creature for longer than it had expected, and the creature decided that, to maintain its mind control, it needed to remain a powerful general. Sensing that its hold on the soldiers was weakening, the creature knew it needed to feed, but the open space of the room would make it difficult. It would have to wait. The silver god had been too careless, leading the creature right to the woman and the vial. The vial contained its genetic material from the planet Arcon. The creature would need the vial to kill Salientian and swiftly conquer the planet.

"Preparing outer shielding for surfacing," said the driver.

"Continue," Khan said in his apocalyptic voice.

The creature had not taken the time to observe the physical qualities of its new form. The black eyes, nearly bald salt-and-pepper hair, tanned skin, and elderly features gave it a look of wisdom. The twenty red chairs in the five back rows were filled with soldiers, and Khan addressed them.

"We're surfacing to capture the woman?" Frior unexpectedly asked, and the creature knew its hold over the soldier was loosening quickly.

"Yes."

"She still has the vial containing the genetic material we need?"

"No, it was taken from her."

"By who?"

"Commander Frior, you're asking me too many questions," said Khan as Frior became silent again. "I just want you to apprehend her. She's confused. Perhaps you must befriend her too first. She is a powerful ally. She could potentially win this war for us."

"Befriend her?" he questioned.

"Yes, she is a powerful ally of our cause. Have you forgotten?"

"No, sir. To crush the hidden leadership of the Harfore and kill the gods, we must bring the woman to our side," he said proudly, "and eliminate the last surviving gods."

"Eliminate? Please use the other word, Commander General," the creature said wearily.

Frior's green eyes intensified on cue when he heard his new title, and he quickly said, "Kill."

"Kill them all!" shouted the soldiers.

The creature realized that it may not need to use any mind control on this soldier, except to suppress his memories. He knocked away, crushed, shredded, and obscured the frequent thoughts of a beautiful blonde and a concerned grandmother.

"Surfacing in three, two, one," the technicians announced loudly. The egglike vehicle shook as it drilled through the usual dirt below the northern prism complex, shifting through protective-foam-covered layers; water, oil, and air pipes; concrete layers; metallic layers; electricity grids; plastic coverings; septic grid; subbasement protective plastics; and subbasement floor. Loud, sirenlike alarms rang throughout the holding bay, but the bright white lights did not dim. The metallic-blue floor cracked upward as the jagged tip of the egg-shaped dark metallic vehicle penetrated the surface. Sharp shards of metal belonging to the floor flew into the air and bounced off the walls and see-through chambers of the prisoners. Half the subterranean vehicle had surfaced, and the debris of the blue-tiled floor littered the surrounding area.

A large half circle on the egg's exterior opened, and out came the soldiers as the creature, the general, cowered in the inside of the egg, replenishing itself on an expendable soldier. Khan pointed them to the woman using his mind. She lay on the dark blue bed ten meters away from the lifted floor, in the airtight chamber. The bullets of the soldiers broke through the thick plasticlike glass that surrounded the chamber. Ignoring the captured soldiers in the upper chambers, the soldiers entered their target's chamber and removed the masklike tube that covered her face as colorless gas could be heard pouring from the mask.

Thirty-two three-meter-long mechanical spiders entered the breached area from the metal ceiling of the prison bay. Khan could not locate the vial but was still satisfied, having retrieved the woman. Their metallic footsteps alarmed him. He had not anticipated such an offensive. He activated the defense system on the subterranean device, and large Gatling-like metallic guns retracted from its exterior. The weapons fired rapidly and blew the spiders to pieces as they approached the soldiers.

Psyy felt her mind surfacing to the waking world. Her eyes opened slowly, and she looked up at the blur of black helmets that looked down on her. She awoke slowly and then somewhat furiously. Her clothes were foreign, meaning she had never chose them. The white gown she wore had many evenly spaced blue squares spiraling around it randomly. On her wrist, there was a light-blue tracking band. "Who are you?" she asked the black-suited soldiers. "Where am I?"

"Don't speak. You've just awoken from an induced sleep."

"Where are you taking me?"

"You're safe. We're here to rescue you. Take her to the general."

"Did you retrieve the vial?"

"Yes, we have, Commander."

The soldier held her hand tightly as they led her to the platform and into the subterranean vehicle. "Could someone please tell me what's happening?" Cassandra asked again as she was led through the vessel and into the passenger compartments.

"General, she's here."

"Good, order the troops to return to the vessel."

"Who are you?" Cassandra asked the general.

"I am Gen. Amar Khan."

"Okay, where am I?"

"In the southern prism, where you've been held captive for the past two days. You've become the collateral target in a dangerous civil war. I commanded my forces to rescue you so that you could aid us."

"I'm confused. Please give me a moment," she said, again fatigued.

Soldiers filed past her and took their seats. "Be seated."

"I feel so out of it. I can't think." She nearly collapsed but regained herself with telekinesis.

"You should be. You fought bravely. Please, Ms. Vyers, refrain from using your abilities in this vessel. The smallest disturbance will damage the delicate instruments."

"Yes, General. Thank you so much for rescuing me. Did you see me defending myself?"

Thoughts of the battle reentered her mind, and she froze with fear. She felt naked; her secret was no longer a secret. She knew hiding her abilities didn't mean anything anymore, but she literally trembled. Her hair was messy and short.

"Please be seated," the creature again requested. "The vehicle is in motion." A large surge of heated light impacted the egg. It shook all that stood unseated.

"How did . . ." She paused in exhaustion. "How did my life get so messed up? I can't believe this happened!" she screamed, reacting to her arm banging against the back seat to the right of her as she held on to her body telekinetically.

Khan's eyes looked at her in amazement; she suspended herself in midair, disobeying his earlier command to not use her powers. The creature could sense its psychic link with the soldiers weakening. Frustration and fatigue became evident on his army. "Get us out of here now, Pilot, at your earliest opportunity."

The cannons on the tails of the six-meter-long scorpionlike robots were menacing and lethally powerful as they approached the subterranean vessel. When fully powered, they could easily damage the spinning blades and armor of the now moving vehicle. The remaining robotic spiders jumped at the spinning egg mindlessly as they tried to slice through its spiked exterior and were torn to pieces as the short-teleporting subterranean vehicle went back into the cold claylike ground. Cannons of light shook the passengers inside the egg.

"I feel trapped! I want to leave! Get me off this!" Cassandra yelled. "I hate confined spaces!"

"Be brave," General Khan said. "These soldiers risked their lives to save you."

"We're already underground," said a calming voice she had never heard before. "Just sit still. We'll be surfacing soon." The helmeted man remembered his mission.

The shock of being awoken from her long drug-induced nap made her unable to contain her anger. She had felt so weak, and this angered her. She could no longer feel the hot sting of lightning. She had not wanted to wake up. The blond hair of the warrior entered her mind. Looking down at her pale wrist and her clear and unmarked legs, she remembered something vain. Her skin was again smooth; all her red scars had disappeared. "Does anyone have a mirror?" she said frantically.

"A mirror? Why do you need a mirror?"

"I just need one. Please, anyone, give me a mirror," she said, turning around to the back rows and then turning to look at the armored soldier a seat over from her. She felt as if she were the only person in the room; everyone else was armored and ranked.

"I don't have one," the young soldier said. She was tired and anxious; she didn't think before reaching over and placing her hands on his reflective helmet. "What are you doing?"

"I need to see your helmet," she said as the soldier assisted her in removing his helmet.

His green eyes met her light blue eyes, and for a few seconds, they admired each other's unobstructed features. She peered into his helmet, at her reflection, and then again at him. Timothy had soft, curly dark-brown hair and five o'clock shadow, and she had curly black hair. His skin was rough and tanned, and hers was soft and pale. He looked strong, though his mind was weak. She looked beautiful, even though she was very tired.

"It's all gone. I've never healed so well without a medic."

"What's gone?" he questioned.

"My scar," she said under her breath. "Nothing. Don't worry about it." She handed him back the helmet, and he gazed on her unmarred face. She couldn't help but attempt to give him a passive answer. "I just needed to see how well my skin healed."

"A powerful warrior as yourself struggling with issues regarding your appearance? Ms. Vyers, you're an accomplished scientist." The general scoffed.

"Don't get angry at him. You were a fighter that day," said the green-eyed soldier. Cassandra was stunned again and realized that she could not read this military man's mind entirely. She looked over to the now seemingly sleeping general and decided not to wake him. "I'm sorry."

"For what?"

"I don't know what's happening anymore."

"What's your name?"

"Ang. His name is Lieutenant Commander Ang," said the general, his eyes opening, interrupting them. "Lieutenant Commander Ang, we're headed for the dense jungles. I thought you'd be very interested in knowing that. Lieutenant Commander, I want you to lead the active missions from here on. Here are your objectives." He gave him a small rectangular black device. "Scientist?"

"I have no skill with weapons and . . ." She never finished her sentence.

"Vyers, you will go with the mission team. I want you to—"

"No way, I won't. I'm still a civilian. This has nothing to do with me, General Khan. Please take me back home. I can't stay here or return the favor. I'm grateful for you rescuing me, but no, I cannot help you. I really think you should take me back to the northern prism," she said, remembering her strength and power. "Before you decide to do anything else, please take me home. I want to see my brother and his wife."

The words repeated through Frior's mind, and powerful thoughts surfaced. "Family," he whispered out loud.

"Ms. Vyers, I would love to do that. Everyone wants to see their families. But as it stands, you are an enemy of the Harfore Empire. We, the Darforians, have risen to overthrow our oppressors and remove the current system. You injured a lot of men, Cassandra. They'll shoot you on sight. They were only holding you in that containment chamber to experiment on you at a later time. We risked our lives to rescue you."

"What?" The large spiders, the dark-blue-suited commandos, the helicopters, the sniper's bullet, the blond man's lightning, the silver one's voice—Psyy could not respond to the general rationally or soundly. He could sense her fear and knew she would do whatever he requested.

"There is an ancient city deep within the jungle. I'll need you to teleport the team of seven soldiers into the crashed ship within the city without damaging its fragile core. You'll need to help retrieve the hard drive of the spacecraft."

"Huh? Wait, how? You know about my teleportation powers?"

"Of course. I knew your father."

"What? That makes sense. Yeah, you're a general. My father was in the military too practically. He was the high director of the HDF. Yeah, you should—you would know him."

"Yes, I did. And I still do."

"Is he alive?"

"I can only hope. He would have died before seeing this war. Seeing you fighting against the regime, he would have been proud."

"I didn't do it purposely. I had no choice, but yes, I'll help you."

"We all have a choice. You have made the right one."

"Please, please I don't care about that. Tell me my father's alive."

"You know I can't do that. I won't venture into that discussion."

"Why? Why won't you tell me? What is left to keep from me?"

"Because I don't know for sure. I'll tell you what I know. What I do know is that if we don't succeed, you'll never see him again. I will tell you more once you have returned from your first mission. Remember, Cassandra, that information is classified to high-ranking officials and military personnel only. Would you still like me to return you to the surface?"

"You're bribing me and manipulating this whole situation, General." The general appeared somewhat startled; her mind was strong.

"Very well, Scientist. I'll return you to the surface to attend your fair trial."

"Fine. All right, I'll help you," she said softly. "I want no credentials in your army. And when this war is done, I'm going back to being a scientist. Do you understand me? I want us to avoid killing, if and whenever possible. Am I perfectly clear?"

"Yes, Ms. Vyers, a wonderful change of heart. A sincere welcome to the force, Special Operative Vyers. Before I tell you any more, take that band off your hand and destroy it," he said, referring to the tracking band on her hand. "You don't have to worry about being found now. What I've heard recently is that your father is on Pylon Six. I believe he's been captured. He is evading the Pylonites quite well and sending in intel every so often. Perhaps he'll return home to us soon. I hope for the best."

Psyy gasped and began to get teary. Her life became a blur, and she selected the easiest alignment. She no longer held on to what she had, who she knew, and where she came from. A new mind had formed inside her. Timothy, the helmetless soldier, was in the orange seat beside her. He stared down at the metal floor, trying to think about something very important, but he was unable to make the connections.

The subterranean vehicle stopped at the side of the deep underground jungle cavern. The half-circle doors to the prism opened, and out came Psyy dressed from head to toe in the black armor of a soldier. The cavern was terribly dusty as the blue lights of the egg illuminated the cavern. Cassandra's short hair was tied back in a ponytail, and she felt little distress having dressed in the middle of a crowded room. The men didn't look at her. She could sense it; they were somewhat absentminded.

Her head spun as she stepped out of the vehicle and into the warm, tropical cavern. She suddenly began to feel the pain of the battle. Large brittle brown roots hung from the high ceiling of the cavern. It was littered with metallic debris and small rocklike formations. The floor was soft.

"Here," said the calming voice that held her helmet.

"Thank you," she said, taking her helmet and placing it over her head.

The group of seven, with their flashlights glaring forward, walked onward as the subterranean vehicle tunneled downward. The six black-suited soldiers moved on as the slow-moving soldier struggled to keep up with their pace as she was uncomfortable with the black boots of the uniforms. Cassandra could not realize how she had come to be in this situation. She thought back to the days before she was just a scientist, far from all the action, and wondered what everyone else was doing. The ground was soft but firm beneath her feet, and she struggled to keep up. Their yellow flashlights led the way through the cavern.

"All right, listen up, people. We're about to enter an area out of reach with the prism's repellent system. So what I'm saying is that we're going to see insects, lots of them." She was too busy with her thoughts to question or discuss. "Leave them alone, and they should leave us alone."

The cavern expanded as they moved downward on a slight slope. Her feet began to pick up, and an arm steadied her.

"Are you okay?"

"I'm fine. I just don't think I'm fully recuperated."

"From what? Oh, the battle with the Harforian warrior."

"The silver warrior struck me with bolts of lightning. But it doesn't look like he did."

"Hmm. No, it didn't," he said, but she didn't realize that he had looked at her while she was dressing.

"It was a clear day. It, the lightning, came from his hands. I didn't even have time to get a clear description of him. His hair was blond. I know, I can't explain how it's possible, but the lightning came from the man that attacked me."

"Yeah?"

"And the scary thing is . . . he's like me."

"He likes you?"

"Yeah. No, he's like me. I can do things like that, not just like that but also seemingly impossible things."

"So can I," he said, imagining her face conforming to the expression of disbelief.

"What?"

"I can shoot flames from my hands and become harder than diamonds when I want to."

"Really? Very interesting. I can make ice crystals and move physical objects with my mind."

"Cool," he said bluntly. "I can go invisible."

"Well, I can also read minds."

"Something tells me that you can't read my mind."

"Let me try. No, no, I can't," she slowly said as the group continued to walk.

The moist ground ended. From their position, they looked down into the sinkhole that was the ancient city. They scanned the city with their flashlights. They saw shattered buildings, broken pavement, flickering glass, toppled monuments and towers, and other decaying debris.

"Yeah, well, I can shoot powerful beams of light energy from my hands."

"I'll believe it when I see it."

"You will."

Their small talk ended quickly. "Okay, sorry, guys, we have to silence all communication frequencies and limit our speech. We're being scanned from the surface."

"By who?"

"Probably your vicious blond friend. The Harforians, the HDF, are trying to find us."

"Why are we fighting them again?"

"Haven't you seen what they've done to us? What they've done to you? They're corrupt, and we have the power to overthrow them, and we will. Now, people, maintain silence."

"But—"

"Maintain," he said, turning his attention to her.

The communication silence was unbearable for Cassandra. She needed to talk about her experience, or it wouldn't seem real to her. A line of thick, freshly spun web descended from the top of the cavern's ceiling. A meter-long furry gray spider was suspended high above them. She stopped herself from screaming.

The group continued to walk down the hill into the battlefield that was the city. The insects could now be seen. Centipede-like insects two meters long crawled across the paved ground, hiding as the light illuminated them. Large beetles raced over the buildings. A horde of tiny flies flew over the group, and spiderwebs were behind almost every building corner. Annoying buzzes colored the dark cavern as hornetlike red-and-black striped insects flew out of the many holes in the wall and could be seen crawling along the dirt walls and floors of the cavern. They were the reason the cavern had not been overpopulated with giant spiders.

"Why are we here again?" she questioned.

"You're here to teleport us down to the crashed ship below the city. Did you forget you could teleport?" he whispered.

The buzzing flies made her feel itchy, and the sawlike fluttering of the hornets made her fearful. They were now in the middle of the city when she sensed a primitive mind. She looked around and saw nothing.

"Did you hear something?"

"No."

"Silence, remember?" said the leader as he watched Cassandra's lustrous black hair shake and her head nod.

The sound of clawed feet alerted Frior, and he tapped the group members to his sides. Cassandra stopped. They stood on the cracked and pot-filled concrete. "What is it?" she asked.

"It's just a pack of nocturnal raptors. Unless someone takes off their helmet, we should all live."

"Sir, they won't stay away from us. We'll need to arm our weapons."

"No, you'll give our position away."

"I totally forgot. I'm sorry."

"That's okay. That's why I'm here to remind you." The words left his mouth, and a two-meter standing raptor appeared before them. Its shiny red eyes were real, and its sharp black claws and yellow teeth alerted them to the presence of slow-moving death.

The group's flashlights illuminated the dark brown and dirty white scales of the raptor.

She reacted before he could hit it. The gloves covering her cold palms melted without sparks ensuing. The raptor was now a solid object. Cries of other raptors that waited for their signal to strike could be heard. It took Frior a few seconds to realize that the raptor was now encased in ice. He was now a believer in her power.

Very glad he didn't have to damage the animal's beauty, he motioned the group onward into a sewer tunnel with a metallic covering. He opened the large cover with one hand, and the troopers entered the hole. The other raptors could not wait, and the sounds of sharp claws scratching against the chalkboard like concrete made the soldiers reach for their guns. She had a gun but didn't know how to use it.

"No! Hold your fire."

The six raptors that opened their jaws to attack the group were thrown backward to the concrete by a wave of energy. She pointed her hands at the floor and began to make a wall around the sewer tunnel's five-meter perimeter.

The walls appeared slowly in the form of blue liquid light around the perimeter loosely at first and then became thick, imperfect walls of white ice. The group was now surrounded by cold ice and could hear sounds of claws slashing away at the exterior of the wall. The sewer tunnel slammed shut as the last of the soldiers entered the dark tunnel and descended the fifty-meter ladder.

The group reached the deeper underground tunnel and found the crash site. Cassandra teleported the group easily into the badly damaged spacecraft and collected the first of seven secret codes they needed to operate the large messaging device the creature sought. She saved them another twenty-minute climb up the ladder and teleported them back to the concrete surface of the sinking city. Unknown to her and the greatly appreciated group, her teleportation carried its own magnetic signal, and it was very traceable.

The spinning robotic subterranean spiders made their way through the soft jungle dirt. On their way, they disturbed the underground hive of the hornets. The soldiers looked up into the underground cavern to see a multitude of hornets flying around the cavern madly. The noise was deafeningly loud and awoke the meter-long sharp, jagged, grasshopper-like brown insects that slept in the damaged city structures. The raptors' screams could be heard as they ate the insects. The large centipedes awoke from their burrows to feed as well, and the entire cave became a feeding ecosystem. Hornets were trapped in the spiders' webs. Chewed grasshoppers clung to the raptors' jaws. Two slow raptors lay motionless on the pavement as centipedes encircled them. Centipedes, spiders, fast-moving raptors, and grasshoppers littered the floor as hornets swarmed and stung them repeatedly. The hornets attacked the soldiers, and they defended themselves with the might of weapon fire, the solidity of ice, the pressure of telekinesis, and the blasting of gunfire.

CHAPTER IX

CITY OF DEATH

The swarms of overgrown insects clustered into close groupings, attacking anything that moved. The movement of the metal spiders that drilled down from the jungle's surface angered the swarm that sought only to protect their queen. The half-a-meter-long black stingers of the red-and-black hornets retracted quickly and easily bored through the exoskeletons of the centipedes. By now, the soldiers had already begun to defend themselves, throwing grenadelike explosives into the air, resulting in the guck and insect parts that littered the moist ground and hard century-old pavement. Large irregular chunks of dry ice were constantly exploding on the pavement floor. High-powered weapon fire from the soldiers' rifles darted through the air at the swarms.

Frior had not lost his cool. His left hand threw grenade after grenade while his right hand targeted the swarms with his massive rifle. He was strong and could hold the large rifle in one arm. Hornets covered the floor of the pavement. Had it not been for the forceful powers of Psyy, someone would have been hurt by the grenades and fatally stung by the hornets. The hornets had tried to advance, but Psyy either froze them or threw them back with her mind several times. The critical green eyes beneath the helmet noticed her failure to use a weapon. He moved over to her position on the pavement, reaching for the woman's weapon from her side pocket. He surprised her, and she tried not to shift her focus. The hornets became louder as they exited their tunnels from every direction, gathering into swarms.

"What are you doing? We're fighting a battle here!" she screamed because she had to.

"You need to use your weapon!"

"Maybe next time! I think they really need my help right now!" she screamed, directing his attention to the soldiers in the foreground who were firing their weapons, set to create a heated, blurry blast. The heat blast took out many hornets in one shot. An overlapping swarm of red and black approached them.

"No! You need to learn to use it right now!"

"How come?" Psyy questioned as he placed the rifle in her hand.

"Hunter spiders are coming from the surface! You'll tire yourself out if you don't learn to use the equipment."

Psyy listened to him and let down her guard as he showed her how to shoot the weapon. She began to shoot at the incoming swarm, but it was too late; they had consumed the man's body as she moved herself from their path. She had tried to take him with her using her mind. Psyy shot furiously at the swarm that shrouded Frior's image. Red-and-black insect debris covered the moist ground. She could see the soldier standing there rapidly being stung. He tried to be calm as the hornets' stingers scraped against his black-armored suit. She got desperate, fearing for his life, and let out a telekinetic blast of air. The hornets were thrown to the ground. He fell over and leaned against his right knee, and when he looked up at her, she knew he had laughed.

"What? What's so funny?"

"You failed your first test. I told you to use your weapon. They can't hurt us in the armor. And oh yeah, we have a COMM signal."

"Well, sorry," she said, looking up just in time to see the newest spectacle.

From the ceiling of the cavern, twenty aluminum-colored legs protruded for a moment and fell from the hard dirt ceiling of the cavern, spinning rapidly onto the pavement.

"They're here. Now start using the right gear." He watched her struggle to guess what gear to use. "Ah, not that one," he said, irritated. "Switch to 'rust bullets.'"

"What's that? Where?"

"It's on your left utility belt. Initiate the right gears on your suit."

"Okay."

"Good. Now aim and shoot. And don't hit any of us."

She had perfect eye-and-hand coordination and would not miss unintentionally. She didn't aim well but slowly and meticulously shot at the robot spiders that engaged them with heated weapon fire.

"I'm moving in close to disable them. Everyone else, cover me," Frior ordered.

He was brave and mysterious to her, and she now knew he had a fiery attitude. She had a very good long-term memory and realized that he had not been pushed as far as he should have been when she blew away the hornets. He was somewhat immune to her sunlike telekinetic and telepathic powers.

Harsh yelling interrupted her perplexing thoughts. "Stop daydreaming and cover me!"

"Oh, okay." She reacted with surprise. As a hornet flew over her, she began to shoot around rapidly into the air.

"Hey, you, the spider robots have repellent devices in them. You don't have to worry about the bees anymore," a soldier said through the COMM system. "And that's why you need to target so you don't misfire."

"Oh, sorry," she said again. "Thanks for the heads-up." Psyy targeted the spiders that were now in a vicious fight with a black-suited ninja. The high adrenaline in her body made her feel alive again. She kept her eyes on the fighting soldier as he threw the two-meter spiders into one another. However, he went invisible. Spiders were thrown a meter off the ground, landing awkwardly as they scraped against the concrete. Metal parts and pieces of the spiders lay crooked on the pavement. Most of the spiders' weapon fire was aimed at the black-suited ninja, who dodged them with aerial precision and speed. He moved faster than the triangular land craft that had taken her to the mountain. Slowly, she realized her weapon fire seemed ineffective. All her latest shots hit their multiple targets yet destroying none.

"How come my weapon fire isn't working?"

"It is. It's going deep into their interior and weakening their armor. They'll fall apart soon."

"What are those ones doing?" she questioned.

To the left of the action, three spiders formed a circle and grouped together in a triangular formation. The spiders transformed into rodlike shapes, and a strange blue light began to glow in the center of the formation. Dark-red-suited soldiers leaped out at such a speed that her eyes barely noticed them cloak. Psyy took immediate action, throwing down her weapon. She leaped into the air, and a powerful blue beam of light left her right hand, destroying the formation. Now in flight, her corona covered her body. It did not tear apart her armor but covered it comfortably.

She looked around, trying to detect the cloaked, sword-wielding commandos. Suddenly, an invisible object slammed into her, and she would have fallen to the pavement had she not suspended herself. She could sense ten separate minds. She reacted by emitting a circle of telekinetic energy, but no noises of moving men ensued. She then felt a slashing impact against her shoulder and instinctively spun around. Her corona protected her from a deep cut. Creating light, she blasted it forward without thinking, and a dark-red-suited soldier appeared, sinking to the crimson concrete.

An explosion near her body threw her to the ground as a large chunk of the cavern's claylike ceiling fell. She held it with her mind as it came closer, spinning it around her like a meteor in a planet's orbit. Psyy could hear motion, and she threw the large claylike rock at the nine spiders in the background. To her surprise, it did not hit them; the soldier reappeared from his natural cloak, having cracked the rocks, and thrown pieces of the rock aside.

"What are you doing?" Frior asked. "You're going to tire yourself out."

"No, you don't understand," she tried to say, but her corona kept the message from leaving clearly.

"You're not going to answer me?" yelled Frior as he watched the woman fall to the ground.

Captured, Psyy began to use her years of hand-to-hand combat training. She kicked blindly into the dark air. Her ribs felt the heavy pressure of a kick and a push. Another slashing sound went across her left shoulder. She tried to fly upward, but a kicking force above her head pushed her down. She released another force of telekinesis and yelled, "Force expansion!" She remembered her childhood attempt to label all her moves.

Nothing happened, and she could sense cloaked figures in every direction. Slash! Slash! Slash! Those were the sounds she heard and just barely felt. Against the cavern wall, she realized a plan of action. Ice fell from her hand and froze the moist ground beneath her. It froze the feet of the floating warriors who levitated inches above the ground. The black ice made the ones who jumped slip as they landed on the frozen ground. They were almost like her, and she felt envious just before she kicked their invisible forms, freeing their feet from the ice. She grabbed the last one and tossed him against the cavern walls, pinning him with ice. She grabbed another commando with her hot hands and hurled him over her head, and he would have hit the floor had there not been a dark water-filled hole where he landed.

Psyy stopped for a moment and walked toward the watery hole to lift the commando out, but she could not sense anyone. To her fright and amazement, the claws of a blue-skinned scorpion crawled out from beneath the water. Its tail struck her instantly in the neck, and she reacted by slicing into its tail with her hot hands and lifting it with her mind. Throwing the scorpion across the pavement was easy. Fearing another scorpion's arrival, she froze the watery hole. Looking down at her hands that had now fully melted through her gloves, she realized her desperation. The sounds of a slash and of reflecting metal caused her face to move to the right and her left hand to strike without thinking. Her hand bounced off the dark object that stood before her.

"It's me!" yelled Frior. "Relax!" He felt some pain in his upper back.

"Ouch! It feels like I hit diamond," said Psyy, nursing her fingernail. "What are you doing so close to me anyway?"

Before saying sorry, he ripped the sword from the cloaked commando's hand and used it against him. The commando appeared and fell to the ground. "Thank me later," said Frior, breaking the sword.

The ululations of an unexpected attack filled the helmets of the two soldiers. He disappeared into the darkness as she flew into the air, and she didn't have time to see the commando who lay lifeless. They both saw the handless soldiers tumble to the moist ground, but Frior arrived first. White flames left his hands, consuming both the soldiers and the commandos. The commandos appeared with white flames covering their bodies. The soldiers on the ground cried out from the heat. She did the right thing and cooled down their immobile bodies. Frior acted out of anger and directed white flames at the four now visible commandos.

The hornets were returning. Psyy gasped at the sight of the melting men; she reacted without thinking and blasted a wave of cold liquid light in Frior's direction. He did not turn to ice, and neither did the steaming remains of the soldiers. The foot of the now invisible commando was covered in ice, and his form could be detected. Frior sped toward the commando, but Psyy's mind moved faster. She pushed the commando backward and blasted a low-energy beam of freeing light at Frior's feet. The ninja tripped.

"Haven't you killed enough? Let him go!"

"What? What are . . . are you . . ." His frustration made him stutter.

"You have to let him go."

"What are you doing, Ms. Vyers?"

"Don't kill him! Please!"

"He killed our soldiers. You're a soldier. They're here to kill us first. Please, Ms. Vyers, don't let him escape after what they've done."

She expected him to fight her as a great ball of white flames circled around his arms; the smell of burning armor did not reach her nose yet. She attempted to gain higher altitudes and began to raise toward the cavern ceiling, but she was paralyzed with fear. The thick smoke that surrounded her, the white flames—they all reminded her of a past situation. Nothing affected her; his attention was elsewhere. The white flame formed around the black waterlike sphere in his dimly lit palms.

She flinched again as a swipe of a sword could be heard whooshing toward her right ear. The ball impacted the invisible commando, and gravity crushed him along with the intense flames that were held within the black sphere. The sharp, heated blade of the long sword sank into the ground, bending under the weight of heavy gravity.

When Psyy opened her eyes and viewed the pile of dark ashes and crumpled metal that lay on the ground below her, the situation seemed heroic. Frior retrieved the sword, and she looked down at him with fear and relief. "I'm still alive?"

"Help me!" a soldier cried. "Help her too! She's still alive!"

The conflict between them would have to wait. Psyy and Frior turned around and hoisted the soldier from the ground as the sound of hornets again began to fill the dark cavern. The able-bodied soldier walked beside them. Psyy's corona faded. She couldn't sense his pain, but she could see it in his movement. Frior hated her. He didn't say anything to her as he aided his comrade and began his walk to the retrieval location. The soldier had lost an arm and a leg. Psyy couldn't move. Failure and fatigue had paralyzed her.

"What are you waiting for?" Frior asked.

"Nothing. I'm not coming. I'm not a soldier or anything like you," she said in anger.

"Start moving right now. You are not deserting your team."

"I don't have to listen to you! I never signed up for this! I'm not doing this anymore! I won't!"

The ground beneath them shook, and he held on to the badly injured soldier. She couldn't think. His heart felt bitter hatred for the Harforians and intense pity for the injured woman, who was a soldier; he didn't confuse the two. Another able-bodied soldier touched her hand.

"You can't stay here."

"Hold on, that isn't our subterranean vessel," Frior said.

"What?"

"Defensive positions, Soldiers!" Frior said, forgetting how few of them there were.

"Yes, sir," one voice replied.

Frior stumbled for a second to find the words. "I suggest you put that blue light back on," Frior said to Psyy as he placed the dying soldier on the soft ground.

"You can't leave him there," she said mistakenly.

"I . . . well, we don't have a choice. Our hands are full."

"Do him a favor," he said, looking up at her seriously.

"How?"

"Like you did the others."

"That was an accident, and they were already dead," she said.

"Sure. Okay, so I guess he'll die slowly."

The scientist's expressionless thoughts consumed her for a moment, and then she stretched forth her hands, knowing that she owed it to the soldier. A reflecting ice covered the dying body of the badly injured female soldier. The walls of the cavern began to crack, and she restored her corona and stood side by side with the soldier. Frior was a few meters ahead of them. She couldn't stop her thoughts and remembered that he had been the cause of the deaths of the soldiers. He set them on fire in his haste to kill the enemy.

With enough warning, the Harforian subterranean vessel—a cylindrical white metallic object—surged through the ceiling of the cavern. More commandos came out and began shooting immediately. She used her riflelike weapon by choice. She was tired, and the soldier standing next to her was trembling. She looked over at him for a second to assess his mental condition. Twelve more subterranean vessels surged through the walls of the cavern. In the scope of a minute, fifty-five HDF soldiers had exited the vessels, despite their attempts to stop them. The three watched, uncertain of how to proceed. She looked over at the soldier beside her. She could sense his fear. He had a family, and they were on his mind.

Her gaze shifted purely by accident, and she saw behind him on the pavement of the cavern the melting ice that covered the sewer entrance. A desperate thought consumed her as a silver flash obstructed her mind's vision. "Let's move, Soldiers!" she screamed because of the corona that surrounded her. "Head for the sewer cover!"

"But no."

"Just do it! I know what I'm doing. Don't look back! Just run quickly!" she commanded as the soldier looked up at her in disbelief beneath the helmet. He hesitated and then took to his feet and headed for the sewer cover.

Her corona came off her in an attempt to hide from the HDF. Hot laser fire burned her suit and stung her skin, and her light blue eyes narrowed. Ascending into the air, she went to retrieve Frior, who was taking out the HDF soldiers with his new commando sword. She couldn't see him, but she could sense him. Flying down through the air as a barrage of laser weapon fire impacted her and flew past her shield, she collected the cloaked warrior in her arms by surprise. His sword dropped, and in his heart, he swore. "What are you doing? Let go of me!"

"We have to retreat," she said as narrowing red light illuminated the cavern.

"No! Put me down," he said, but she ignored him without fear.

"We need to go down into the sewer again."

"Sewer? Put me down. If you put don't me—"

"We'll die if we stay here!"

"Ah! The sewer has no exit!"

"You don't know that," she guessed. "We'll find an exit. I promise." She did not know entirely how they would do that. Flying unto the pavement, she used her telekinesis to lift the running soldier underneath her arm and grabbed on to him.

Timothy had stopped resisting her. He sensed some logic in her plan of action. She dropped the two soldiers to the pavement, and they rolled in somersault positions. She shot a beam of blue light at the sewer entrance, melting the ice around it and breaking open the barriers. The unknown soldier jumped down into the sewer and slid down the ladder. Timothy waited for her to go down the sewer first but knew it was her plan. He jumped down the sewer feet first. She dived into the sewer headfirst.

With her hand stretched back and her head looking upward to the sewer opening, she released a large ball of liquid light that covered the exit of the tunnel in a thick layer of ice. Slowing her fall in midair, Cassandra caught the ladder and started to descend slowly. He looked up, waiting for the two soldiers to make it down the ladder. His heart pounded. She had a headache. The unknown soldier slipped. Cassandra slowed his descent, and Tim caught him. They now waited for her at the bottom. The two falling elements now fought together against the ruler of the floating station.

They ran through the green-walled copper tunnels aimlessly, searching for an exit. She wanted to go lower, while he wanted to search the rooms for anything that looked like a good weapon. They had opened a few doors and found badly damaged pipes, and then the tired soldier took her side. They went down the ladders, deeper and deeper into the cold tunnels. The HDF had melted her ice barrier and were now searching for them within the tunnels.

After placing several beacons in the tunnels to guide the subterranean missiles, the allotted two hours of searching the mile-long and miles-deep tunnels ended. The soldiers were recalled to their vessels. Their mission was a success; they had forced the scientist into the tunnels that led to the buried city. There, the silver one, Salientian, expected her to meet the tunnel dwellers and achieve enlightenment, which would aid her greatly in accomplishing his destiny. As the blond knight thought his actions were unknown to the silver one, he ordered the explosives to be set to such an intensity that they would blow the cavern apart and open it to the rays of the sun. He had a score to settle; no warrior had ever defeated him in battle, but for the moment, the hornets reclaimed the cavern and feasted on the corpses that covered the hard pavement and sank into the moist ground.

The dustless air of the tunnels began to suffocate them, and they drudged on down the ladders. Timothy was always the first to get down, but even he was getting sloppy on his landings. The lack of oxygen affected everyone. The three began to descend the next ladder. Cassandra paid particular attention to the soldier.

"We'll never get out of this tunnel."

"Yes, we will," she said, trying to sound optimistic.

"I haven't breathed fresh air in over an hour," Tim said.

"I hate your negativity," she said.

"I say things like I see them. How are you going to get us out of here? I trusted you. Please tell me."

They continued to climb down into the tunnels and would have become completely engaged in one another's lives had the creature's powerful hold over them diminished.

"How long have you been in the military?"

"A few months."

"And you're already commanding everyone?"

"Yes, it's not how well you perform in the military. It's who likes you," the soldier joked.

"No, I did really well on all my missions. I deserved this. No, this situation, my rank," Timothy said.

"So this isn't your first real mission?" Cassandra said sarcastically, not meaning to offend him.

"I didn't mean to burn those soldiers. It was an accident."

"I know, I didn't mean it like that," apologized Cassandra, but he never accepted it. "When did you know you were so gifted?" She breathed deeply, trying to distract herself from complaining about the lack of oxygen in the tunnels.

"Always."

"Always?"

"Yeah, but I didn't know how to use them consciously. I had to learn. It's like knowing you have hands, but then you need to learn how to use to them to hold a pencil and write with it."

"Um, yeah, I understand," she said, truly confused.

"We better stop talking and concentrate on breathing, okay?"

"That's really wise."

The tunnels went on and on in a bottomless spiral of black tunnel ladders. The tunnels were pitch black, and their flashlights guided them. Truly, everyone was tired, hungry, and mentally exhausted. A shock wave of energy vibrated down into the tunnels. They felt the shaking. Psyy heard it first; she felt it first. "Guys, something's happening up there."

"Obviously, the tunnels are shaking."

"You're right. They're probably blasting through the tunnels or sending spiders after us."

The sound of shaking pipes filled the tunnel, and the soldiers' hands began to shake with the ladder.

"Should we . . . Let's let go of the ladder. Get ready to jump."

"Okay, on my mark, one, two . . . three."

Rocklike debris fell unto them, first in the form of small particles and then larger chunks. The tunnels were filled with fast-falling debris. A bright flash of blue light encompassed the three as the heated wave of energy approached them. Speechless in the sphere of light, the two soldiers looked at the woman. The sphere began to fall. The walls of the odorless sewer tunnel began to melt. The sphere fell through the floor of the sphere, and their stomachs lurched. She tried to steady the vehicle of teleportation, but she couldn't breathe. There wasn't enough air inside the sphere.

A glittering bluish-white light surrounded the breaking ladders and melting floors. Their skin began to burn underneath their suits; they were not hidden from the temperature outside. The sphere's shape changed. An arbelos of glittering bright-blue light encompassed the soldiers, and they continued to fall through the remaining levels of the tunnel.

Within the light, Timothy remembered everything. His girlfriend awaited him. He knew his grandmother grieved over the failure to act on her premonitions of danger in the southern prism. Timothy felt at peace in the fall.

Cassandra knew everything and reflected on it again. Her hands gripped onto the fabric of time, holding on to the two strangers as they fell. Tim fell in the largest half sphere, while the other soldier considered his freedom in the other. Cassandra had the full sphere, and they were all contained in the half circle that was the arbelos. Her mind could not grip onto time for much longer, and all the bubbles of energy burst as they should have.

Frior's mind became conscious of the free fall into the darkness. He bounced up with the sticky material. He struggled to free himself from the thick web that saved his life. The soldier landed on the webbing behind him and ripped through it. The soldier glittered wildly and fell past the ground until his death. Cassandra fell nearest to the large spider's web den. The large black spider ran out to retrieve her. She still glowed of the faint, glittering light. The spider gripped her arm, struggling to break through the black armor. She was lifted from the web, the silk sticking to her. The real spider spun another web around her.

The ninja's heated armor melted the thick patch of spiderweb, and he fell. Landing on the skyscraper's rooftop, he looked up at the struggling figure that was now covered in thick white web. The web was secured from the ceiling of the new cavern to the larger building beside it. Frior could see the many red-and-black hornets that were also captured in the web at a previous time. The giant spiders had protected the tunnel dwellers from the mindless, hornetlike insects.

He didn't love the woman, but he cared for her, and flames gathered in his palms. Again, sparks left his armor. A red fire formed in his hands. He felt deathly weak. Fast-moving black figures approached him, but he could not make them out clearly. Shiny green eyes were transfixed on him, and strange dark markings on their foreheads and arms made him stop to look. He could no longer move his hands to defend himself as ropes were tied around his arms and feet. He lost his balance and fell, and losing his will to struggle, he just lay still. The giant black spider released the freshly wrapped saint and lowered him onto the concrete rooftop.

CHAPTER X

TIMELY EVENT

nside the deeper, carbon-filled caverns, the tunnel dwellers lived. They were protected from the numerous insects by powerful spiders. The spiders needed warmth from their fires and learned to obey the dwellers' telepathic commands. They lived in the ancient cities of the Darforians. They were all telepathically inclined persons, capable of predicting future events and the outcomes of almost every action collectively and independently. They worked together and settled disputes by randomly selecting a decider, and therefore, they lived carefree lives. Their population was less than nine hundred, and they lived in small bunches and groupings of forty to sixty members, spread out throughout the deeper underground caverns of the jungles and ancient ruins.

The tunnel dwellers loved to adorn themselves with metals and minerals. Gold, silver, diamond, emerald, and ruby commonly adorned their bodies. Silver was once their most precious metal. Silver, harder than gold, reflected their desire for solitude and protection from the outside world. Silver possessed the highest electrical and thermal conductivity and optical reflectivity when exempting aluminum. Silver still meant very much to dwellers, but they thought twice before wearing it. They shunned the color for its legacy of betrayal.

Forty years ago, a silver visitor came to learn from them. His purple eyes and silver skin made them instantly desire to help him. They made him a member of their society and taught him the secret powers of dwellers. The god was given the ability to glimpse the future, but still, he wanted more; he wanted the power to change the future and therefore the past, but they would not teach him that. The half-ancient-Darforian tunnel dwellers believed it was far too dangerous to tamper with the past because they believed that one single changed event would affect the entire shape of history and create perpetual chaos. They believed through their learning and stories from their culture, which valued knowledge and power, that thoughts flowed out of people and cascaded throughout the temporal universe, giving energy to other forces, and similarly flowed into the temporal universe, giving people thoughts and dreams from an unknown place.

The silver one, Salientian, desired to change one short but powerful moment in his life and explained this to the people. Then and now, the god was much stronger than the dwellers but knew their dangerous potentials; he feared their foresight. Uninvited, Salientian approached the throne of the elderly matriarch of the dwellers and revealed to her his request, but she rebuked him. The matriarch warned him that, had he not been considered a son to her, she would have banished him, never to return to the caverns. A mad anger swiftly consumed him, and Salientian soon endeavored to destroy the tunnel dwellers.

He started the fight. A fight in the realm of their minds resulted in the matriarch's momentary death and Salientian's victory. The matriarch's eternal presence disappeared from the plane of time, but because of her death, he would not get his wish. However, he did gain so much that day. Salientian now had the power to see clearly into the future and increased his control over the cells of living things. He depleted the tunnel dwellers' population when he left, taking with him a group of gifted followers. They were the strongest minds and bodies the dwellers had ever trained. With their counsel, he wished to one day achieve his attainable wish of altering the future and therefore the past, for he knew that anything he desired he could achieve.

The sleeping body of the new matriarch lay in the whit-sheeted bamboo hammock, the product of simple materials harvested from the surface. Two necklaces of pearl and gold lay on her neck. She was dressed in red silk, and her long hair flowed down her head. Lots of time had passed since she fell onto the web. Her mind felt the pain of holding on to the hot fabric of time.

In the darkly lit diamond-walled room below her chamber, the soldier lay sleeping. Every bone in his body felt numb, and his teeth felt loose. His armor off, he lay in a gold-clothed native attire, and his pale skin was free from strange markings. The room looked like a luxurious hotel suite, when in fact it was a prison. Many died for the diamonds; they were villainous. Unconscious, he pondered the last days, and he remembered everything about his life. Although he was very strong, he healed slowly.

She was awake hours before him and toured the upper chamber with her handmaids. The granite flooring of the chambers was soft on her ruby-sandaled feet. She didn't feel threatened by the gold-cloaked female servants who led her around her chamber, showing her various treasures. She had seen many gems and jewelry that appealed to her but refused to try any of them on. She saw the doorway and thought about leaving. The telepathic women sensed her will and led her to the exit.

Looking up at the passageway as she left, she admired the living gold statues of warriors. As she approached the exit, she could not detect the very awake minds of the gold warriors. Interrupted by the high priestesses beside her, she stopped. She could barely understand them until they began to think at her pace. "Matriarch, you cannot go outside. You lack the ability to breathe carbon." It took her a while to understand.

"Matriarch? There's no fresh air out there? Oxygen?" Cassandra responded.

"Yes. We would speak verbally, but you cannot understand our language."

"Okay," she said, realizing how trapped she felt again.

"We're not trying to keep you captive here. You can leave as soon as the high priest Pages arrives."

Pages? What a silly name, she thought. "How do I get out of here? I want to leave now." Cassandra had not wished to think those thoughts to them, but she did, and they fell silent for a moment. Even with all their precious minerals that surrounded her, she still wanted to return to the surface world—the world that had damaged her and taken so much from her.

"We understand, Matriarch."

"Will you stop calling me that? Please call me Cassandra."

"Yes, Cassandra," the servants said.

"Where is the other guy and the other guy? I can't remember their names, but they must be alive if I am."

"There is only one man now, and he is in the holding cell."

"He's in a prison?"

"Yes, Matriarch Cassandra."

"Remember what I told you. Please call me Cassandra."

"Yes, Cassandra, it was an unforgivable accident. How shall I be punished?"

"No, no, no, don't worry about it. You're forgiven or whatever it takes to not be punished. You know what, call me whatever you want to call me."

"Thank you for your mercy. The man we've found, his mind responds to the name Timothy. He is infected with an illness of the mind."

"What?"

"You were also, but your illness is temporary compared with his condition."

"What? He's sick? I was sick? How did that happen?"

"Yes, Cassandra. You had a metal parasite in your mind. Every thought you were thinking was being transmitted to a receiving mind. Very complex situation. Someone's seeing through your minds basically. He or she is a very powerful telepath. We can't tell the creature's gender."

"I don't understand. Unbelievable. What does this all mean?"

"Cassandra, the creature has been manipulating your mind and the mind of the man you claim to know."

"I do know him. His name's Frior. He talked to me. We talked. He likes me, and I—"

"Indeed, his condition is much worse than we first believed."

"What? Am I okay?"

"Yes, the mental probe has been deactivated and severed. Also, we have increased your telepathic potential for you to understand us, and it should help you evade the creature's detection."

"Okay, what about Frior—I mean, Tim?"

"His mind is perfectly intact, which is unusual for the duration you traveled through time."

"What? This is getting confusing."

"His body, however, is struggling to survive the teleportation."

"I can't scream anymore. Explain this to me slowly."

"Are you wondering how you survived the explosion?"

"Yes, the explosions in the tunnels. How? How did I survive?"

"You survived the explosion by creating a teleportation frequency that bordered on time travel for about six or seven minutes. Your mind is tired, but your body appears to be unaffected by the travel."

"Time travel? I thought that was impossible. That's the one this science cannot do."

"Cassandra, you are the matriarch. We have been awaiting you for over sixty years. Your powers over time have nothing to do with your other powers."

"So is that why I couldn't freeze you when I tried."

"Yes."

"Can you take me to Tim?" Cassandra said, unintentionally mocking their foreign accents."

"Yes, yes."

"Where do we go?"

"We go nowhere. He shall come to you."

The large burly white-chalk-covered guards dressed in red native attire came to her waiting room carrying the body of the soldier on a smooth wooden plank. "Tim. Is he awake?"

"No."

"What happened to his hair? It was so long."

"It fell out, Eternal One" came the voice of a broad-nosed black-haired man. He had the noble features of a lion, and his age could not be seen, for a large furry red mask covered his face and eyes. He was painted red, and his native garments were that of bright gold.

Oh my, what's that on his face? she thought.

"It's spider skin from my first spider."

"You ate it?"

"No, Matriarch, I rode it. Please take the man outside," he said to the servants. "He is not worthy to face the throne of our guardian." The guards began to leave.

"He's not worthy? What makes you worthy?"

"I do not know, but I know that I am meant to speak with you."

"What? How do you know that?"

"For centuries, my ancestors and I have possessed the ability to see into the future. I have seen you in my mind since I was a child of two years."

"Oh? Here we go."

"Please don't get impatient with me. The sooner I reveal the past to you, the sooner you can leave."

"Okay, tell me. I want to know everything," said Cassandra as her light-blue eyes rolled.

"May I approach?"

"Yes, yes. What are we doing?"

"We need to be closer. I must transmit highly sensitive thoughts to you, thoughts you cannot share with outsiders."

"I'm an outsider," she said as the masked priest firmly gripped her hand, and the priestesses left the room.

A powerful flash of white light filled the room. The past revealed itself to her. The enslaved and captivated Darforians, the great war, and the hidden planet beside Darcon appeared in her mind. "The silver one's desire to have the treasures of this planet became apparent. Do not help him."

"Why?"

"Because he wants to gain his own power and return what cannot be."

"I hate riddles." The surface world appeared to her.

"This is not your ancestors' true home. The planet Hier is."

"I'm confused." The ancient people appeared in her mind's eye. "They look like giants compared with us."

"Yes, they were large." The shattered remains of the tunnel dweller appeared before her. "This was our home."

"Wow, everything looks so bright but smoky."

"Yes, we should have known it would not last forever like that. We now breathe the dark air."

"Oh, okay." The other planet in the far distance of the two appeared. "It's huge. It's massive." The red planet was Arcon.

"Yes, indeed."

"What could stand the gravity on it?"

"Only those that beat the game. Do not play their game."

"What?"

"You'll understand in the latter pages of your life."

"Okay, that's your name. Pages? You're Pages?" The blond child, Thunder, appeared in her mind.

"He will be approved." The adolescent silver one entered her imagination. "He is the one you must hate, for his desires would have killed your soul."

"He looks almost like you, the ancient people."

"Yes, Salientian is a powerful half-breed." The black-haired man who handed her over to the red-eyed woman entered her mind.

"Who's the man? Who's the woman? He looks like my . . . father." The experimentations were revealed. "What's that?"

"It is your beginning, the reason you have power." The chaotic death of the strongest god and the banishment of the red-eyed woman became vivid.

"Who is she? Why is her face masked?"

"You will battle her and the other three rulers of the red planet, Arcon."

"Wow, I'm lost."

"Your mind will remind you when the time comes. Behold the importance of the past." The silver one laughing among the tunnel dwellers appeared in her mind.

"Is he bad or good?"

"He is against us and just as evil as the rulers of Arcon." The fight between the white-haired matriarch and the bald silver youth was seen. "Salientian destroyed your processor. You must not underestimate his power. She did not have your other abilities, but she battled bravely, having mastered temporal energy, and she did win, for you exist."

"I'm getting a headache. He will not have the destructive power of time control." The immortal creatures of light that were hidden on the planet Hier appeared before her eyes; they were captured behind glass on the surface of her true home. "What are they? I've seen them before."

"They are in your genes. You reflect their power the most. You have the power to change the past, and that is your claim to the throne, but just because you can doesn't mean you should. Let life unfold."

Their powerful psychic bond broke, and Pages fell down. It took her what felt like a few moments to reach consciousness.

Forty days had passed by in a matter of moments particularly because her travel on the spider's back was comfortable. Placed on the cool desert floor, Frior lay beside her in his black armor. The desert ground was harsh even underneath the shade of the high rocks. Without her helmet, Psyy could see the spiders running away in the distance of the horizon. Looking around, she could feel her cool black armor around her body. Her destiny had been revealed to her, and she knew the tasks outlined would be difficult to achieve. She didn't feel lost anymore; she had purpose in her individuality.

From the floating station in space, a rectangular shimmering blue vessel left Darth's orbit, reflecting stars as the red propulsion engines moved it slowly toward the second planet.

"King?"

"Yes," said the hidden god.

"Where is Cepheus?" the silver one said.

"His last known location was at the southern prism. I can't keep looking after him."

"Yes, you can. And you will. You must. He is too scheming to be left unwatched."

"You're right. I will keep a watchful eye. Who will accompany me to Hier?"

"The only one left to help you."

"But the station will be under your command alone."

"I know. I am capable of multitasking. If you do find him—"

"I will find him. And what when?"

"Tell me."

"Yes, you'll also need to transport Communar to my vessel before I am out of range."

"Of course, brother." The comm signal from the station ended.

"He's looking for me. He might think I'm here, but he won't assume anything. Why couldn't you speak for me? I can't pretend to be you for too long. Your voice is so colorful."

"Don't try to distract me from your foolishness. He'll find you soon."

"And so what? We can't stay like this forever. Is that what you want, to live on a weak planet among the weak?" Cepheus said, his bright hazel eyes flashing in the dark lighting of the spacecraft.

"No. I want to go to Arcon and live among the strong," King said, his fear hidden behind his stern black eyes.

"Salientian is the only one that wants us to stay here. Had it not been for him, we would be far from here with our real brothers, gods on Arcon."

"What will we do when Communar arrives?"

"She must make her final mistake."

"Must it be this way?"

"Yes."

"You would murder her?"

"No. Of course not. We'll store her on Hier until we're ready to leave for Arcon."

"In that icebox? That's just like killing her."

"That is true, but this way, we can resurrect her when we've reached the red planet without expending too much energy."

The starry, golden-eyed, and red-caped female god who personified an ideology that ruled the planet Darth appeared on the vessel, and Cepheus took her form and voice after greeting her.

It took several hours for Frior to awake, and she stared down at him and into the desert foreground. She admired the blurry haze the sun had cast on the lightly sanded desert ground. The land was barren, except for a few cacti. The sky was a cloudless light blue, and she saw no insects. This location was far from the jungle surroundings.

Time went by, and it was midday, but she was not restless. He pondered her life and her new destiny. Had she not seen the spider run off in the distance, she would not have believed the encounter with the tunnel dwellers. Her situation was sad, but she did not cry.

Psyy waited for the stranger to wake up, but he slept on. Her strength made her believe she could walk through the desert, but reality kept her in check. Looking at the stranger's black armor, she knew she needed his helmet again. She took off his helmet, bypassing her reflection. Inside the helmet, she heard a yelling voice. "Where are you? Can you hear me?" the apocalyptic voice said. "Soldier? Respond. State your position." It was the creature's voice.

Knowing her destiny, she feared it, and she felt compelled to respond. "Hello."

"You are there. What took you so long to respond to me? Where is the commander?"

"He's unconscious."

"How come you took so long to respond to me?"

"We're in the desert, and I don't know how we got here."

"The desert? How? You must have teleported out when the caverns were bombed."

"Maybe."

"Ah, very well, I'm glad you're still alive, Soldier."

"How are you going to find us?"

"Stay awake and hold your position. I'm coming for you within the hour."

"Okay," Psyy said. The comm signal ended before she could respond. "Hello? Aw, he's gone."

Her eyes shifted over her situation and now watched the soldier who struggled to stand up. She slowly walked over to him, placing his helmet down beside him. His hair was low and rough, but he looked well rested. "Where am I?" he asked. "Who are you?"

"I'm Cass—" She stopped herself. "It's me, Psyy."

"Oh, you. My head hurts."

"You'll be fine. I've contacted the general. He'll be here soon."

"What? I don't want to go back there. I'm done with the army," he said, about to stand up.

"I thought you were a soldier."

"No, I have other things I need to do. I have to go back to the southern prism. People are waiting for me."

She knew she shouldn't have stopped him from leaving, but what other choice did she have? Using her now twice-as-strong telepathic powers, Psyy knocked Frior out with a powerful psychic frequency that even his immunities could not repel. She felt awful again.

Minutes later, the ground began to shake. The creature was coming, and her important thoughts were now fading to the background of her mind. The creature had control once more.

CHAPTER XI

THE LAST CHAPTER

Throughout their pleasant rest and revelations, a war raged on. The creature's forces were being hunted down by the HDF. The blond knight, Thunder, was relentless, and he used almost all the resources available to him; however, the creature's mind control was powerful, and it invaded the knight swiftly. The conflict between Thunder and the creature was an entirely different game to play, for it was a simple story of objectives and killings. The western prism lay in ruin, and the northern prism remained badly damaged from the missiles. The western prism was completely destroyed; it was the creature's main base of operations. The subbasement of the blackened northern prism could be seen clearly from the surface.

The creature reclaimed its two treasures, Frior and Psyy, in the desert and knew it would be victorious. The egglike subterranean vessel tunneled toward the location of the long-range satellite tower. Its silver dish spanned thirty meters in diameter and the six-story towerlike red building supported it effectively. Psyy and Frior were only partially under his control, and he would have to wait to begin the mission.

Khan, the creature's host image, chose to make the event very real to them and would introduce them to his best warriors. On the edge of the desert, the vessel surfaced a mile from the satellite tower. Off-loading the vessel, he assembled the remains of his army. Astonishingly, fifty out of a thousand soldiers survived his leadership, and he wanted to make the best use of the rest. Sunset approached, and he allowed his six chosen warriors to gather together.

"Soldiers, this is your last mission. You have fought bravely. Your objectives are to protect the tower. Regardless of the overwhelming might of the enemy, you must ensure my survival. You have one hour to set up the defensive perimeter."

The soldiers were off-loaded, and the subterranean vessel moved onward to the tower. The remaining occupants of the vessel were scientists and computer technicians from the western prism. Cassandra could sense what was occurring but could not break the creature's control over her mind. A powerful tension commanded her movements.

The subterranean vessel surfaced meters from the satellite tower. Dressed for battle and recognition, the creature wore black armor and a thin black metallic cape. The scientists were also in black armor and helmets. The technicians wore thin orange suits that displayed their skills of knowledge and comprehension. They disembarked quickly, and Cassandra's newfound control of the weaponry helped open the large rust-covered doors of the towers.

The creature and its entourage entered the empty building and climbed the gridlike metallic stairs. The creature barked orders to have the fuel cells connected to the tower's outdated electric system. The satellite on the tower was not powered. It ordered its decoys in the southern prism to activate the armed bombs, which drew all attention away from the creature's location for the next twenty minutes while the HDF struggled to deactivate the creature's intense postnuclear heat-wave-creating devices. It needed to set the complex coordinates of the biological satellites on Pylon. These satellites were the most powerful receiving minds in the galaxy. In the nebula of Pyl, where the Pylonites lived on their worlds, thousands of insectlike black-covered warships awaited the location of the lost planet Darth. The creature could taste its promotion among Pylon and longed to reunite with its living brood.

Her feet were heavy as she followed the creature's body and other technicians up the staircase to the control room. She looked around the dusty metallic room and watched the dark screens that covered the outdated control panels. The screens opened in a sliding action, and the creature ordered the technicians to type a massively complex code. With the creature's tone desperate, it again looked at the woman. She could not move. Her life flashed before her mind; she knew she should have tried harder to rebel against the creature, knowing its true intentions, but she didn't. Something inside her told her to wait. She wanted to see what would happen next.

She didn't hear the words that entered her mind as she reached for the control panel and began to type something very important. It was the two unique frequencies of the biological molecules she and other scientists had worked on earlier. In a matter of moments, the satellite would transmit the gods' genetic frequencies across the galaxy where they would be reconstructed and experimented on. When she had completed her task, Cassandra remained seated. Fervent loud words reached her ears but not her mind. She knew she was doing the wrong thing, but she had to see the enemy. If she was this "matriarch," perhaps her past self would save her from whatever fate awaited this body.

"Didn't you hear me? Move from the seat and exit the room, all of you," said the powerful voice of Khan.

"Okay."

"Whoa" came the voice of a technician, having watched her unblinking stare moments before.

"Where am I?"

"My head hurts."

"Leave! Now!" commanded the creature.

She could feel her thoughts reentering her body as she walked down the stairs. She could hear the psychic vibrations of arguments inside and outside the tower. A war was raging outside.

"Commander Ang, just follow my orders and attack the enemy!" commanded the creature.

"There are too many of them! You'll get us all killed!"

"This is war, Commander. I promoted you to protect and accomplish this mission," said the heartless creature as it ended the conversation. It had lost all control over its army, but its purpose was complete now. He had transmitted the location of the lost world. Darth would once again become a battleground and a world free for the taking.

The creature returned to its true form. Its insectlike frame was frail, and now it needed to feed. It regretted asking that they all leave.

Outside the structure, a hundred helicopter-like aircraft approached the defensive perimeter. The scattering frequency and the will of Salientian prevented bombardment from the floating station. The now sleeping Communar, the only female god of the planet, would have ensured the satellite was destroyed by any means, as would be her instructions, and this was precisely why he allowed her immobility on Hier by her fellow gods. Communar's black hair reminded him of many people.

Returning to the ensuing battle, the three-meter metal spiders ran across the desert ground toward the tower. The magnetic mines buried underneath the sand grabbed on to a few of them, preventing their movement. A thousand flying and gray-suited soldiers wielding flaming swords landed in the sand as the weapons of the tower became activated.

The defenses of the tower were simple. A frequency-jamming device prevented weapons from aiming correctly. The robotic gunners hidden in the sand fired at anything that breached the perimeter of the tower. Sand-dune-creating machines were already part of the tower's subterranean defenses and pulled in enemies by surprise. The tower's shield system was old but functioning perfectly and would retract the tower into the ground if the fighting became too intense. The first red gunfire from the hidden gunners signaled the end of the creature's two-hundred-year plight.

Jeremiah had polished his silver armor hours before the battle. He once again had a full head of hair. His bones were firm and did not crack. He could once again dream. Happy thoughts of him burying the deserters deep in the caverns of the jungle, he had such pride, but the last target remained. He was fully healed. Four months of rest and revengeful thoughts made his plan of action perfect.

The silver god, Salientian, was at peace with the creature and Thunder's handling of the situation, so he thought he should be also. He would not need heavy weapons this time. He placed his mask over his dangerous face and withdrew his light steel sword from the wall behind him. His camouflaged zeppelin followed the subterranean vessel unnervingly for days, and he was only minutes behind the first wave of gleaming robotic spiders. It would be the final battle at sunset. He eyed the red tower.

In space, not far from the planet, a ball of subspace unraveled, and hundreds of seed-shaped black ships that looked like large insects moved toward the planet Darth. Salientian braced himself. His purple eyes showed none of the fear that filled his heart. The truth of his power to see the future as it was would be tested to its limits, and he feared the chants that mocked him as a fool. In his dark lair, he gathered his invisible guards to protect himself. His cloaked vessel began to drift toward the sacred planet of Hier.

Frior fought bravely, destroying the spiders swiftly. The turrets on the tower shot unendingly at multiple targets. The battlefield was covered with red, white, and blue blasts of energy, but the highly advanced technology prevented friendly fire. His anger motivated him. He didn't know how or why he was fighting this enemy, but he had to defend himself. White fire left his hands, melting the spider's metallic exteriors. The desert night was setting in, and flames covered the ground. His agility and speed made him the best weapon in the field. He was hit directly by many projectiles, but his black covering protected him better than Psyy's blue light corona, and combined with his ability to shoot a gun and throw a melting punch, he was in no danger.

The flying soldiers slashed at him with their swords and missed. He broke their suits' armor. He threw grenades. He sliced through them with their own weapons. He kicked away the spiders as if they were made of thin wood. It took five days of manufacturing to create a single metallic spider and five seconds for him to destroy one. The other soldiers were falling quickly. He was invulnerable but could still be pushed. He couldn't protect them forever.

He moved closer and closer to the tower and then looked up into the starry sky the moment the moon took rule. It was now night. The shooting stars flew through the desert sky. He made no wish. The soldiers fought bravely, but their abilities did not match their desires. They were also confused with their whereabouts and struggled to fight offensively.

Fighting at night was dreadful, and inside the dark tower, Psyy looked around for some window to the outside world. She thought about going to the room that held the creature, but she feared a confrontation. She had not seen a technician for almost an hour and could not sense their minds either. The creature was rejuvenated with the strength of its hosts, and it prepared itself for the arrival of its leaders.

Thunder fought without the guidance of a conscience, slaying the infected soldiers with lightning slices. He dropped the temperature around the soldiers to a bone-chilling degree as he approached their position. The spiders were formidable, but he was stunned by the rate at which they were failing. He kept having to call for more reinforcements. His gray eyes looked up to scan the terrain. His nearsighted eyes identified the cause of the chaos.

A common soldier threw heavy metallic spiders meters into the air. Thunder watched him carefully before withdrawing his sword. White flames shot from his hands, leaving a blur of warm air. Frior looked up and saw the silver warrior in the background of his battle. He took aim. The knight turned to lightning and reappeared before he could shoot his weapon again, slicing it apart. The ninja punched. The knight dodged his fist and reacted with a slicing motion. The ninja's shadow vanished, and the attack missed.

The two most powerful forces were now fighting. A punch landed on the knight's chest as he turned to light. Frior wasn't electrocuted as volts of electricity ran around his smoking shield. The knight regained his true form and slashed away at the ninja. The temperature was dangerously low, and he could not understand how this common soldier could fight against him. White flames fell on him, and they quickly turned red as they were blown away by disruptions in the subspace that created a windlike effect. He struck the soldier with lightning, casting him to the ground. Frior stood up and was blown down again. A piercing point pressed against his heart as he tried to stand up again. The sword would have touched his heart had he not had the layer of dark gravity surrounding him. He looked the gray-eyed warrior in the eyes from beneath his helmet as he secured the blade of the knight's sword. He broke it, causing the knight to turn to lightning again and allowing him to stand. The knight retrieved his real sword.

"You are a worthy warrior."

"I don't need your praise. I don't know why you people want to fight me anyway, but I'll fight every last one of you."

"You're infected, and we can't cure you all."

"Shut up and fight!"

"That's what I like to hear."

A powerful bolt of lightning left his free hands as the soldier charged at him. The ninja's flexible body transformed to lifeless black diamonds, and then in the darkness, he vanished. Thunder was speechless as he missed his target. He swung his sword blindly. A hand reached out of the darkness, gripping his shoulder, intending to toss him into the twisting dune. He changed to light again. Wicked air left Thunder's open hands, causing cold fog to cloud the air. He was now invisible also. They fought intensely. He kicked, and the other blocked. He punched, and the other punched. Frior missed, and the Thunder landed his punch. The freezing cold air did not affect the ninja.

The moon was not in the background, and they both took their time to acknowledge it. The hand-to-hand fighting was intentional. Thunder's strength did not match Frior's, but his abilities to strike with lightning and wind made him the aggressor. Frior's innate shield was impenetrable to all contemporary forms of attack, but he could feel the cold air whenever he let down his guard.

Frior tried to take the other sword from the hand of the colorful fighter, but his grip was strong, and the jolts of electricity caused his muscles to seize up. Frior threw him or attempted to repeatedly, but Thunder reversed his toss or changed to lightning almost immediately, slashing away with his sword. This sound reminded Frior of the past, the same sounds that haunted him. He swung a punch that hit the knight's face immediately. A howl of pain left his mouth. Blood dripped. A crack of lightning sent the ninja to his knees for a moment. His mask had shattered. Several sharp slashes landed on the ninja's helmet. He reacted with a clamped, swinging fist, knocking the knight's sword from his hand as he turned to light to retrieve his weapon.

The ninja withdrew his grenade. He tossed it. The grenade touched the place where the lightning would recombine and exploded as the lightning struck it. The knight took his human form and fell closer to the tower. The spiders attacked the ninja. He melted them and threw them into the swirling dunes. It became cold again. An electrically charged kick hit him to the sand as a sword sliced through the thick skin of his arm. He bled for the first time in years.

Thunder's features darkened, and his hair did not suit him. He looked worse than a commoner pretending to be royalty. The ninja moved quickly; using his martial arts training, he disarmed the knight and pushed him to the sand. Lightning left his hands and seemingly decapitated the ninja. The knight looked stunned as the smoke cleared. Frior's head was still on, and a blackness covered his face, full head of hair, and upper neck. His angry green eyes met the gray eyes of the trained swordsman. Red fire encircled him just before he stomped the ground, forcing the knight to change to light and reappear above him. He kicked against the top of his head, lower neck, and back as the knight kicked down on his spine. Frior stumbled for a moment as he moved forward, touching the ground; he did a half-cartwheel movement and faced his enemy.

Large objects fell from the sky, which smoked from the flaming remains of the station. They both could not stop themselves from looking up. The falling extraterrestrial debris fell to the planet. The warriors surveyed the scene—his bloody mouth, his bleeding left arm. Words could not express the shock within them. The remains of the station looked like large meteors in the sky, falling awkwardly as they rolled.

Reflecting, insectlike objects filled the cloudless dark sky. Frior began to count the dots consciously. Bright lights filled the dark night sky as nearly a thousand unidentified objects flew over them. Explosions could be heard in the background of their battlefield. The turrets of the tower stopped spinning and shooting. Thunder's zeppelin no longer responded to him.

The ninja took advantage of the knight's concern as he slammed him against the hard red wall of the tower. The knight jabbed against him with his sword, intending to draw blood. The intensity of the strike was so hard against his shield of gravity that the sword broke. The ululations of regret filled the night air, and pure light energy left his hands. It bounced against the dark shield, shattering the light on the sand and against the wall. It sliced through the dark gravity; it defied Salientian and mortally wounded the soldier. It pierced the vulnerable tendons at his wrists and ankles.

Great happiness overtook the knight as an unexpected effect of the broken field of gravity swept over him. The gleaming black liquid light radiated from the ninja. Jeremiah's body felt the crushing force of a weight he could not lift. His spine broke in several places as the bright light that left his hands faded. Jeremiah's thoughts of immortality were dying along with him. Timothy fell to the dusty floor, trying to stand. He would not accept his fate. The knight tried to turn to light again, but his body would not respond to him. The centipedes and other creepy night things would have too much to consume.

Inside the tower, the woman waited and moved around frantically. She could hear the regretful screams of dying minds. She ran through the darkness of the tower, looking for help. She did not want to go outside. She did attempt to create a teleportation sphere, but the space was far too crowded, and she couldn't think. She grew frantic. She burned the walls helplessly, trying to melt the heat-repelling inner walls of the tower. Cassandra did not want to be a participant of the war. She no longer wanted to see the outside world as she heard the footsteps of a technician. "Who's there?"

"It's me, a technician," said the creature. "I think the building is about to fall. You should leave with me."

"That explains why the power's out."

"I know how to get out. Follow me."

"Follow you? Why?"

"I know how to get out."

"Wasn't your suit orange?" The pink suit of the technician made her skeptical.

"No."

"Oh, yeah, of course, my mistake," she said, believing his alteration of reality.

She followed the creature to the door of the tower, and the creature walked with her out in the mayhem that was the cold desert. Without having to think, tears began to roll down her cheeks.

"Why are you crying? Isn't this what you wanted? Peace?"

"Yeah, but I also wanted freedom," she said, looking up at the many dots that filled the sky.

"What's freedom? You know what, I'll let you live," it said, walking toward her. The flaming corpses of metallic spiders were behind it.

"No! No! Get away from me!" A forceful blast left her hands, sending the creature flying into the desert sand. The creature's full stomach forced its reversion back to its insectlike form. It stood up slowly.

"It's too late. I've won. You've lost. Accept it."

"No," she said, looking around at the creepy things in the background.

You've lost. Come to terms, the creature's mind told her. *You have lost.*

"No."

"My people have come to claim this world as they should have years ago. You do value rightness? You can still be great. Merge with my mind. Allow me to be your master. I will make your form great."

"No. You've only won on this plane, in this reality," she began to think and say.

"Don't fool yourself. Take my offer. With your power, the Pylon will be able to compete for survival against the Arconians," the creature said, standing up. "We are the lesser enemy. If you don't help us against our common enemy, Arcon will find you soon and put every last one of you in the game. No one would survive, not even you."

"I don't care," she said. "It's not for you to decide."

"Who do you think you are?" The creature hissed.

"I'm not sure, but I know it's my decision to make."

"You don't have a choice," the creature said slowly, curling each word as he walked toward her.

"Yes, I do. I always have a choice," she said as the creature began to hiss loudly, building up its charge.

As the Pylon vessels circled the creature and the new changer of time, preparing to descend lower to the surface of the desert, she felt the harsh wind against her face. Her cheeks were now warm. She was alive. The warmth she felt traveled to her fingertips. Psyy looked at the creature in its evil eyes. "I'm the matriarch, and I will stop you."

A sparkling light covered her body, and the creature's jump was frozen in time as its jaws opened to brutally close. The timeless blue light left her hands. The whirling motion of the bluish light caused the tower to shake and bend. She didn't know where she wanted to go or how to do get there, but she was moving. The creature disappeared. She was in motion, not the matter around her. The sand beneath her shifted. The sky changed color; it was brighter. She had left her body behind. She could see the invisible ring of white light that surrounded her mind. Her clothes were gone, and her mind appeared to be like gains of salt. Her saltlike white hair swept over her face as it blustered in the flow of time, transforming to a saltlike white as well.

The war rewound before her eyes. It was Frior and the unknown knight. The two had fought. They were fighting before her open eyes. She touched them with her mind, but her glowing and shaky form seemed out of phase with their reality. It caused her to doubt herself momentarily. The bright, glitterlike blue light expanded and covered the entire planet. The fight scene vanished, and she appeared in the darkness of gravity.

Everything began to hurt. She was no longer a glittering fairy. Her body vanished into the darkness of the night. She was in a familiar place. It was her mind. She was warm but felt comfortable. She had arrived at a moment that required action. The last chapter became her new beginning to life. Her knowledge and abilities would no longer dictate her actions. The new matriarch would evade death just this once and suffer the consequences of tampering with time.

The silver one was the first to become aware of his survival. He breathed a sigh of relief, felt anger in the failure of his guards to protect him in another time, and commanded them to leave his chambers and return the cloaked vessel to its correct orbit. No one understood his behavior.

CHAPTER XII

POST PREDICTION

A flash of white light covered the planet; all the telepathically inclined beings sensed it. Time had suddenly stopped for the two minds that were in darkness. Timothy reached his body first and dropped to his knees in confusing pain. Jeremiah dropped his sword, never slicing into the weak soldier. He felt the ticking again; he could hear his heart. Salientian had ordered the spiders to retreat and to disable the containment field around the tower, which had prevented Cassandra from leaving. Her older mind was yet to reach her younger body. Cassandra's hands were once again touching time, and this time, the fabric felt comfortable. It was only as she entered her place in time did she feel the pain of a onetime feat. He entered the room with computers the moment the yelling started.

"Didn't you hear me? Move from—" the creature said, its sentence ending before its time.

From inside the badly injured mind, a forceful energy left her body, sending the technicians through the walls of the circular room into the outer hall unintentionally. The functions of the computing device ended as electromagnetic energy fried the circuits. The creature was instantly furious. The woman began to speak as she fell to the floor. Her black armor glittered. Her helmetless face expressed utter mockery and defiance.

"There's your victory. You thought you had won. But didn't you?" she declared, stumbling off the black chair.

The creature shrieked as its body changed from that of Khan's. Its insectlike body was weak. Its ridged and flat face with protruding jaws returned. The creature's knees bent, and its dry greenish-black eyes opened wide to stare at the woman as if to say, *What have you done?* The creature's plans to leave the planet had been ruined in a matter of seconds. Its meekness had all been in vain.

Its claws struck her instantly as it leaped at her. She was pushed out of the narrow doorway. The creature's reptilelike body impacted her unexpectedly. Her skull had chipped the doorway exit on her way out. The creature snapped at her, but its sharp teeth seemed to go right through her hands. She impacted the metallic floor and rolled down the stairs, her nothinglike hands dipping through the stairs. They were glittering. The creature's feet landed on her rib cage, and she looked up in pain. Her powers were not working. No ice came from her hands to stop the creature's fury of slashes. The glittering blue light around her seemed to protect her from scarring.

The creature picked her up by the shoulder, throwing her down another flight of stairs. She did not bleed, but her skin was bruising. Her hair flew around rapidly as she tumbled down the staircase. The creature leaped down to crush her once more. She rolled to dodge his crushing stomp and finally landed a blow with her feet. The creature winced and retaliated with a swift claw against her armor. Her helmet was off her face, and she was vulnerable; the creature slapped her. Her nose bled, but her fist punched the creature. Her hands were not returning to their cold state. The creature was stronger than her and threw her against the railing. Her back slammed against the rail.

Her mind reached out to the soldier. The creature hissed so loudly that the entire tower echoed. The creature secured her right arms in its rows of sharp teeth and clenched its jaw. She screamed, feeling the arm cracking. Slapping the creature's cold-blooded skin, she screamed helplessly. The telepathic mind of the creature spoke to her. *You may have defeated me, but you will die. I shall rule this world in your flesh.*

The creature's teeth had bitten through her armor and marked her tougher, bleeding skin. She punched the creature repeatedly, but it would not release her. A powerful blue light left her hands, slicing through the creature's chest; however, the creature continued with its viselike grip. She thought she would die as she began to lose consciousness. Her blurred vision took hold, and her weakening blows proved that. The purple blood of the creature dripped unto her armor from the wound she had made.

In space, the Pylonites awaited the messages and, after the appointed time had passed, knew that their operative had failed them. The creature would be doomed to die on Pylon no matter its success. The connection between the hive and its mind was now severed. The Arconians would still maintain their dominance over the brood. Deep within the dark jungles of the Pylon home world, an execution took place. The spy from the lost world remained locked in his prison cell and gathered his thoughts for the next phase of extraction therapy, but the creature's brood would pay the ultimate price for his failure.

Outside the tower, the ninja heard her cry for help; and remarkably, so did the knight. Somehow they had become connected to one another on a narrow frequency of danger. The three now shared a permanent link and a glimpse into a possible future where they had all died together. Rapport existed between her and the ninja, so their connection was stronger.

Timothy heard the shout, while Jeremiah ignored the whisper as he did many others. Instead of looking at each other as they did before, they looked up at the tower—the source of the noise. Frior ran toward the wall, pounding it with his fist. The wall didn't move. He kicked the wall. She attempted to climb the wall but had no grips. He acknowledged that he was too weak to climb, and then he saw the door.

Lightning struck the tower's satellite dish, and the knight appeared on the narrow walkway at the top of the tower. He disabled the turrets with an electromagnetic pulse and opened the orange door that led inside the structure. He summoned his zeppelin, which was high above the tower. He heard the screams of the badly injured woman. Jumping down through the gap between the winding staircases, he turned to light.

The creature's jaws squeezed the woman's arm with killing force. A flash of lightning appeared behind the two, and a loud silencer click sounded. The creature's jaws released her. The creature slumped against her, and she pushed it off to rest on the next staircase. Her boots were cold and bloodied.

Too exhausted to think, she looked at the beautiful warrior who stood before her. His gray eyes looked deeply into her light blue eyes. He admired her face for a moment and realized that she was still alive. His bombs had not buried her beneath the tunnels. He was somewhat glad watching her struggle to look past the barrel of the gun and analyze his face. The silver pistol pointed at her unstable mind, she felt a pressing pain against the targeted spot. His blond hair was the first thing she noticed and remembered about him. Her blurry vision was the reason she did not flinch. Jeremiah's nerves got the best of him, and his head jumped in surprise. He didn't pull the trigger.

"Drop the gun," said the uncloaked ninja who continued to walk up the staircase below him, his larger rifle aimed at Jeremiah's masked face. "I won't say it again." Timothy armed the weapon again.

"The blast will kill us both. Don't give me ideas to do things I shouldn't. I wasn't going to hurt her."

The rifle's bullet caused the silencer to flip over the railing. Cassandra had now fallen on the ground beside the creature's body. The bullet hit its target, and the silencer flew from Jeremiah's hand.

"I wasn't giving you a chance."

The two met for the first time. Their gazes added to the sense of death that lingered in the room. Frior looked down for a second to see the creature's dead body. His face grimaced at the sight. Thunder admired his reflection in the soldier's helmet.

"Step away from her," Timothy said, "now."

"Whatever you say," mocked the knight. He did not fear death. "Just don't do anything hasty."

"Stop talking."

"Very well," Jeremiah said, realizing that he had reached his limits of energy usage, and there was little static in the air.

Jeremiah's hands began to electrify; he was about to do something hasty. The short electromagnetic pulse left his body, and the soldier's rifle was made useless; also, the visuals inside his helmet ended. The knight retrieved his sword to the sounds of many rifle clicks. Revenge could have been his, but he stabbed the still living creature instead of the woman. Timothy's emotions nearly got the best of him; he threw off his helmet, and his hands were very heated. Psyy looked up at the two revived warriors.

"Prepare yourselves. I'll assume this is the first time you've left the planet," the blond knight said mockingly.

The brightness of the flashing red light that transfigured their forms to the zeppelin brought fear to Timothy and relief to Cassandra, for the knight was ordered not to harm them. The three had no real alliances, but their lives were now forever intertwined.

CONSEQUENCES OF A WORTHY CAUSE

On the Harforian station, the wounds of the warriors were attended to, and the truth about the planets' histories were revealed to the two prism-raised visitors. The Harforians did not reveal experimental origins of the perfect three. The complex genetic codes that were engineered into their cells were the cause of their powers. Salientian's power freed Frior from the powerful spell of the dead creature without meeting him. Psyy's mind was strong enough to heal itself and remember the important past.

Having only a few hours of rest on the station, Frior desired to return to the surface to face the disaster. Psyy was anxious to find out what had become of her brother and sister-in-law during all this time. Sitting on her new bed aboard the massive Harfore station, Psyy embraced her new destiny and shed many tears for the people of the past. Her trip through time drained her both physically and emotionally.

Salientian realized his mistake. The trouble of his plan only dawned on him slowly. Deep in Arconian space, a large sensor constructed for the purpose of detecting temporal energy emissions emerged. It detected a sharp vibration in time. The vibration usually meant that another energy well had sprung up in the large galaxy. Several large cylindrical ships destined themselves for the hidden planets. The silver god, Salientian, made the mistake of assuming the planets' gravitational-temporal energy displacement shields which protected the lost planets, Darth and Hier, from all forms of detection would mask the new matriarch's trip through time.

The godlike being feared the strength of the Arconians. Their immunity to his powers of control made him no god to them, particularly the four rulers of Arcon. Yes, his wisdom preceded theirs, but he was older now. His goals to resurrect the beings on Hier would need to proceed much faster than he had first planned. The planet Hier was rich in minerals, massive energy supplies, and technology that the Harfore-Darcon alliance could integrate for use in defending themselves from the coming invasion. The strange radiation on the planet Hier made him unable to attain it without the three: Psyy, Frior, and Thunder. In a week, the vessels would reach the lost planets and lay waste the worlds' resources before he had time to assess the other gods' progress on Hier.

Salientian would not forget the traitors' scheming plan. The immortal and wise warriors on Hier awaited his commands but, for now, were drifting in an unpowered ageless sleep, waiting for him to command them to destroy Arcon and create his new universe . . .

GLOSSARY

Ancients: The mostly dead race of beings that have imprisoned their created race, Darforians, on the planet Hier. Their highly advanced technology is now stored in the tunnels of Hier. Their exposure to a sustaining radiation has made them unable to procreate efficiently. Their genetically engineered descendants are the half-bred gods that rule Darth and Hier and the nobility on Arcon. The ruling gods of Arcon are Zeus, Odin, Sekmet, and Sobek, all in competition and cooptation.

Arcon (Arconians): Race of aliens who possess incredible strength and mental defenses. Telekinetic and telepathic powers are powerless against them. On their home world of Arcon, only the strong survive. They have very dark or light complexion, no in-between tones, and look very much like the Harforians and Darforians.

Darth: The battlefield of the war between the alien races and the planet the Darforians were transported to from the planet Hier. The climate of the planet is hostile, and the wildlife is too savage for the inhabitants to survive unprotected outside their prisms.

Harfore (Harforians): Race of aliens possessing powerful telepathic and telekinetic abilities. Their intelligence and ability to communicate quickly makes them a threat to the Arconians.

The Harfore have fought a war against the Arconians and Pylonites, with the help of the Darforians, in a one-hundred-year galactic battle under the leadership of the gods.

Hier: The planet of the Ancients and rightful home world of the Darforians. Its climate has once been free from predators, and its very cold nights and warm days have repelled visitors. The tunnels of the planet have been the former home of the Darforians. The planet has eventually been claimed by the half-bred gods.

the game: The warlike challenge mandated by the leaders of Arcon to ensure that only the strong survive to rule and conquer the known universe.

the gods: Half-Harforian descendants of the Ancients with much less power than their ancestors. There are four remaining gods: Salientian, Communar, Cepheus, and King.

Salientian (half-bred god): The silver god. He has the power to control living cells and, therefore, minds. He has the power to see the future, but the complication of this power will eventually complex his mind beyond his limits. His past is shrouded by his betrayal of the tunnel dwellers and the murder of his former master.

Communar (half-bred god): The golden-eyed god and the brilliant multitasking controller of the Harforian station. She is titanlike in height. Her disappearance signifies the breakdown of the socialist structure of the planet.

Cepheus (half-bred god): The hazel-eyed young god with little mental powers who has become aware of the complexity of the universe and has been embedded with thoughts of surpassing his elder brother and leader, Salientian.

King (half-bred god): Traitorous and colorless god whose power to change appearance makes him deadly and cunning. He has filled his younger brother's head with thoughts to challenge Salientian. He has helped the creature's plan succeed and desires to live on Arcon.

Athor (Sekmet) (full-bred god): The red-eyed god is one of the few Ancients still living after banishment from Darth. The location of the planets, along with her relation to the gods, is stolen from her by Salientian. She lives on the planet Arcon as an all-powerful champion of the game. Her adoption of the blond child (Thunder) forces Salientian to raise him as close to godhood as possible and treat him like a real brother.

temporal energy: The force that causes time to move. Unlike gravity, it is only sensed but unfelt.

the communion of the gods: An adopted ceremony of their ancestors that allows the gods to view the leaving of their bodies defenseless in the solid world and refuel on purified temporal energy, which sustains their minds and generates their power.

the matriarch: A destined person, usually a woman, who has the power to feel the force of time, predict the future, and change it. The last matriarch has died protecting the past.

the tunnel dwellers: A rare half-breed of the Ancients and the Darforians. They live deep within the caverns of Darth and possess great agility and intelligence. They have successfully socialized with spiders. Their culture is one of wealth and providence. Most possess the power to see events before they occur or if they occur, but usually, only one can see the unlived past and alter it.

psionic: A term referring to psychic energy.

Pylon (Pylonites): An insectlike race of aliens that possess the ability to steal the genetic traits of most animals. They have powerful telepathic abilities collectively. They feed off the biochemical and telepathic energies of their hosts. Their home world is located in the galaxy of Pyl. They are no longer countable with their physical features because of a failed adaptation of the Ancient alien traits. Their race has created the Arcon as a result of the failed adaptation.

Lightning Source UK Ltd.
Milton Keynes UK
UKHW041618181218
334174UK00003B/70/P